In Zanesville

Also by Jo Ann Beard

The Boys of My Youth

In Zanesville

a novel

Jo Ann Beard

Little, Brown and Company

New York • Boston • London

Little, Brown and Company
Hachette Book Group
237 Park Avenue, New York, NY 10017
www.hachettebookgroup.com

First Edition: April 2011

Little, Brown and Company is a division of Hachette Book Group, Inc. The Little, Brown name and logo are trademarks of Hachette Book Group, Inc.

The characters and events in this book are fictitious. Any similarity to real persons, living or dead, is coincidental and not intended by the author.

The publisher is not responsible for websites (or their content) that are not owned by the publisher.

Library of Congress Cataloging-in-Publication Data
Beard, Jo Ann.
   In Zanesville : a novel / Jo Ann Beard. — 1st ed.
      p. cm.
   ISBN 978-0-316-08447-5
   1. Teenage girls—Fiction.   2. Nineteen seventies—Fiction.   3. City and town life—Illinois—Fiction.   I. Title.
   PS3602.E248716 2011
   813'.6—dc22   2010041808

10 9 8 7 6 5 4 3 2 1

RRD-C

Printed in the United States of America

For Scott

The wind is rushing after us, and the clouds are flying after us, and the moon is plunging after us, and the whole wild night is in pursuit of us; but, so far, we are pursued by nothing else.

Charles Dickens, *A Tale of Two Cities*

In Zanesville

We can't believe the house is on fire. It's so embarrassing first of all, and so dangerous second of all. Also, we're supposed to be in charge here, so there's a sense of somebody not doing their job.

"I told you to go up there and see what they were doing," Felicia says.

"I told *you* to go up there," I reply.

We've divided the kids up, three each, and two of hers were upstairs playing with matches while the third, and all of mine, were secured in the backyard.

The smoke isn't too bad at this point; basically it smells like a campfire. We still can't find where it's coming from, although the third-floor bathroom is a pretty safe bet, if we listen to Renee, who is accusing Derek of setting a toilet paper fire in a wicker wastebasket.

There is no sign of Derek anywhere; he set the fire and moved on to the next thing. Renee, loitering in the hallway, had played Barbie until the last possible moment and then gave up when the smoke began swirling, calling out, "Fire!" in an annoyed voice.

"He said if I told, he'd murder me," she trilled, loping down the stairs and out, eluding us.

We've been babysitting for the Kozaks all summer, five days a week, eight hours a day; six kids—Derek, Renee, Stewart, Wanda, Dale, Miles—and various other, easier-to-control creatures: a tarantula, a python, a rat snake, some white mice, and an elderly German shepherd with bad hips who lies in the dirt next to the doghouse all day, licking his stomach. We each get seventy-five cents per hour, which doesn't sound like enough when we're here but blooms into an incredible bounty on the weekends, when we're lying around trying to decide how to spend it. Almost a dollar an hour, accumulating slowly and inexorably, in a revolving series of gagging diaper changes, nose wipings, placing of buzzing flies in the tarantula's terrarium, assembly-line construction of baloney-cheese-mayonnaise sandwiches, folding of warm laundry, chipping of egg crust off the vinyl tablecloth, benevolent dispensing of Sno-Kone dimes, helpless shouting, appalling threats, and perusal of their porn library.

We are fourteen, only three years older than Derek, who is the oldest of the Kozak children. Derek isn't much work because he disappears for most of each day, showing up only when the parents are due back home, which is fine with us. He won't mind, he cusses, and he once threw a handful of worms at us after a rainstorm. The other five kids range in age from one and a half to nine; some in fact claim to be the same age, although none of them look even vaguely alike. We can't figure it out, but then again, we don't try to.

*   *   *

"Man, are we in for it," Felicia says, panting.

We're evacuating the pets. She's struggling with the smaller snake aquarium, which houses, along with the python, the python's furniture—a bent log, a plastic bowl, and a rock for the mice to hide behind. The snake, a young albino, is gently probing its ivory nose at the jumbo box of ice cream sandwiches we've put on top to hold the wire mesh lid in place.

I've got the tarantula cage under one arm and all seven white mice, which are riding in a pillowcase. Once outside, I go through the gate, past the semicollapsed garage into the alley to where the sticker bushes are, set the pillowcase down, and give it a poke. The mice nose their way out and disappear into the bramble.

"The mice just escaped," I announce to the kids as I come back through the gate.

"Wanda ate gum off the fence," Dale reports.

Wanda is hanging upside down from the rusty jungle gym. She opens her mouth and something purple lands in the dirt. "Dale stole money," she calls out.

"Shut up and stay there," I tell them.

"Our mom said if you told us to shut up one more time, she'd shut *you* up for good," Renee informs me. This has the unmistakable ring of truth to it—her mother has a thatch of black hair that she sets on hot curlers every morning, and once when she was taking out the curlers, she said, "Look," and when I looked she had popped out her false tooth and was leering like a jack-o'-lantern.

So far, no smoke is visible outdoors, but when we go back inside, the hallway is swirling, and it stinks quite a bit, more like a toilet paper fire now than a campfire. It takes both of us to handle the rat snake aquarium; we're staggering, trying not to breathe, but we both hate the rat snake and are scared it will get loose, so we stop and rescue some food to pile on top—a box of cereal and some flat packages of cheese—and then lug it toward the door.

The snake, agitated, puts his head under a corner of the lid, and about four inches of him leaks out, right near my hand. I start screaming and then Felicia sees him undulating there and starts screaming too. For a moment, we revolve in panicked circles, holding the aquarium between us and screaming. The sound is so loud and frightening in the narrow, smogged hallway that we calm down and use a package of cheese to direct him back inside where he belongs.

"Now what are we supposed to do?" Felicia asks, once we're outside.

The children, clustered by their swing set, stare over our heads. Behind us, like a dragon, their house has begun to exhale long tendrils of smoke.

Forget fathers, forget teachers: our mothers are the ones with the answers, the only people who know something about everything, although it's true that the answers are never that great and that both mothers are incredibly bossy and both have at least one disturbing trait. For Felicia's mother, it's a bad back that can go out on a moment's notice, freezing her in place; for my mother, it's a deep manlike voice that frightens people. Felicia's mother, Phyllis, works downtown at an optometrist's office, answering the phone and polishing eyeglasses; my mother works near the river at a cement company, typing and doing accounting.

We call Phyllis about any issue involving the kids and their behavior, and call my mom about anything having to do with food or household troubles. Both mothers are in the dark—obviously—about the snakes, the furred spider, the pink-nosed mice, and the occasional late-afternoon visits by a rival motorcycle gang called the Cherry Pickers.

We call the Kozak parents about nothing; we don't even know where they go during the day, each of them riding off on their own motorcycle. Yvonne wears green hospital scrubs and black leather chaps; Chuck wears jeans that fasten somewhere underneath his stomach, and tall clanking boots with buckles; they both wear leather jackets year-round that say *King Dong* on the back.

"Sand and Gravel," my mom says in her at-work voice. "How may I help you?"

"Hi," I say. I'm in the back hallway with my head out the door, the phone cord stretched as far as it will go.

"Uh-oh," she says over the sound of typewriters, her own and that of her co-workers, Trish and Char, women my mother mentions incessantly around the house. "Now what?"

Once I tell her, there's no way around something hideous happening. I knew we should've called Phyllis, who is more erratic but also pliant. A toxic cloud of smoke is starting to come out the doorway, swirling past us into the bright summer air of the cluttered yard. Felicia raises her eyebrows at me and steps backward, down the porch steps.

"What, quick, I'm busy," my mom says, lighting a cigarette into the telephone.

"Well," I say. "Something's on fire here."

"What do you mean, something's on fire?" she barks. All the background typing stops.

"There's *some* smoke, not too much," I say.

"Don't say *some*," Felicia hisses. "Say *lots,* but that it was Derek, not us."

"I heard that," my mother says quickly. "Where are the kids?"

"Out," I say.

"Where are you?" she asks.

"In," I say.

"Get out *right now*," she tells me.

"Don't call the fire department," I plead.

"Out," she says. "And get those kids far away from the house."

"This is embarrassing!" I cry, slamming the phone down.

We move the children to the next-door neighbor's yard, a place so beautifully mowed and toyless that it might as well be in another dimension. The man, Mr. Vandevoort, uses a table knife to make a narrow moat between the grass and the sidewalk; Mrs. Vandevoort grows rosebushes along the side of the house and petunias in a painted tire. She wears white ankle socks and comes out briskly clapping her hands whenever a crow settles on the lawn. It's a good thing they're at work, because they would not like knowing that the Kozak children are standing on their grass. We set the snakes and the spider under their picnic table and frantically call Lurch, the German shepherd, over and over, until he gets to his feet, hobbles across the yard, and stares through the open gate.

"You're gonna get burned up!" the children shriek at him. Stewart sprints over, tugs on the dog's collar twice, and then gives up and sprints back. Lurch sits down and cocks his head, listening, then points his nose into the air and makes a high, thin howl.

A siren can be heard off in the distance.

As it turns out, the firemen, who we were afraid of, are nicer than my own mother, who we both are and aren't afraid of. She pulls up in the Oldsmobile, smoking a cigarette and accompanied by Trish and Char, also smoking cigarettes. At that point the firemen have already unrolled their hose and carried it inside the house. They haven't even bothered to latch their boots, and in fact behave more like garbage men, swinging on and off their truck, banging things around, and carrying on conversations that aren't about fire.

Right as my mother and her friends pile out of the car, the firemen begin breaking all the windows in the third floor. My mother stares upward, through dark green sunglasses.

"Goddamn it," she says.

Felicia and I have now joined the ranks of the children; we stand side by side on the Vandevoorts' grass, me holding Miles in his wet diaper, Felicia with her hands over Wanda's ears. Shattering glass and shouted orders for two minutes and then it's over.

"Hi, I'm responsible for these two," my mother explains to the fireman in charge, pointing at us. "They're only fourteen."

You can tell he's the chief because he looks like a fireman from a television show. He has carried forth from the house the charred skeleton of a wicker wastebasket and a molten hunk of turquoise plastic that used to be the diaper pail.

"The fire was contained to the third-floor bathroom," he tells her. "And it wasn't even a fire, actually, although we soaked the room pretty extensively—you just have to," he explains apologetically. "It looks like what they said: matches and toilet paper. This thing"—he inclines his head toward the melted plastic pail, a hunk of brown diaper still visible—"is where the noxious smell came from. Second and first floors, they need some fans going for a couple of hours and it'll clear out okay. We gave them free air-conditioning on the third floor."

My mother and her friends talk in low voices while the men roll up the hose and kick the shards of glass off the driveway. One of the ones wearing his rubber coat open over an undershirt points to the bare feet of the children and then to the glass. Feet, glass. Get it? The children nod obediently, struck dumb by the dazzling celebrity of all this.

Miles, clasped against my dampening T-shirt, takes a plastic shovel out of his mouth and points it at the big red truck in the driveway.

"Fire fuck," he whispers.

My mother takes her colleagues back to the office and then returns with two old, clattering fans to add to the ones that are already going, and a grocery sack full of worn-out bath towels. When all the fans are set up it's like a terrible, rattling wind tunnel, smelly, and then my mother makes me and Felicia wipe down the front hall with damp rags.

The kids sit at the kitchen table while my mother scrubs the vinyl tablecloth and then makes them lunch from what she finds in the icebox.

"We're having chicken!" Stewart cries.

"It's tuna fish, poophead," Wanda says. She looks at my

mother with a mixture of challenge and awe. "Huh? He's got poop on his head."

"*Hey*," my mother says. She stares down at Wanda until Wanda closes her eyes, picks up her sandwich, and takes a bite, then sets it back down, half on the plate and half on the tablecloth.

"She's blind," says Dale helpfully. "She can't even see the poop on her *own* head."

"If I hear any more of that, you'll all be spanked," my mother says. "I don't fool around."

"They're finally gonna get it," I whisper to Felicia. Our bucket is full of black, oily water now and we're done cleaning, just waiting for my mother to leave, slapping at the walls and the baseboards only when she walks by the doorway.

"*We're* the ones who are gonna get it," Felicia whispers back. "We burned up their house."

For a moment, we both have an image of Chuck, in his boots and cracked leather jacket, the overhang of the stomach, the walrus mustache, the way we have seen him grab Yvonne by the waist in order to say something in her ear. She's not exactly petite, either—Felicia saw her pick up Stewart by the neck once and give him a toss. In going through their dresser drawers, we've come across black-and-white photos of Yvonne and Chuck and some of their friends, all stark naked in a variety of shocking tableaus. The pictures are mostly of couples and groups, squirming around on gray bedclothes or outside on blankets with rocks in the background—all except one, of an older woman wearing a sailor's hat and nothing else. She's lying on a bed grinning into the camera and saluting. We used to stare at it every few days for a long time, trying to make sense of her pose, her expression, the deep dirtiness of the whole endeavor. Then one day she showed up at the house, with a very large teenage girl in blue jeans. The two of them sat on the back steps, smoking and drinking Pepsi, and ended up leaving right before Yvonne and Chuck came home. The older woman was wearing a tank top and she didn't have on a sailor hat, but it was definitely her.

We can't even anticipate what these people are capable of. Derek is missing, my mother is trespassing, the house is coated in soot, the ice cream bars are melted. Felicia begins to cry.

"Don't cry or she'll never leave," I beg in a whisper.

"W-w-w-we're deh-heh-head," she sobs. "*Deh*-heh-head."

A crowd appears in the doorway, the kids clustered behind my mother.

"No use in crying, Flea," she says briskly. "This isn't your doing, it's theirs." She means Derek, Yvonne, Chuck, the entire crew of Kozaks, for calling all this attention to themselves. The children gaze up at her, a tall, sandwich-making woman with a deep voice who can make the babysitters mind.

"She better go home," Renee suggests to my mother. "Right?"

"Wrong," my mother replies.

Go home! Home, where it's somebody's job to babysit *us*. We wish fervently that we'd listened to ourselves and not taken this job. All to get clothes! Specifically, a pair of tweed wool culottes with a matching jacket for me and a navy blue sweaterdress for Felicia. Those are the outfits that started the whole problem, which has now expanded to fisherman's sweaters, Nehru shirts, two-toned Capezios, a plaid wool miniskirt, green corduroy flannel-cuffed shorts, et cetera. And all on layaway at the Style, a store we wouldn't even have the nerve to go into if we weren't hopped up on all this income.

We do enjoy our Saturdays, though, after a hard workweek. Our pattern is to sleep late, at one or the other of our houses, and then walk uptown to eat at Weigandt's, a soda fountain run by a family with prominent noses. Even their littlest kids have to work there, counting jelly beans and putting them in Baggies with twist ties; their grandmother sits slumped at the cash register with her hands tucked in her armpits; one of their teenagers waits on us. I always order the same thing: iced tea with sugar and two bananas sliced into a bowl of mayonnaise. Felicia gets navy bean soup, fried baloney, and the same thing as me to drink. From there, we walk downtown to shop at the Style, picking out new items and laying them away along with the old ones; then we go to Carlson's, our downtown's depart ment store, to use the bathroom on the fifth floor, which has pale blue carpeting that I once threw up on. Then we go to the dime store and poke through bins of crap—buttons, hairnets, shoehorns, clothespins—until we're in a bad mood; then we go to Felicia's mom's office and wait to get a ride back up the hill with her.

The optometrist's office is grubby and stale, with withered, dusty plants climbing all over inside the front window, and the optometrist himself wears thick, smudged glasses; it's like peering into a pond to look him in the eye.

"Here they are again," he always says, leaning out from behind his curtain. "Frick and her friend Frack."

Felicia's mom's working at an optometrist's office is why Felicia had contact lenses before anyone else had even heard of them. They are virtually invisible and yet still have to be located when they pop out onto the floor or float off their mark, drifting like unmoored rafts into the farthest bloodshot reaches of her eyeballs.

My mother disapproves of the whole concept of contact lenses—the idea of putting a shard of glass in your eye! "I don't know what Phyllis is thinking," she said. "This doctor has her over a barrel."

"It's a new thing!" I tried to explain.

"Yes," she replied, arching a brow. "They've got to have the crème de la crème over there." She'd never forgiven Felicia's mother for buying a blue fur couch and armchair. Not fur like a real animal, but fur like a stuffed animal.

Right now the smoke and the crying have irritated Felicia's eyes to the point where she has to switch to glasses, turning her into an earlier horn-rimmed version of herself. She immediately resumes the unconscious habit of wrinkling her nose upward to reset the heavy glasses when they slip down.

"Here comes the witch of witcherton," she says, staring at herself in the hall mirror. Actually, if one of us is good looking, it's her. She's tall and elegant, green eyed, although her teeth are slightly out of order, and she isn't particularly neat.

I, on the other hand, am neat, but that's about it. The body is wrong, scrawny; the face is pale and nondescript under its suntan. I talk with a faint sibilance that people think comes from the gap between my front teeth but that actually comes from me trying to be like Dee Jurgenmeyer, a girl from my childhood who had a real lisp. Once I started it, I couldn't stop, even when they sent us both to speech therapy and Dee was cured. The hair is the best feature, limp but long and silky. I don't particularly like having nice hair, though, because it gives people the wrong impression about me.

It's like a mysterious stranger I saw in a movie once, who everyone thought was a beautiful lost child in a red cape. From a distance all you could see besides the swirling cape was a head of lustrous hair. A man finally grabbed the child by the hood and turned it around and it was a leering dwarf; the man screamed, and everyone at the movie screamed too. That's why I mostly wear my hair in braids.

In fact, my mother does finally return to work, after taking it upon herself to leave her phone number and a note of explanation on the kitchen table. She also put the kids down for naps, something we never even bothered trying before.

"That's a good way to get a fire started," Felicia says as they troop upstairs.

As soon as my mother's gone, we tear up her note and the phone number. One by one the children drift back downstairs to stare at us.

"That lady was mean," Wanda says admiringly.

Dale is staring out the window. Suddenly he bolts for the back door. "Here come the cops!" he shrieks. "Here come the cops!"

The children disperse like vapor, all but Miles, who clings to my leg, sobbing.

There's a cop on the front porch, fitted out with a gun and holster. Felicia and I open the door together; Miles goes limp and lets me lift him off my leg and onto my hip.

"Who's in charge here?" the cop asks.

"The parents are, but they aren't home," Felicia says in a whisper. "We're here right now, but her mother was in charge." She gestures toward me and quickly retreats behind her hair, the straw curtain.

"She stepped out," I lie. Felicia nods vigorously at the floor.

"So, you the babysitters?" he asks.

"We were, we aren't sure now," Felicia says evasively. She looks steadfastly past the barbered edges of his head. Behind him, next to the door, is a round leaded-glass window with a number of BBs lodged in it.

"You didn't call the fire department when you had a fire," the cop states, as though he's reading it off a police report. "Out of 'embarrassment,' that right?"

"No," I say. "We did call." He's slightly fat and has got several things swinging from his waistline, including a radio, a leather nightstick, a long-handled flashlight, and a pair of handcuffs.

"Well, next time keep in mind," he says, "you could end up literally dying of embarrassment."

"We called!" Felicia insists, looking at him directly for the first time. In fact, glaring. "How else do you think the firemen got here?"

He stares at us, chewing a thin strand of gum, one hand resting on the knob of his nightstick. We stare back for a while and then give up and look off to the side. "I need to talk to the boy who started the blaze," he says finally.

"We don't know where he is," I tell the cop. "Nobody knows."

A voice comes ringing down from above. "He's at Victor's!" Renee calls out. A moment later she appears on the landing, wearing a swimsuit and a pair of boots. "He thinks the whole house is burned down."

"Well, I'll be sure and let him know," the cop says generously, "if you tell me where Victor lives."

She stares down at us, scratching at her leg inside the rubber boot. The cop looks at me.

"Tell him, Renee," I order her.

She turns and runs up again, into the farthest reaches of the ruined house.

Felicia sighs and heads outside the back way; Miles puts his hands on my cheeks and turns my face toward his. "Cah?" he asks moistly.

"Cop," I tell him, and then feel confused. Is that wrong, to say cop? "Policeman," I clarify.

Felicia returns in half a minute with Stewart; she's got his arm twisted behind his back so he has to walk sideways up the front steps.

"Okay, I don't like to see that," the cop tells her. She lets him go.

Stewart's face is streaked with tears, and his white hair is pressed against his pale pink head. His shorts are a size too small. He tugs at the front of them.

"Let me ask you, pal," the cop says to Stewart. He moves closer and then tries to crouch, but his gear rides up on him. He puts a knee down to steady himself. "Can you tell me where Victor lives?"

Stewart nods.

Normally, right before the parents get home we do all the housework we were supposed to be doing during the day, dividing up the tasks and either bribing or forcing any of the kids we can get our hands on to help us. Today all we can do in the final hour is walk around in circles, eating the last of the bag of chocolate chips.

"Them are for cookies," Wanda says, appearing in the doorway of the kitchen.

"Here," Felicia says. Wanda holds out her hand and receives a pile.

"Mr. Vandevoort wants to talk to you," Wanda says, putting all of them in her mouth at once and then holding out her hand for more.

"Why?" I ask her.

She holds out the hand insistently.

Felicia and I go into the backyard, pick our way barefoot across the glass-strewn lawn and over to the driveway, where Mr. Vandevoort is standing in his work clothes—a short-sleeved shirt and a narrow necktie—staring at the upper stories of the Kozak house.

"I got glass everywhere," he informs us. "It's clear out on the street."

We don't know what to say.

"Those kids said there was a fire," he goes on. "Normally I wouldn't believe it, but I see where all the windows are knocked out up there."

We turn around obediently and look along with him. The third floor is gaping.

"There's liable to be slivers where I parked my car," he says, shaking his head. "And I don't know what was done in my yard—I hope nothing—but I see over there where somebody has left some empty aquariums under the picnic table."

We follow him over and sure enough: empty aquariums under the picnic table. The wire mesh has been pushed aside.

"What are empty aquariums doing under my picnic table?" he asks.

He's got to be crazy if he thinks either one of us is answering that question. We remain silent, watching our bare feet carefully as we lug the aquariums into the Kozaks' garage and throw a tarp over them. The tarantula cage is nowhere to be found, but then we find it. The tarantula is sitting on his Styrofoam boulder as usual, waiting for someone to feed him flies.

The kids have scattered, all except Miles, who is right where I left him, clasping the porch railing. He climbs onto my lap when I sit down on the steps. I rest my chin on his head and try not to think about how all this looks — the sopping, blackened bathroom, the mound of smoky sheets that were peeled off the beds and kicked downstairs, the grimy rags hanging from the banisters and doorknobs, the skyline of dirty dishes stacked along the kitchen counter.

"This is all Derek's fault," I say tentatively, trying it out.

"Maybe," Felicia says uncertainly. The problem is, since Derek hasn't been spotted since before the fire was even reported, he seems somehow the least guilty of all of us.

Lurch staggers to his feet and teeters across the yard, his tail waving. We listen. Off in the distance is the angry buzz of an unmuffled motorcycle.

"That's my dad's hog," Renee calls down from the third floor.

Both parents arrive at the same time, and the children materialize at the curb, talking and shoving. Chuck and Yvonne, climbing off their bikes and unfastening their helmets, ignore them. Yvonne shakes her flattened hair and then pauses.

"What?" she says, grabbing Renee by the shirt.

Renee is instantly struck dumb.

Yvonne makes her way toward us, her dark-circled eyes

scanning the front of the house, the porch, me, and then past me, to Felicia. "You," she says. "Explain."

As Felicia talks, the rest of the world gets quieter and quieter. Next door, Mr. Vandevoort stands holding a broom, his back to us, listening. Wherever Mrs. Vandevoort is, she's listening too. *Matches, Derek, toilet paper, smoke, her mother*— their eyes flicker to me, and my mouth goes as dry as kindling—*firemen, hose, glass.*

A long pause. Mr. Vandevoort resumes sweeping.

Yvonne looks at Dale. "You," she says. "Get my cigarettes."

Dale races from the porch to her motorcycle and flings open the saddlebag, races back with a pack of Old Golds and a lighter. He's panting.

Chuck has been standing silently, staring two burn holes into Felicia. He suddenly glances over at Wanda. "You," he says. "Get my gun."

Wanda edges uncertainly toward the house, her eyes on Yvonne's face. "Should I?" she asks.

Chuck barks out an unpleasant laugh, and the children begin sidling away. Yvonne lights a cigarette on her way into the house, letting the door slam sharply.

"It's not our fault Derek won't mind," Felicia says suddenly, loudly, to the porch.

Chuck stares at her in disbelief, unfolding his arms. Suddenly he stops, glaring past us.

"Cah," Miles says, turning my face toward the street.

The patrol car glides to a stop in front of the house, lights whirling. The siren burps once, summoning all the neighbors to their front windows.

"You got the law on me?" Chuck asks, his voice low and

poisonous. He hesitates for just a second and then walks slowly toward the cop, who is pulling Derek out of the backseat.

Inside the house, Yvonne has dumped the sheets down the basement steps and then gone upstairs to change. She comes back down wearing cutoffs and a halter top. Her hair has been raked back into a rubber band and it looks like she's crying a little.

"He stinks," she says to me, nodding at Miles, who is still on my hip.

I go upstairs with Miles while Felicia goes to the basement with the sheets. Even though it isn't a bad one, I linger over the diaper change, peering out the bedroom window to the curb, where the cop is talking to Derek, whose head is down, and Chuck, who is staring into the distance and nodding. Miles points to the soiled diaper, to the clean diaper, to the powder, and to me.

"Me," he says.

I can't tell whether we're fired or not, but I'm starting to hope we are. Down in the living room, Yvonne is smoking and watching out the window. When the cop climbs into his squad car again and Chuck turns Derek toward the house with a hand on the back of his neck, we all scramble to the kitchen. Yvonne lights a cigarette off the one she has going and then gets a can of beer out of the fridge. From the back hall comes the rustling of children, quietly congregating like birds on a telephone wire.

The front door slams and Miles clings more tightly to my neck, like a baby monkey. A jostling from the back stairs, a sniff, and then silence.

Derek enters the kitchen first, landing against the far wall like a discarded boot. He remains hunched there, head down, hands in his pockets.

"Is this the one you can't make mind?" Chuck thunders at Felicia.

She glares at Chuck, her hands balled into fists at her side, refusing to answer. He never even glances at me—one of the benefits of being a sidekick—but snaps his fingers at Yvonne, who opens the refrigerator and sets another beer on the table. He pops the top, takes a leisurely swig, and stares at Derek's bowed head.

"Com'ere, you little turd," Chuck says.

Derek shakes his head no.

We've always thought of Derek as a large, overbearing kid who shouts out words we've only seen in spray paint. A shin kicker, an arm twister, a worm flinger. In fact, we see now, he's a lot smaller than we are, a narrow-shouldered boy with a big head and Yvonne's dark circles under his eyes.

"Com'ere," Chuck says again.

From the back stairs, Renee's voice: "Dad, no!" she cries.

Back when I was eight, a tall, skinny girl in my gym class named Alma Rupes flung herself into a cartwheel and landed right on top of mc. It was like being whacked in the side of the head by the long wooden paddles of a windmill—I was stunned, literally, and for an hour or so afterward everything I looked at was in high relief, like a 3-D movie. I kept saying to the school nurse, "Everything looks funny," my voice hollow and loud, as though someone had their hands over my ears.

That's what's happening now; the kitchen has become distant and silent, more like grainy footage of a kitchen. Stark, depressing details are suddenly visible: the window propped open with a Pepsi bottle, the light switch surrounded by a black halo of grime, the crumb-filled toaster with a Wonder bread wrapper melted to its flank. Everything. I swing Miles around to the front so he's facing me, and I'm seeing it all through the blond fuzz of his staticky hair.

Chuck takes one step, grabs Derek by the upper arm and lifts him off the floor like a stick. Derek is stiff and resistant, and his eyes are closed.

"You don't know how to make this one mind?" Chuck asks Felicia.

The evening sun has moved down a notch, glinting off the metal edge of the counter, the sweating can of beer, Felicia's glasses. She thrusts them back up where they belong and continues glaring at Chuck.

He drags Derek by the wrist over to the stove and turns the burner on.

"Don't!" Felicia cries.

Yvonne turns her back on the scene, opens the freezer and takes out an ice tray.

Chuck yanks Derek's hand over the flame and holds it there while the boy struggles, like a worm on a hook.

"Stop it," Felicia gasps, crying helplessly.

The boy's face is twisted into a breathless grimace; he kicks at his father's legs and Chuck plunges the hand into the blue part of the flame. Derek starts shrieking.

In the flame.

The hand is cooking.

Still in the flame.

The screams are like sharp blasts from a horn.

Suddenly, there is a fuming, scorched smell in the kitchen, and Derek collapses on the floor. Chuck strides out of the house. When the door closes behind him, a chorus of crying starts up in the back hall.

Yvonne cracks the ice tray and empties it into a dish towel. A motorcycle roars to life and Felicia stumbles out of the room. Yvonne claps her hands once, summoning Miles out of my arms.

Derek is slumped on the linoleum, the dish towel in his lap, staring at the hand—brick red up to the wrist and strangely tight looking, like an inflated rubber glove.

Yvonne claps again, sharply, and holds out her hands, but Miles grips my waist and won't let go. She pulls him away, like taffy, as he fights to hang on.

"Me!" he cries out in desperation, searching my face. "Me!"

I peel his fingers from my neck, one by one.

His cries, hollow and lonely, follow me as I join my friend outside and walk quickly away, past Lurch, who stands trembling next to his doghouse, past Mrs. Vandevoort in her white socks and pruning gloves, and past the blond snake, waiting in the green crew-cut grass at her feet.

We live in a factory town, Zanesville, Illinois, the farm implement capital of the world. This means nothing to Felicia and me; we care only about our own neighborhood, everything between our two houses, a handful of potholed streets and alleys lined with two-story homes and one-car garages. We have a couple of busy intersections with four-way stop signs, a red brick barbershop, a corner tavern, a taxidermist, a family who paved their backyard and painted it green, and a house where the garage has been turned into a tap-dance studio. Otherwise, it's all the same, every block, through our neighborhood and the neighborhoods beyond.

My mother can't stand the tap-dance teacher, who wears her hair in a tall unstable beehive and has a daughter named Shelley who was in my class all during elementary school, a tiny, dazzling creature with kinky tresses and an overwrought personality. During our early years, Shelley had wild, seizure-like temper tantrums—she would utter a series of sharp shrieks and then for three minutes became a blur of hair ribbons and pistoning Mary Janes. Everyone adored her because she was out of the ordinary, but nevertheless she was sent away at some point, to a distant grandmother.

"They sent that little girl to live on a farm," my mother said at the time, not to me but to someone on the telephone.

Shelley's mom's studio is where Felicia and I part company to go to our separate houses. Felicia's route is stepping through a hedge and sliding down a steep terrace; mine is a scurry along someone's back walk, past their windows, eyes averted, and down their front steps.

Over on my block, the semi-interesting people include a woman who comes outside and washes her dog's face with a dishcloth every hour or so, and a widowed man who is so gigantic he needs a kitchen chair to get to his car, alternating between using it as a walker and sitting on it to rest. He calls himself Pudgy, and we call him that too. One coincidence: we also have a neighbor named Fudgy, or Uncle Fudge, a barber with no hair of his own. Next door is Old Milly, whose middle-aged drunken nephews come over and make trouble at her house. My sister and I, from our upstairs bedroom, can look down at night into Old Milly's kitchen and watch what's going on, the staggering and shoving. Once very late at night we saw her niece, a stout, red-faced nurse named Shorty, kissing a man in a way that made us sick.

Otherwise, not much fascinating. A lot of dogs: the clean-faced Jeffy; a white dog with a blue eye named Chief; a black toy poodle named Trinket; our own dog, Tammy, a rat terrier who bites when cornered; and Curly, Old Milly's thick-shouldered, bowlegged, and unpredictable dog. All the dogs in the neighborhood are tied out, so there's a lot of ambient barking and animals on their hind legs at the end of chains, staring at back doors. Curly is the only one who never gets to come inside. He's pumpkin colored with a gnarled head, and he lives in a four-foot dirt circle underneath an apple tree, with a lean-to for cover. Old Milly is the only one who goes near him, feeding him every morning from a rusty cake pan. A few times each winter, if it's going to get thirty or forty below, she'll snap a leash on his collar and drag him to the cellar door and push him down there for the night. That's his entire life, twelve years and counting.

He lifts his orange face as I go up the back walk, and then settles it back on his paws. Our dog, Tammy, is inside, tethered to the basement door, up on her hind legs watching everyone eat dinner. She runs immediately under the table when I unclip her leash.

Dinner is fried chicken, mashed potatoes, creamed corn, hot rolls, et cetera. My dad is sober, it looks like. He's wearing lawn-mowing clothes, listening to my mother tell him about the fire. She stops, chicken leg in hand, when she sees my face. "Now they've had *you* crying?"

"No," I say. My older sister, Meg, looks me over briefly and then goes back to her book and her sculpted tower of mashed potatoes. My brother has a full plate but is eating from a bowl of cornflakes and milk. Tammy has stationed herself underneath him so he can pass things down to her — a dinner roll, a glob of potatoes, and a leaf of iceberg lettuce, which she is standing on.

"You should've seen this crew," my mother tells my dad. "Kids running loose everywhere. Boy, she must be a real doll, that woman."

"Uh-oh," he says.

My dad is a door-to-door siding salesman. He is tall and tanned, with the haunted brown eyes of someone who does something terrible for a living. Some days he can't even bring himself to leave the house, but sits at the kitchen table clearing his throat and making notes on a clipboard that he keeps pushing back and forth, lining it up with different edges of the table.

"Don't ever be afraid to call the fire department," my father says to me. "It's those guys' job, they don't mind."

"Firemen can do kung fu," my brother, Raymond, says. He is seven and has a light brown forelock and the same warm, shattered eyes as my father.

"That older girl was a snot," my mother continues, reaching behind her to the cluttered counter to take a drag off a cigarette. "And the baby looked half-anemic."

The front of my T-shirt is stretched out from Miles gripping it. I'm childless now, and unemployed.

My mother looks at me, cigarette held above her head with the elbow cupped in one hand. "I'll bet you ten bucks they didn't even bother disciplining that kid, did they?" She exhales and the top third of the room swirls with smoke.

"Did they?" she asks again.

After the dishes, I'm heading over to Felicia's to stay overnight; we're going to make a pan of fudge and try to figure out how to get our clothes out of hock. I press my spoon into a bowl of red Jell-O, carving out a big shimmering piece for myself.

"That's fine, but it isn't your whole dinner," my mother says.

I've had other bad babysitting experiences, once locking a scratching girl in a bathroom, once eating five jars of blueberry buckle baby food and claiming to the parents that their baby ate it, and for several months being the Saturday night babysitter for a four-year-old named Daniel who couldn't move or talk—a large, beautiful child with creamy white skin and black hair. Before they went out for the evening, his parents, Trent and Lisa, would carry him out and place him on a stack of quilts on the floor in the living room so he could stare at the ceiling while I watched TV. I did have to change his diaper, which was disorienting at first because of how big he was, but eventually it was just the same as changing a baby—even easier, because he never struggled at all, just watched me with his wide, damp eyes.

Anyone would have thought it was the perfect job, but it began to get to me, the way his slim, pretty mother, who looked exactly like Daniel except for her lipstick, would hug him and arrange his legs on the quilt, then the long evenings of television shows, broken only by me kneeling next to him on the floor, checking for drafts and dabbing his mouth with the soft bib that was snapped to his collar. They bought special food for me, each week something different—boxes of Ding Dongs, bags of corn chips, cookies—and would send what I didn't eat home with me. They paid me more than anyone ever had. "Daniel just loves you," Lisa would say insistently, as I stared uncertainly at the cash.

After a few months I began to feel a terrible skin-prickling loneliness as soon as they left, in the shadowy house with nothing but a bowl of Bugles and the champagne music of *Lawrence Welk*. I was unable to quit and needed my mother to do it for me, but she wouldn't. It was just the idea of hurting Lisa's feelings—of her thinking I didn't love Daniel as much as he loved me—and the thought of her there every day, all day, in her sneakers and apron, hair tied in a bandanna. The last time I babysat for them, I got so lonely and upset that I called home so my mother could hear how unraveled I had become, but my parents were at the tavern—it was a Saturday night—and so my sister walked over in the dark and kept me company. We sat eating caramel corn out of a bucket-size tin until the parents' headlights swept across the ceiling, at which point Meg got up and put her shoes on, leaving through the front as they were coming in the back. We passed her when Trent drove me home a few minutes later, a tall girl in a white blouse, walking along in the dark.

"At least these ones weren't retarded," Meg says now, of the Kozak kids, dumping silverware into the rack and spraying it, and me, with scalding water. Meg's style of dishwashing is all sleight of hand—swishing, spraying, and summoning clouds of steam to confuse my mother.

"The dad is," I tell her. That's all I'm willing to say. She can take my own arm and beat me with it, but right now she's in neutral mode, which is where she'll remain until her girlfriend arrives to spend the night, at which point she'll switch over into mean.

I actually like her friend, Edwina, a girl with an extraordinarily long face and shiny, palomino blond hair. Grown-ups call her Edwina, Meg and her other girlfriends call her Whinny, and everyone else calls her Mister Ed. Although my sister has a number of questionable friends, Mister Ed isn't one of them. She rarely tortures younger kids even though younger kids have been known to torture her.

"How's it hanging?" she asks Meg upon arrival.

"It's hanging down," my sister admits.

"How's it hungigungadin?" I say inanely, just to insert myself in the conversation.

Meg reaches over, takes my wrist with both wet hands, and twists the skin in two different directions. Mister Ed diplomatically looks away as I struggle silently against the pain and then give up and holler out.

"Company will go home if you can't get along in there," my mother calls from the dining room.

I go to the doorway. "I'm sleeping over at Felicia's," I tell her.

"You don't tell me what you're doing, you ask," she says, without looking up from her sewing. She's remaking a wool shift that I made last winter in sewing class.

"Can I sleep over at Felicia's?" I ask.

"No," she says, holding up the dress, which she has cut down and removed the darts from. "See? I could have told her: you needed darts like a hole in the head." She believes the home-ec teacher at our junior high to be incompetent. Besides the sleeveless shift, we also learned something called huck toweling, which is a made-up name for a cross-stitch design on a dish towel, and how to make a reversible three-cornered scarf. The shift my mother is working on actually has a matching scarf made out of wool, which gave me a rash under the chin.

"I'm leaving now," I tell her.

Right at the halfway point, Felicia materializes out of the darkness.

"I thought I was coming to your house," she says.

"No, I'm coming to yours," I tell her. From where we're standing—on a sidewalk shielded by a hedge—we can see right into the Casper house, where another kid I went to elementary school with lives. A boy with the ruinous name Milton, and a buzz cut to go along with it. Inside the Casper living room, a man is sitting on the sofa folding laundry.

"What did your mother make for dinner?" Felicia asks.

"My mother made french fries out of a bag."

Her mother makes the food I like and my mother makes the food she likes. All the extra fried chicken Raymond didn't eat and I didn't eat is back there, sitting on the counter, waiting for my dad to get hungry again. Nevertheless, we can't go back to my house because there are too many people over there. We have to sleep on the living room floor when Meg has a guest, and last time we did that was in the spring, and Felicia fell all the way down the stairs after a trip to the bathroom in the middle of the night. She cracked her tailbone, had to be taken to the emergency room, and was then made to carry around what looked like a foam rubber toilet seat for a month. At school she shoved it in her locker first thing in the morning and winced her way up and down the halls, sitting on the side of her hip in class and crying in the bathroom. Only at home and at my house would she use the rubber donut, which made a discouraged sighing noise when sat upon.

She's fully recovered now, able to slide down the mossy terrace in a yard patrolled by a bitten-up cat named Zero. We cross the street and go into her house, the bottom half of a rambling duplex. Felicia's father works the night shift, but her mother is here, still in the white optometrist's dress, lying on the sofa with her shoes off and a cool cloth across her eyes.

"Girls?" she calls out. "Girls? Is somebody there?"

Felicia crosses the room silently and leans over her mother's still form. When Phyllis calls out again, she says, WHAT? scaring the washcloth right off her mother's face.

"Hi there, honey," Phyllis says to me. She gets up on one elbow. "I'm going to tell you like I told Flea: call the fire department if a fire starts in *any* house, I don't care whose."

"We did," I say.

"Well, you did and you didn't," Phyllis says firmly. She settles back onto the couch and drapes the cloth again. "Get yourself some french fries if you're hungry."

"We're sleeping in the camper," Felicia tells her. She puts the afghan across Phyllis's feet and tucks it in. She looks at me and pretends to punch the feet. I pretend to poke her mother's eyes out.

"What are you laughing about?" Phyllis asks. "And I will look out there at eleven o'clock and if I see a light on, you're coming in here to sleep."

"Don't worry," I say. "You won't see a light on."

*   *   *

The camper is a dented metal box on wheels that cranks open and pops out into a half trailer, half tent, with canvas walls, zippered screens, a table nook, a foot of damp carpeting, and a tiny efficiency kitchen. We sleep in the popped-out ends, on wide bunks covered with foam pads, outfitted with sleeping bags and pillows that smell like rain.

We get the lantern lit and zip everything up so nobody can see inside, and then we creep out, down the pitch-dark alley to an abandoned garage, cobwebby and collapsing, where our kittens live. There are three of them—a sick one, a friendly one, and a wild one. I don't even know why we went in there in the first place, just looking to see what they had, and the friendly kitten came running up to us. We've been feeding them and playing with them all summer with no one finding out, and we hope to keep it that way.

The wild one is named Ruffles; it has long spiky fur and has to be caught using an old T-shirt. The sick one is mine, a rickety little tortoiseshell named Freckles who has something wrong with his fur. The friendly one is Felicia's, pure shiny black with an intelligent, trustworthy face. We named him Blacky Strout, after a man running for sheriff, whose name and face are on billboards all over town. Once we catch Ruffles and get him tied into the T-shirt, the other two are easy; when they're released inside the camper they go crazy for a while, clawing their way up onto the benches and bunks, attacking our feet.

"Yours is drooling," Felicia says.

It's true, there's more foam on him than usual. He doesn't seem to notice, though, and sits purring on my lap for a few minutes, running his claws reflexively in and out as I pet him. I have an affinity for anything that has peeled-off fur or looks terminal, or, for that matter, for anything that seems to notice me, which this kitten does. When he finally hops down, he turns his freckled face to look up at me. His nose and the rims of his eyes are a tender, sore-looking pink.

"He looks a little bit like the Rebabbit," I tell Felicia. This was her sister's former pet rabbit, which had black-and-white fur and pale pink features. About a year ago the Rebabbit hopped away while we had it out of the cage, went under a series of sticker bushes, and was never heard from again. For a while we'd been able to see it in there, pretending to eat grass, whiskers trembling, crouched over its long velvety paws, waiting to be pounced on either by us or by something worse. Every time we tried to reach it, we got scratched by thorns and the rabbit took a further hop, until eventually all we could glimpse was a disappearing blur of white. The stickers went on for some ways and then blended into the tangle of a dense neighborhood ravine. In there were festering communities of garter snakes, looped over fallen logs, draped haphazardly along the reeds, et cetera. We wouldn't go down there if it were our *own* rabbit.

Felicia's younger sister, Stephanie, had gone predictably berserk. "He was *mine* and they let him *loose!*" she sobbed determinedly, assessing us from behind her fogged glasses, strands of blond hair stuck to her face.

You'd never have guessed Stephanie had not paid one bit of attention to this rabbit and left him moldering in his cage for days at a time, a rubbery uneaten celery stalk poked through the mesh.

Stephanie finally threw a handful of marbles at us, chipping a mirror, and was carted away to the pet store, where she was given the first in a series of doomed goldfish, which suited her much better—the frenzied sprinkling, the eager nibbling, the pomp and circumstance of the funerals.

"What if he's dying?" Felicia says. She holds her toes still as Freckles sniffs at them, his sides heaving back and forth. He produces a wet sneeze and then sits down to clean himself. In the middle of it, he closes his eyes and just sits motionless.

"Uh-oh," Felicia says.

We stare at him together, willing him to perk up. Eventually he opens his eyes again and settles into a catlike crouch, purring and watching us watch him. I feel such an immense and sickening love for him that I panic and have to get out of the camper.

"Food," I say.

Felicia unsnaps the window, peers at the house, and snaps it back up again. We get our berry cups, pour more milk in the kittens' saucer, and tiptoe forth. We forgot shoes, so we have to sneak into the house and get them, then sneak back out again. Phyllis is in the same spot, sound asleep on her side, the washcloth soaking into the blue stuffed-animal fur of the sofa. There's a record player going behind Stephanie's closed door, an off-key voice singing along.

The mulberry patch is four blocks away, in the perfect nighttime yard of some people we've never seen. A neat house, a span of swept patio, a flower garden with a six-inch fence around it, and the mulberry bushes hulking in a black patch of shadow. We crouch on either side of the laden bushes, Felicia in the yard, me in the alley, filling our tin cups silently. Recently we've seen a movie about little English boys who steal out of necessity, and ever since then we've felt better about taking people's fruits and vegetables.

"Plee suh," Felicia says, thrusting her cup through the branches at me, "may oy hev samoa?"

By the time we're done, both of us are purple. We go through alleys to get home, eating berries and listening for cars, stopping only once, at the end of Felicia's block, at the house of a parochial school teenager who has no curtains in his bedroom and does strange things that can be viewed from the street. So far we've seen him hanging from a bar in his underwear, hauling himself up and down in a flurry of desperate chin-ups; we've seen him with a nylon stocking on his bushy hair, pressing it flat; we've seen him doing his homework, tugging at his earlobes and probing gingerly inside a nostril with the point of his pencil; we've seen him talking on a telephone, lying on his stomach across a bed with one leg bent coyly, its sock foot up in the air. It was a girl's pose, actually, although when he hung up he plunged around the room for a while with a Nerf ball jammed in his fist, bobbing back and forth and making leaps. Eventually he stopped and stood there listening, then opened his mouth and yelled something back. Tonight, the whole house is dark.

"Woy, ee ain owm," I say.

We walk along.

"Ay," Felicia says. "Way fugoat to mike the fudge. Fudge. Fudge." She thinks about it and tries again. "Fudge." It can't be said with a British accent.

"Ellow, ow abowt some fudge?" I try. It's true, they must call it something else in England.

Back at the camper, the kittens have worn themselves out

and are in their various states of repose—hiding, dozing, or trembling. At the table sits Felicia's sister, a small smug apparition in shorty pajamas and kneesocks.

"You're in for it," Stephanie says quickly. "In for it. Dead. You've got kittens that you aren't supposed to." She points to Freckles. "That one's sick, and you're probably catching it." She nods, up and down, and waits. "Its eyes are sticking shut," she adds.

Nothing. Some glaring back and forth.

She bolts up and tries scrambling out the door, but Felicia puts her knee in front of it. The camper is pretty small. I do know Stephanie's a fierce fighter when the situation calls for it. She's been known in rare instances to lay Felicia flat, due to the fact that she's fighting out of desperation instead of for recreation. I've seen it happen over at my own house, with me going unexpectedly nuts on my sister.

"Do you want one?" I ask casually. "Because we have an extra."

I pick up Freckles and set him on my knee; he turns his face toward me without opening his eyes and makes a hoarse purring noise for a couple of breaths, then bows his head again. Felicia reaches for Strout, who climbs nimbly up her front and begins kneading, cradled against her T-shirt. In the corner, Ruffles has jammed himself between a cushion and the canvas wall and is staring resolutely at nothing. Long spiky fur frames his face like a lion's mane.

"That one is extra?" Stephanie says uncertainly. "He isn't anybody's?"

"Ruffles is his name," I tell her.

"He named after a tater chip," she says childishly, pursing her lips into a sly, annoying pout. This is not one of her best traits—that she reverts to baby talk anytime she's pleased about something. Fortunately, she isn't pleased that often.

"Your kitten," I explain quickly, "is not like these ones, which are friendly. Yours is *independent*." I try to make it sound like a good thing.

"He my kitty," she says, curling her fingers over so her hands look like blunt little paws. "He my baby kitty." She hops up on the cushion and crawls toward him on her paws and knees, at which point Ruffles rises up with a hiss, bats her about the face, runs up on top of her head, and leaps to the ceiling, where he hangs from the canvas, growling.

There's a knock on the camper first thing the next morning. Before we can answer it, Phyllis pushes the door open and sticks her head in.

"All right," she says. "Show me these cats."

Felicia is on one side and I'm on the other; we crawl from our bunks and shake out our sleeping bags, pick up the pillows and hold them under our arms. Felicia nudges open the cabinet under the sink and Phyllis glances in.

"She was scratched," she says in a scandalized voice. "So I don't want to hear that she made it up. If there were cats and one of them is sick, you better tell me about it right now. I'm waiting."

The carpeting is orange and gray, a loud, spongy pattern. Felicia's sleeping bag slumps but nothing falls out of it. There are no kittens here.

"You cannot keep cats in a camper, and you cannot keep them in the house. We have people who are allergic to cats here." Namely her.

Cats, cats, cats, cats, cats. Cats.

"I'm sick over this," my mother says when I wander through my own back door. It's Saturday, so she's home stirring up a domestic crisis: homemade noodles hang everywhere in the kitchen, from the towel racks, from the curtain rods, over the backs of chairs. She's got a cigarette in the ashtray and one between her fingers.

"You have two cigarettes going at once," I tell her.

"Yesterday I'm calling Phyllis and today she's calling me," she continues, "and you two are supposed to be teenagers. If you don't have any more sense than to harbor some kind of feral cats, I don't know. And neither does Phyllis. We're both fit to be tied."

I take a long, limp worm to eat—the floury dough looks somehow like sugary dough, even though I know it isn't.

"You eat raw noodles, they'll make you so ill you won't know what hit you," she says. This isn't true; I've been eating raw noodles for years, every time thinking they're going to taste good. "Phyllis's of the opinion you're late bloomers; I told her the hell with that. I want you to quit pulling this kind of shit and act your age, both you and Flea."

I hate the phrase *late bloomers*. It sounds old fashioned and vaguely rank, like something a prairie woman would wear under her sweaty calico dress.

I curl my fingers under and hold out my paws. *Me little baby.*

She stares, smoking, until the phone rings. "Oh, I'm just standing here talking to this kid of mine," she explains to the caller, still eyeing me, "telling her she better watch out."

I take my bird outside to the picnic table to clean his cage. My dad is staking tomato plants, tearing a sheet into narrow strips.

"He was sure singing this morning, honey," he calls to me. "I took his cover off, and boy, did he go to town."

I've had a lot of birds in my life — green and blue parakeets, zebra finches, and singing canaries like this one — which is one reason I can't have a kitten. I did have a temporary cat once, a stray from the neighborhood named Inky, who came by of an evening and let me wrap him in a pink doll blanket and put him to bed in an empty window box on the front porch. Eventually he broke into the house and was discovered by my mother, draped over the bird cage, one long black arm inside, groping for the canary, who was clinging to his cuttlebone.

That cat Inky was never seen again, and a determined, unapologetic silence would settle over my parents whenever his name was brought up. I still have the pink doll blanket with his hair on it in a box that contains other keepsakes — a little hat I wore in kindergarten that had yarn pigtails and a girl's face embroidered on the back of the head, a drawing of my grandfather in heaven sitting across from God at a two-legged table, and a fan letter I wrote to Tramp from *Lady and the Tramp*.

The canary loves the sunlight, although he can easily bake in it, and begins trilling wildly as I replace the newspaper, sprinkle gravel on it, sand off each of his perches, and pry the hardened crap off his swing. On second thought, I remove the tray again and put a bowl of water in there. My dad comes over and we watch the canary take a series of blustery, cage-soaking baths.

"Now he's really going to sing for you," my dad predicts, but he actually doesn't, and my dad goes back to tearing the sheet into bandages. It's 10 A.M. and he's already been drinking.

*   *   *

Since it's Saturday, Felicia and I are walking downtown to look at our clothes. We've fallen into a vast pit of depression over our troubles—collapsing kitten, burned boy, incarcerated outfits—and barely talk most of the way. At Weigandt's we order our food and sit silently until it comes, carried aloft by the teenage waitress, who looks as miserable as us, her dirty hair crammed into pigtails. The bananas are clumped at the bottom of the mayonnaise, and I pry them apart, one by one.

At the Style we page rapidly through the things on the racks, overcome with the usual desperation to have all of it, even the things that don't fit. Today they have mix-and-match sweater-vests made to go with items we already own. We stand in the fitting room talking for a long time about whether to add them to our roster of unpaid-for outfits. The saleslady at some point comes in and asks if she can help us.

"No, thank you," we whisper through the slatted door.

When we leave, the sweater-vests are back on the table, folded into soft candy-colored bundles. Outside, there's a bright headachy glare and a snarl of pedestrian confusion—a gang of grubby boys on Sting-Ray bicycles have hopped the curb and are weaving erratically down the sidewalk, terrorizing the townsfolk. Right in the middle of them is Derek. We brace for the worst, but instead of coming after us, shouting cusswords, he gives a shy surprised grin and, steering with one hand, extricates himself from the snarl of bikes, turns around, and rides back to us.

"Hi," he says, still smiling, lifting his free hand in a sheepish wave. The hand is thickly and inexpertly bandaged, already dirty and unraveling. The tips of his fingers look pink and exposed.

"Um, are you coming to babysit us on Monday?" he asks. He smiles again, a strange and compelling sight—Derek Kozak smiling!—and then waits for the answer.

"We were fired," I tell him.

"And/or quit," Felicia says.

"No, no," Derek explains. He looks nervous and eager. "We-we-we want you to babysit us again. If you don't come on Monday, my m-m-mom is leaving and never coming back." The smile creeps wider across his face, stretching everything in the wrong direction and making a white ring around his mouth.

"My mom says that all the time," I tell him.

"Ha," he says flatly.

Silence. Derek's friends are circling in the street, trying to knock one another off their bikes. While he's waiting, he tries wrapping his bandaged palm around the handlebar but can't bend the fingers. He winces, then places it gingerly in his armpit.

"She said if you show up, you're getting a raise and my dad has to pay it," he says dully. "And if you don't, she's leaving with Wanda to go down to Wanda's mom's house in Arkansas. And will not come back."

We walk, and he pedals slowly alongside us for half a block, the wounded hand tucked under his wing. At the corner, he takes the bike over the curb and pedals slowly away, no-handed, steering with his shoulders.

"I thought *she* was Wanda's mom," I say.

"Food," Felicia says wearily. Thin chocolate mints from the Candy Shoppe, stacked like dominoes. We buy an eighth of a pound, which is five each, and—it's boiling hot out—eat them under the awning of a store that sells medical devices and shoes for people with legs of varying lengths.

" 'I stand corrected in my orthopedic shoes,' " I quote.

" 'I see butts, says the person under the bleachers,' " Felicia answers.

She can't even remember the jokes from her own joke book. *Under the Bleachers* by *I. C. Butts.* Get it?

"No," she says pointedly, and sets out walking again.

We go up the hill on opposite sides of the street, both of us starting out stomping and ending up crawling. At the top we wave at each other.

"What're you having?" she yells.

"Dumplings and homemade noodles," I yell.

"Can I come?" she yells.

"I want to come to yours," I yell.

"Yours," she yells back.

"Okay," I yell.

She crosses.

My dad is asleep in the backyard, sitting semiupright in a lawn chair with a beer bottle in his hand and his head dropped forward on his chest. We walk past silently, Felicia staring diplomatically sideways at the neighbor's shrubbery. Inside, my mother is smoking and setting the table.

"There," she says, putting down the final fork. "You can all go to hell."

"What did *we* do?" Meg calls from the other room.

My mom smiles at Felicia and takes a swallow from a glass of beer. "Here's somebody who'll eat my dumplings."

"Yeah," Felicia whispers nervously.

"Tell your dad dinner's on the table," my mother says to me.

"He knows," I say.

"Raymond! Help get your father."

Out in the backyard, Ray gets one arm and I get the other and we pull, sending him dangerously over to one side. Ray braces himself against the lawn chair, grunting theatrically.

"Dad, *get up*," he croaks.

"Huhrr," my dad says.

All the neighborhood dogs are watching this with interest, including Tammy, who is on her hind legs at the end of her tether. The dogs' owners are watching from behind their curtains, out of respect for my father, whom everyone likes.

"Dad," I entreat him. "Dad, Dad, Dad. Mom has noodles." Even if we get him on his feet, we'll never get him in the house. "Go tell her we can't do it," I hiss at Ray.

"Unh-uh," he says, jamming his cowboy boots into the dirt and pushing with his back.

"Dad!" I yell it directly into his ear, causing him to jump dramatically and grimace. I feel sick and terrible now, like I stabbed someone in their sleep.

I cup my mouth and speak in his ear: *"Get up and get in the house, it's dinner."* And then, because I can't help myself: *"I have company!"*

We tug and he comes off the chair, then gamely lifts one foot after the other as we steer him across the grass and up the steps into the house. At the table, he settles heavily into his place and looks around.

"Why, hello, Flea," he says faintly, and falls asleep again.

My mother ladles food onto everyone's plate from what seems like a boiling vat of sweat socks. The mood is such that even Raymond takes a few bites. My nerves are shot at this point. I know it's entirely possible my kitten has died by now — when we put them back in the garage at dawn, the other two ate but Freckles just crawled onto a stack of boards and sat there, shuddering.

I love that kitten, and if he dies it's my fault. I will have killed a kitten at age fourteen; the whole rest of my life will be ruined. I get up and go outside to where Tammy is still hovering expectantly at the end of her chain. I unhook her and we walk back in, past the long-necked bottle tipped over in the grass. I fix myself a bowl of cereal and take my place again.

"She can't eat a bird with a bird watching," Meg explains to my mother, who grabs a dish towel, walks through the doorway into the dining room, tosses it over the canary's cage, comes back, puts my bowl of cereal in the sink, and adds another wad of chicken to my congealing plate.

"You want to act like a three-year-old? You can sit there until it's gone," she says, lighting a cigarette.

My troubles are accumulating. The dying kitten, waiting in the cobwebby dark for me to come and do nothing, and now the canary, put to bed while it's still light outside, trapped behind a dish towel, encased in the terrible fate of a bird who has never flown, but who watches all day through the dining room window while other birds land and take off from the clothesline. Sometimes he sings so elaborately and desperately that I have to put my hands over my ears.

And there's no way Yvonne can take Miles with her to Arkansas; even if she felt like it, he wouldn't be able to hold on. A tiny boy in a bad diaper, abandoned in the backyard, fingers gripping the chain-link fence as it gets darker and darker, as Lurch shoves his empty bowl around.

"She's bawling," Meg says, and gets up to remove the cloth from the birdcage. The canary resumes swinging and looking out the window.

My father wakes up for a second, lifts his fork, and puts it back down. My leg starts shaking and I can't get it to stop. I start hiccuping, violently.

"All right now, that's enough," my mother says. She removes my plate and makes me a fresh bowl of cereal. "What's the matter with you?"

Felicia eats her dumplings carefully, not looking at anyone.

A half hour later, we have no trouble getting out of dishes or out of the house, although my mother calls me into the dining room before we leave, to ask why sleeping in a canvas box is so appealing to me when I have a bed right upstairs. Also, she doesn't want me going over there and acting like nobody fed me dinner.

"And let me ask you this," she says, whipstitching a hem, squinting against her cigarette. "Don't you two ever get sick of each other?"

"We're sick of each other right now," I say.

We stop at the end of her block to rest for a while, lying back against someone's mossy terrace. It's a stagnant Saturday night in Zanesville, velvety black and hot. The parochial kid's light is on and everything is visible but the boy himself—a desk lamp, a picture of Jesus, the top of a cluttered bureau, part of a mirror with a palm frond behind it.

"His mother should get him some curtains," Felicia says.

On a different Saturday night, back when I babysat for the

big quiet boy Daniel, his mother had shown me the new curtains she had hung in his bedroom. They were crisp white, with bright farm animals appliquéd on them. They looked like they had been bought at a store, but in fact Lisa had made them herself.

"He loves anything from a farm!" Lisa had said, bending over Daniel in his railed bed, smoothing his curly hair. When he had a cold, she had demonstrated how to clear his nose, using a pointed rubber ball and a warm washcloth.

"Okay," she told him, pressing on the bulb to create a vacuum and then poking it into his nostril. "Big sniff!" she said in a lilting voice, releasing the bulb and drawing out the contents of his nose, which were deposited in a tissue. It was actually an interesting tool, but I never got good at using it.

If my kitten had ended up with someone like her, he'd be playing with a ball of yarn right now instead of dying.

"Hey, wait," I say, sitting up.

The camper is dark and mostly silent. Felicia has a habit of sighing in her sleep, like her dreams are disappointing her, and she does that now—sigh, sigh...sigh, sigh—on her back with one arm flung over the edge of the bunk, the inside of her wrist untanned and vulnerable, and the other draped over her forehead. With the sighing, the theatrical arms, the occasional donkey kicks, she has as big a personality asleep as she does awake. I, on the other hand, sleep like a sidekick—on my side. All limbs are kept close to the body for safety reasons, and a tube sock is laid across my face, a holdover from sharing a bed in childhood, when I had to sleep with a pillow over my head, then just the pillowcase, then a hanky, now anything that symbolically makes me think I won't be hurt while I'm sleeping.

Footsteps.

A foot of door is unzipped and Felicia's dad sticks his head in to look around.

"Asleep," he whispers.

"Poke them," Phyllis whispers.

"I can *see* them," he whispers.

They switch places.

"Girls!" Phyllis whispers.

Nothing, just the faint couplets of sighing.

"Girls!"

I startle up onto my elbows, my sock falling to the floor. "What?" I say, squinting. I can just see the shape of her upper body and head, the moon shining through her teased, Saturday night hair.

"Oh, nothing, honey," she whispers. "We were just back and wanted to make sure you were here and all."

"We're here," I say sleepily, and crawl farther into my sleeping bag.

Zip.

One, two, three, four, five.

A creak and a snap as the back door opens and shuts.

Six, seven, eight, nine, ten. Flea kicks off her sleeping bag.

"Nice sighing," I say.

Three minutes later, we let ourselves inside the dusty blackness of the vacant garage and wait. A soft thud and the padding of paws, a meow. Blacky Strout. After a moment, a muffled clatter. Ruffles.

Silence.

He's always come to me, no matter what, as soon as we stepped inside. I sit down right where I am, on the mangy dirt. Oh, please, he can't be dead; he cannot have died alone in a jumble of roofing supplies and empty motor oil cans. My legs have started trembling like crazy again.

In one final sweep of the flashlight, we find him, up on a shelf jammed with rusted paint rollers and empty jars. He looks tiny and moth eaten, blinking into the light.

"Whew," Felicia says.

We have to go eight blocks, through her neighborhood, through my neighborhood, and then into Monroe Park, a neighborhood where the shrubbery is denser. Any potential benefit of this—for people who might be out after curfew, carrying a cardboard box full of cats—is more or less undone by the fact that a number of teachers live in Monroe Park. I don't care to see teachers anywhere except in their classroom and perhaps the hallway outside it; in Monroe Park I once saw my fourth-grade teacher on a step stool, painting a downspout while her husband stood there talking to her, drinking a beer. Another can of beer sat on the stoop, next to the open paint. Everything pointed to its being the teacher's.

It isn't that I don't know they're regular people with regular lives; it's that I find it confusing to think of them that way. A case in point is the time when I was a second grader and went to my friend's house for lunch and her mother was in bed with the mailman.

Me and Dee Jurgenmeyer, walking into her mom's room to ask what there was to eat, and there was the whole confusing scene: the messy-haired divorced mother in a pale blue night-gown, sleeping in the middle of the day, the mailman's familiar face with strangely red lips like a woman's, and the mailbag itself, hanging on the bedroom door. For a long time afterward I would suddenly think, Dee's mother takes a nap with the mailman, and I'd feel strange about it. And yet a mailman would get tired too, just like anyone else. Maybe more tired, with the bag.

We trade off carrying the box. Felicia is starting to cry a little. We have no idea how we ended up dragging these cats down with us—they were perfectly happy in their garage when we met them. Now one is dying and the other two are frantic. Everything we go near gets ruined. Somewhere there's a boy with a damaged hand and a mother possibly riding a motorcycle to Arkansas, a bowlegged baby teetering on a top step. Before putting Blacky Strout in the box, Felicia had taken a long time saying good-bye to him.

She's crying pretty hard now, which somehow makes me feel better.

"Don't cry," I say kindly, lugging the box. Inside, the kittens are sliding around.

She is silent for a while, walking along. "I'm not," she says finally.

The house is low and composed, with green shutters, all dark except for a faint light way back in the vicinity of the kitchen. On the porch is a basket of trailing ivy, a white wicker chair with a cushion, and an antique crank-type doorbell. We creep up and set the box on the porch floor, untie Ruffles from his T-shirt, close the flaps loosely, and tiptoe away. Along the edge of the yard, in the black shadows, Felicia stops so abruptly that I run into her.

"What if they're on vacation or something?" she whispers.

Vacation! While we're pondering this, there's a thump and the cardboard box starts moving. A paw pokes through the flaps, thrusting around in the air; then a head squirms through alongside it and Ruffles is out, scrambling across the porch, up and over the railing, into the night.

Gone.

"Shite!" Felicia hisses.

She shoves me forward and I dart across the lawn and up the steps. On the dim porch, I can barely tell the remaining kittens inside the box apart, which one is dying and which one is running for sheriff. From this view, Monroe Park looks exotic and sinister, with its moonlit teachers' houses and over-grown bushes. There's a narrow garage next door, made of crumbling brick, with ivy framing a small, dirty window. From here I can see that the side door is ajar, and that's where I direct Felicia. Over there, over there. She run-walks across the lawn and shimmies inside.

Freckles doesn't seem to be breathing. I put one finger under his chin, and his head seems limp. But then he lifts it toward me without opening his eyes, and I lean into the box and kiss him. As he settles himself deeper into the towel, I give Strout one last pet and close the flaps. I ring the doorbell and sprint, down the steps and across the lawn.

The garage is junky but it smells good, like gasoline. I squeeze through the door and grope my way over a fallen bicycle to the dirty window, just as the porch light goes on and Trent comes out, wearing a pair of striped pajama bot-toms and nothing else. He looks down at the box and then toward the street, shielding his eyes from the light. Lisa comes through the screen door then, in a white nightgown and bare feet, her hair loose and curly on her shoulders.

There are cobwebs all around us, one of them stretched like a shroud across my face. Felicia has a death grip on the bottom of my shirt. The garage has a dirt floor; anything could be living in here, including a snake.

Lisa kneels and lifts each of our kittens out for a moment and then sets them back inside the box. Lisa and Trent talk quietly, at one point both of them pausing to stare penetratingly out into the night.

When Strout pokes his head up and starts looking around, Trent lifts the box by its flaps and carries it inside while Lisa holds the screen door. She starts to follow and then changes her mind and walks to the edge of the porch, shielding her eyes and looking out toward the silent, empty street.

Her nightgown comes to just below the knee and seems made of gauze; in the porch light we can see right through it. Her eyes are dark and calm, like Daniel's. She gives a little wave, out into the summer dark, and then turns and follows her husband inside.

We can't bring ourselves to go back to the camper. Too dank, too claustrophobic, like being zipped into a gym bag for the night. Instead, we lie on someone's terrace and look at the sky. There are a million stars, and it's warm. On the other side of the street, the parochial kid's window is open and there's a low lamp on somewhere in the room.

It was strange seeing Lisa and Trent like that, in their pajamas.

"They were definitely letting it all hang out," Felicia says.

The only signs of life I ever saw in their bedroom were the tracks the vacuum cleaner left in the pale blue carpet. Nothing in the drawers but folded clothes, nothing on the nightstand but an alarm clock, nothing on the dresser but a cluster of glass grapes and a padded jewelry box. Nothing to alert you to their nighttime selves, his bare shoulders and chest, the precise line of hair running down his abdomen, disappearing into the waistband of his pajama bottoms, the dark smudges visible through her gown, the frank way she looked up at him, kneeling. You could somehow see that it wouldn't be that big a leap from them inspecting a box of kittens together to an activity closer to what Yvonne and Chuck might be involved in.

We lie there for a while on the sloped terrace, looking up at the black sky. This is how poor Daniel would look up at the ceiling, no matter where you put him. Just gazing upward, chin wet with wonder. I hope they take him outside sometimes, in the warm months, because this is so interesting, the immense galaxy looming overhead—billions of stars, ringed by the oak trees and slanted roofs of Zanesville.

Felicia cracks her knuckles, one by one, while an airplane blinks its way across the sky. We both know the Kozak family has won. At least we'll be getting a raise.

"We're just finishing out the summer," she says finally. "And then no more babysitting, ever again."

I've always mentally kept track of them by cataloging the whole clan in descending order: Chuck, Yvonne, Derek, Renee, Stewart, Wanda, Dale, Miles, Lurch, whatever snakes they've been able to round up, and the tarantula.

"If you're doing size, Lurch is bigger than Miles," Felicia points out.

She's right, it should go Lurch and then Miles, but I hate to see Miles followed by a snake. "I'm doing it by species," I say.

"Oh," she says.

I'll be able to pay for the things I've already laid away plus new things that haven't even arrived in the store yet. Besides what I'm going to wear to school once it starts, I wouldn't mind having a new nightgown, something delicate and gauzy.

In the future, I want something more interesting to happen than normally happens to me. "I'm sick of being a late bloomer," I say.

"Ha," she says. "You should be."

"We both are, according to your mother, who said it to my mother," I inform her.

"I hope she doesn't mind getting her head smacked off," Felicia says to the sky. "I mean mine, not yours."

"Ha, we're a *pair of bloomers*," I say. "Late and crusty."

In our weakened state, this sets us off. We laugh hyenically, rolling around on the terrace, slapping weakly at the grass. Suddenly the boy materializes in the window.

He must have been in bed, reading. We can see only his back at first, and a froth of bushy hair, as he roots around at his dresser for something, then sidles to the window, lifting what looks like a pirate's telescope to his eye. He turns slightly, focusing it...where? On the upstairs window of the house next door? No, that house is completely dark. He continues to turn, inch by inch, until the telescope is pointing in our direction.

"Uh-oh," Felicia says.

We freeze against the grass, our white tennis shoes throbbing in the darkness, as the boy stands still for a long moment, a pirate looking for land. He seems to be seeing us seeing him, but we aren't sure. Suddenly, he holds the telescope as though it's part of his anatomy and starts yanking on it.

Now we're sure.

We scramble back up the terrace and then crawl through some shrubbery, dust off our shorts, and wander down the alley toward the camper.

"Ee ain too noice," Felicia says at some point.

"Ee ain," I agree.

Over the past summer while we were distracted by Kozaks and kittens, Felicia has grown even taller, causing her to feel towering and uncertain and me to feel like it isn't so much that one of us is growing but that the other is shrinking.

We were supposed to try on our band uniforms a week ago, after school, but the music room was crammed to the hilt with folding chairs and music stands and there was nobody to guard the door. Just holding them up over our clothes, it was hard to tell how they'd fit. Now we know.

"Do I look like Uncle Sam in this?" Felicia asks.

The jackets are thick blue wool with bright brass buttons and yellow braiding; the pants are white with knifelike creases down the front and adjustable waistbands. The hats are hard blue cylinders with a short white brim, on top of which a hunk of braiding is secured by two brass buttons; a white strap buckles under the chin. You're allowed to wear your own shoes, but there's a black felt flap that buttons over the instep, creating the illusion of spats.

First problem: the hat is resting on my ears, which means they are exposed. Second problem: the entire uniform is too large and too stiff for me—it looks like the person has withered away and the outfit is there on its own. Third problem: Felicia looks like Uncle Sam.

"Do I?" she asks again.

The hats are at least eight inches tall. There is a spot on the top for a metal-tipped plume to be inserted; it will be worn by the first-chair band members and the band teacher, who marches ahead of the whole pack, setting the pace by raising and lowering a gilded scepter. Since we have neither talent nor leadership capabilities, we weren't given a plume.

"At least you don't have to wear one of their ratty feathers, which would make it even taller," I say, and we stare at ourselves, standing on my parents' bed, looking in their big vanity mirror.

Raymond follows us downstairs and partway down the street. He's starstruck and imagines he's going to the parade. "I'll go like this when I see you," he tells us, chopping the air in front of him and kicking sideways.

We've both been in band for as long as we can remember— fourth grade for me, third for her—but we're in ninth grade now, and neither of us has risen through the ranks at all. Instead we've each maintained a spot somewhere in the middle of our respective rows, neither first chair nor last. Felicia plays clarinet, an instrument my mother wanted me to play because Old Milly had one in her attic, but I couldn't play an instrument with a reed—anything soaked with spit made me gag. Also, the clarinet's case was too heavy; the flute was the only instrument I could carry to school when I was nine.

I like the way the clarinet sounds, like a clear cellophane ribbon unfurling, better than the flute, which has a narrow, harassed sound. I do enjoy the flute itself, the beautiful silveriness of it and the fact that it goes against your lip instead of inside it, the brown leather case with the velvet-lined depressions where the separate pieces are laid to rest, the flexible stick with a wooden handle that you wrap a rag around and run through the tubes to clean them. Altogether, band is a pleasant experience— Mr. Wilton, the teacher, pays attention only to the first-chair musicians and the percussionists, a gang of unruly thick-waisted boys wielding drumsticks, gongs, and triangles. Everyone else comes under the category of Others and gets to follow.

"Percussionists will *listen* and will *count*," he says to the ceiling, arms raised. "Miss Chambers: *tenderly*. Mr. McVicken: *crisply*. Mr. Waddell: *lilting*. Others: follow."

He closes his eyes and begins pawing at the air, and suddenly the sound of "Greensleeves" is rising up and wheezing around us as we labor along. I like to play hunched over, with one elbow resting on a knee, the flute pointed down at the floor. Not everyone gets into marching band, and we have no idea why we were chosen.

"You two are the long and short of it," Wilton said one day after the bell rang and people were shuffling out of his cluttered room, trying not to knock things over. Later that day he posted a list for marching band and our names were on it. Even though Wilton is well known for his high-strung personality and depressing body malfunctions—platter-size armpit rings, foam collected at the corners of his mouth, dandruff—he's right now our favorite teacher.

The annual Zanesville parade is always in mid-October and

always has a Halloween theme. It's a hectic, gargantuan affair, fifteen blocks of Elm Avenue devoted to it and people standing ten deep all along the way. This time, instead of watching from the sidelines, we'll be marching in formation, behind the majorettes and in front of the football players and the floats.

"I can't play and walk at the same time," I confess to Felicia.

"Ha, me neither," she says.

Wilton's wife is there in the John Deere Junior High School parking lot, helping people fasten their top coat buttons and referring to Wilton as Jim. She's blond, friendly, and pregnant, wearing a big black wool tent and a pair of nurse's shoes. When we walk up, she tries to give us each a plume, sorting through a flat decaying box to find two that aren't bald.

"No, thanks," Felicia says, alarmed.

"Jim?" the wife calls, pointing at us.

Wilton shakes his head and she smiles warmly. "You're fine just how you are," she says.

It feels very strange being in the dark with people from school when it isn't schooltime. Wearing the uniforms has pried us all loose from our normal selves and we're wandering around disoriented. Some people are randomly blowing into their instruments, creating an angular, cacophonous noise that is causing my heart to pound.

"People, people, people," Wilton calls tonelessly from the bumper of a pickup truck. "Please, people. People, please."

Off to the side, things are quieter. The float looks like a giant sheet cake on wheels. All those Kleenexes stuffed into all those holes. A skeleton is working on a special effect while a witch hands him tools. They have the overcheerful, pious look of involved parents, trying to make a cauldron belch smoke.

A group of cheerleaders walks past, followed by a group of football players, one of whom is Danny Powell, who lives in my neighborhood and was my friend when we were five. He and I used to play a game under the picnic table where we pretended to be Vic and Gin, friends of my parents who hosted my family's yearly fishing vacations. The real Vic and Gin owned a motel in the Wisconsin Dells and once gave me something off the check-in counter in their lobby—a black plastic thing that held a card for the vacationers to fill out when they registered. Attached to the black plastic thing was a chain and a pen, which had run dry. Danny and I used it in our game of Vic and Gin, which consisted of one of us pretending to be a traveler and the other pretending to be a motel owner. The game gradually devolved into Gin making Vic plates of food out of sticks, grass, and maple seeds, which he would then pretend to eat. Eventually we drifted apart. Now he's become suave and massive, his head sitting like a pea atop his shoulder pads.

He nods as he passes.

"Hi," I say.

The cheerleaders are their usual glossy selves, wearing letter sweaters over turtlenecks, short pleated skirts, and leg-colored tights. They stretch and mill around, talking to one another while absentmindedly doing the semaphore signals that go along with their cheers. Two of them move off the gravel into the grass and spot each other doing backflips.

The football team has momentarily turned its attention from the cheerleaders to the band's majorettes, who just took off their coats, unveiling sequined leotards, fringed wrist cuffs, and white ankle boots. They are all ninth graders, like the rest of us, but the whole corps seems to have developed quite graphically overnight: they look middle-aged and lewd, parts of them drifting out of the packed leotards.

"Band people!"

From a distance Wilton seems small compared to his wife, and he keeps losing his balance and having to jump down from the bumper. Felicia is standing in a cluster of clarinets, but so far I don't see any flutes, just an ocean of ill-fitting wool. Everyone I look at seems to be scratching their neck.

In the same way people can resemble their dogs, the flutes are a thin and tremulous bunch, led by Larue Varrick, a pale, cautious girl with red-rimmed eyes. I join them, somewhere in the middle, with the woodwinds right behind us. Felicia reaches over and taps my shoulder.

"This coat is itching me," she says.

The cheerleaders and the football players are waiting for the band to take shape so they can get into formation behind us. They're standing around, some with arms folded, some with hands on hips, watching the proceedings bemusedly, the same way grown-ups might stand in a doorway and watch a cartoon.

"What's wrong?" Felicia asks me.

The giant kid on tuba straggles up, his pants dragging, and stops to apply Chap Stick to the bottom half of his face, chin and all. Two cheerleaders gape at him and then abruptly turn their backs to compose themselves. When they turn back they're poker faced, deliberately not looking at each other. Suddenly I'm flooded with the same feeling of humiliation that I get when someone from school accidentally sees me with my parents.

"What?" Felicia says curiously. In the hat, she looks as tall as the Empire State Building. I can feel my ears standing out like tabs on either side of my head.

I hadn't realized before, but now I do: We've made a terrible mistake. Band is weird.

I'd like to be the kind of person who can do something weird and not become weird because of it, but that's out of reach for me—I am what I do at this point, and if I do this I'm done for. Once I march in their parade, I will be in it forever, uniform or not.

Felicia, unaware, has gone back to her spot. She's been stationed in the very middle like a tent pole, and I'm on an end, where everyone in Zanesville can get a good look.

Help.

Drum roll.

Help.

Cymbals.

With that, Wilton sweeps his arms upward and then downward, sending the band shuffling forward, out of the parking lot and into the street, toward Elm Ave and the IGA parking lot, where the rest of the parade is forming.

Right, left, right, left, right, left, right, left, right, left, right, left, right, left, right, left, right, left, right, left, right, left, right, left.

The neighborhood looks haunted, with wet leaves clumped in the gutters and streetlamps creating cones of light high in the air. At the corner, instruments are lifted to lips and blown into, and a big misshapen sound comes forth. The song of the weirdos. Somewhere behind us, cheerleaders and football players follow along wryly.

As doom descends, panic rises, and a vampire motors past in a golf cart, smiling with plastic teeth.

* * *

In retrospect we probably should have quit band after the parade instead of during it.

"In *retrospect*, we never should have been in band in the first place," Felicia says. "I was only doing it because you said to."

"You played the clarinet when I met you!" I say indignantly.

"Remember I said, 'I play the clari*not*'?" she reminds me.

"Remember I said, 'My playing is *flut*ile'?" I reply.

"That's when we first knew each other was funny," she says dispiritedly.

We're carrying our instruments and our hats. We tried to take the jackets off to be less conspicuous, but it was too cold. So we're a block off Elm Ave, where there are no elms and where the parade is roaring along at one mile an hour, thousands of people lining the route, just as we feared. A car swishes past us and pulls up at the curb, and a man gets out balancing a pizza box and a six-pack of pop.

"The parade's thattaway," he says cordially.

"We know," Felicia answers.

He stares at us for a moment, resting the pop against his hip.

"Which school is that uniform?" he asks.

"John Deere," I say.

"I went to Walt Whitman way back when," he says. "Worst years of my life—just kidding."

Now that I'm not in the parade, I have nothing against it. We decide to cut over and watch it from the Grassy Knoll, a hidden spot about ten feet above the sidewalk, where a gently sloping hill meets an eight-foot retaining wall. From up there, if one were so inclined, cars going by on Elm Ave can be bomped with soft, rotting vegetables, preferably ones that splash, like tomatoes. We've never done it ourselves, but we know of certain others who have.

"I hope your sister and her friends aren't there," Felicia says.

The Knoll is on the far side of the RF Charity Home for the Infirm, where the old folks have been bundled up and put out on the sidewalk in their wheelchairs. Some of them are waving and clapping, some of them look angry, some have already faded into sleep.

When I was young, the RF was an actual house with tall, shuttered windows and a cupola, donated by Miss Jemima Rosen of the Rosen Fertilizer family after her death. It was a place for old schoolteachers and nurses, mostly, but then they tore it down and built a facility, low and brick. Once, years ago, a demented woman came up on our porch, knocked on the door, and, when my mother answered it, told her that they were trying to kill her over at the Fertilizer Home. My mother brought her in, put a housecoat on her, and called one of her friends to discuss it before giving up and reporting it to the home's staff. When they came to pick her up, the old woman was at the sink drying dishes that I was running water over and handing to her.

I felt so strange about that woman, her dark eyes and cottony hair, the thin, pilled nightgown she was wearing. Off and on for a year afterward, I would ride my bike in their circular drive, watching for her, but she was never let out again.

The Grassy Knoll is empty and has a perfectly framed view of the parade route: A series of floats with macabre themes is under way, each appearing and then making way for the next, like Pez, followed by a cluster of boys on dirt bikes weaving in and out of one another in some kind of Boy Scout formation, one familiar kid in the middle of them, bigger than the rest and hatless. Derek Kozak, revving his engine. Before we can process that, we're seeing our own majorettes, in their leotards and fishnets—from this angle they look young again—then Wilton with a whistle in his mouth, followed by the band, loud and brassy, and so tightly bunched that the two holes we left are gone.

The band members are indistinguishable under their hats and behind their instruments. Next the cheerleaders swim by in their neat cable-knit sweaters and short skirts, the football players following trancelike in their wake. Suddenly I feel desolate in my queer wool tunic and limp, electrified hair; I might as well be one of the zombies out there broadcasting Tootsie Rolls into the crowd. Two leather-vested women ride by on palomino horses with a banner stretched between them. Right as the horses clop past, one of them slows down, arches its tail, and churns out a road apple.

"Trick or treat," Felicia says.

A half hour later, back at John Deere, people are getting their cases out of the gym and turning in their plumes. Wilton wanders through the ranks, exhausted and euphoric, blue coat open to the elements.

"Good work, girls," he murmurs as he passes Felicia and me taking apart our instruments.

For just a moment, we think we've gotten away with it, until I glance over and see Varrick, the first flute, staring at me. Her nose is running from the cold, her blond hair wisping out of its long, sullen braid.

"Hey," I say weakly.

"Hay is for jackasses," she replies.

* * *

Detention is held in one of the science rooms, where there are lab tables instead of desks. Felicia and I walk in together but pretend not to know each other so the monitor will put us at the same table. She barely looks up from what she's knitting, something green and tube shaped.

"Do your homework," she says to her needles. "If I hear talking, everyone in here will have another detention added."

"God!" somebody exclaims, a hoodlum in a red sweatshirt and a jean jacket. He has a sneering baby face, with jet-black shiny hair that he tosses sideways, like a nervous horse.

"That's talking," she says. "So, once more for everyone in here."

Another kid raises his hand as we take our seats. Knitting, she doesn't see it until he clears his throat raspingly, several times.

"What do you want, Mr. Prentiss?"

"Um, I was wondering if I could not have more detentions added, because I didn't say anything and if I get any more my dad is going to take away my dog, and all I did to get in here was nothing...I missed health class, but it was because I had a doctor's appointment and I went to it, but my mom never called the office and I thought she was going to, and so I left without permission but I thought I *had* permission. It was to get my arm rewrapped." He indicates his wrist, which is haphazardly wrapped in a dirty Ace bandage.

"Why would he take away your dog?" the monitor asks, looking over the top of her glasses at Mr. Prentiss, who isn't quite cute.

"Because," he begins slowly, thinking it through, "my *dog*...

was given to me by my friend's brother...this guy who found him down running along the river when he was fishing, and for some reason no matter what my friend's brother did, this *dog*..."

"All right," she says shortly. "I don't want to hear about a dog and I don't want to hear talking, period. Starting right now, *anything* I hear will lead to another detention for everyone."

The original kid raises his hand. She looks at him.

"God!" he exclaims.

"One detention for everyone, thanks to Mr. Nelson," she says decisively. Mr. Prentiss waves his hand again, clearing his throat, but she ignores him, stabbing away at her project.

Felicia has her head bowed over her math book, writing carefully into a notebook. She tears the page out without looking up, folds it and turns to a new chapter, begins writing again. The folded page disappears and then materializes on my lap. I open my English book and thumb through my binder, finding my assignment, which I unfold and place in front of me, where I can read it. It says:

THAT GUY LIKES YOU!!!!!!!!!!

I work on my assignment, fold it, and send it next door, where it is found to say:

NO HE DOESN'T!!!!!!!! (WHICH ONE???)

She sighs, flips around in her book, and then settles down again, yellow hair swinging forward. She tears a corner from her page and rolls it absentmindedly as she reads. Two seconds later, a tiny scroll lands in front of me.

DOG ONE, it says.

I write in my notebook and then push it far to the side to

make room for my grammar book. Flea glances at the open page, which is next to her elbow.

RED SWEATSHIRT ONE LIKES <u>YOU</u>!!!!!!!

Eyes on the monitor, she reaches over and erases the *r* in sweatshirt.

I don't know why she said that guy liked me, because he doesn't, but just having had it said and then seeing him every day in detention makes it seem vaguely true. To my knowledge, I've never had a guy like me before.

"Rodney Feldsquaw," Felicia reminds me, ear to the door. We're in her room, hiding from her mother, who has a Saturday off and is making her way through the house in a robe and rubber gloves.

Rodney Feldsquaw materialized last summer, at her outdoor family reunion, when I got cornered by an uncle who took me aside to show me how to throw a horseshoe. According to this uncle, he couldn't stand watching somebody who didn't know what they were doing...in anything, not just a game. The uncle had taught people things I couldn't imagine—one person, how to fix a merry-go-round that had a slight hitch in it.

"This was over at the state fair," he explained. "It wasn't dangerous, no, but it sure as hell wasn't right. The guy didn't have a tooth in his head, and I just said, 'Listen, hobo, get a wrench and I'm gonna show you something that will help you.'"

At that, the uncle had held a horseshoe directly in front of his face like a hand mirror and glared into it. "You go like this . . . ," he said to me, sweeping his arm backward, "then you go like *this*," and he let it fly. The horseshoe landed in the dirt right where he had gouged out a mark with his heel. He handed me one. "Now I want to see you do that," he said.

I wanted to see me do that too — for being not good at any game or sport, I am nevertheless very competitive. At one point in my youth I was stopped from playing the big neighborhood games that required running and tagging because I would get short of breath to the point of reeling. Everyone thought it was from asthma, but it wasn't. It was hyperventilation brought on by losing.

The uncle's coaching had no effect, but he kept me there practicing and listening to tales of how he had successfully demonstrated other skills to other people. "I said to the guy, 'Don't *stab* at it. Rather, you put the shovel under it and *pry*. . .' "

Eventually horseshoes broke up and Felicia came to rescue me.

"I have to go," I said to the uncle.

"We're done here anyway," he answered.

As I went to walk away, he loomed for a moment, tall and thick, with gold frames around two of his teeth, and asked me one last thing. "Now, you have a boyfriend, don't you?"

That tutorial I couldn't begin to fathom, so I just nodded.

"You better!" he said.

"I do," I lied.

"What's his name?" he asked.

While he stood there expectantly, I stared at him, my mind as white and flat as a bedsheet pinned to a line. Name. Name?

"Rodney Feldsquaw," I said.

"Feldsquaw?" he asked. "What kind of name is that?"

"I don't know," I admitted.

"Well, he sounds strange," the uncle said.

He would have to be, wouldn't he? And even stranger is the fact that once I conjured him up, R. Feldsquaw wouldn't leave. Blurry and unspecific, he lounged around the edges of my daydreams, admiring me.

Unlike Rodney Feldsquaw, Mr. Prentiss at least has the sense to not pay any attention to me. All he's ever offered me is the back of his head, which, the more I look at it, the more I realize how attractive it is. The silky brown hair that kinks sideways in one spot, the way he puts it behind his ears before talking and then shakes it loose again when he's finished. The army jacket with a ballpoint design on the back, possibly made with a Spirograph, the flannel-shirted shoulders, the sneakers mended with duct tape.

"He looks at you," Felicia insists. "When you walk by, he swivels around and watches you."

"It's the gargoyle effect," I say.

Meanwhile, we were only given five days of detention and we're down to the end, unless I can think of a way to get more.

"I actually don't want more," Felicia says.

Her closet door has a mirror on it and there's another mirror above her dresser, so if I stand on a chair I can see what I look like from behind. A knock on the door. Felicia flattens herself against the wall.

"Who is it?" I say.

"Stephanie," Stephanie says through the door, and then sniffs, a loud, loose sound that makes me feel like going home.

"What?"

"You guys are supposed to help, my mom said."

"I'm busy," I tell her, staring into the mirror. I feel a surge of affection for the back of me, trim and unsuspecting in its pink sweater and corduroy pants.

"Doing what?" Stephanie asks.

"Lookin' at me arse," I reply.

"I'm telling," she says automatically. And then, because she can't help herself: "Where's Flea?"

Felicia throws the door open and yanks her inside. She resists, just for the sake of it, and is pulled across the carpet, stiff and grimacing.

"Did I hear you say Step On Me?" Felicia asks her.

"No," Stephanie says primly, shaking herself loose. Before we know what's happening, she whirls and starts kicking wildly, which is her new thing. The whole younger generation is suddenly into kung fu fighting, inspired by a TV show.

"Get out of here, you little skrizz," Felicia says, stepping back.

"Ha!" Stephanie cries, kicking inefficiently in all directions. "Now you're scared of *me!*"

"I'm scared that you're an idiot," Felicia answers, closing the door behind her.

The back of Mr. Prentiss and the back of me seem like a perfect couple. If relationships were that easy, we'd have it made; instead, I have to somehow get a padded bra.

"That's what books are for!" Felicia insists. "You walk in holding your books across your chest. You look at him. You smile. You say hi."

She stares at herself in the mirror and then smiles, to demonstrate. "Can you do that?"

"I can do the books-across-my-chest part," I tell her.

Just at that moment there's a commotion, yelling and the sound of a clattering bucket. Her mother has had it. Even my name is being taken in vain: if I'm not willing to help clean up this house, which I was more than willing to help destroy, then maybe it's time for me to go home. She bangs open the door.

"I'll take the bathroom," I say quickly.

I love cleaning; it gives you time to think. There's nothing better than thinking. Thinking about detention mostly, how romantic it is: The rustling sound of note passing, the way the monitor periodically lifts her knitting high in the air to loosen another length of yarn from the skein, the clock jumping along, the science smell of sulfur and dissected worms. Mr. Prentiss's foot in its sneaker, hooked around the bottom of his chair.

What if he just spontaneously started talking to me and I just started talking back? What if I talked to him first and he started talking back? What if he said something to me and I went completely dormant and didn't say anything back? What if I said something to him and he didn't say anything back? What if I go in clutching my books and smile and say hi and he is sickened and embarrassed? What about when I was a kindergartner and had on my favorite little hat with yarn pigtails and a face embroidered on the back, and a sixth-grade boy who I was enchanted with started teasing me by speaking only to my hat? What about how I sobbed until he begged me to stop? What if I do something like that again?

"You don't have to put your arm in the toilet," Felicia's mom says, standing in the doorway. "There's a brush."

"I like to," I tell her, scrubbing. It's the only way you can really get in there.

"Well, it might not even be sanitary," she says, continuing on her way.

There are several surefire ways of getting detentions: anything having to do with a fire alarm, destruction of school property, tampering with school property, misuse of school property, launching of projectiles, physical aggression, and possession of smoking materials. I wouldn't mind committing any of the crimes, but I can't bear the idea of being caught for them, after all the lecturing and disappointment we inspired getting the detentions we already have.

A less surefire way would be to skip a class, but we can't hurt another teacher's feelings, which rules out everything but Special Sports, taught by a traveling teacher, Mr. Pettle, who doesn't bother learning people's names from school to school, just calls everyone either Bub or Dolly. We don't care any more about Pettle's feelings than he cares about ours, but the fact is he doesn't take attendance. Right now Special Sports is medicine ball, a gloomy game where we all lie on our backs in a circle and kick an enormous leaden ball back and forth.

"I'll talk to you while you hurry," Felicia says, stepping gingerly across the floor I'm washing to sit on the edge of the tub. She shouldn't be done yet, but she is — one of the reasons you can write your name on every surface in this house.

"I think we should skip medicine ball and walk around in the halls until somebody catches us," I suggest, rinsing the toothbrushes in hot water.

"I'm not getting more detentions," she says testily, "and neither are you. We're wasting our lives in there."

"That one kid likes you!" I say. "*He likes you.* So if you want to forget it, fine with me." I'm talking about the black-haired boy who tosses his head like a horse.

"The blurter?" she says skeptically. "I doubt it."

"Well, I don't! He stares at you all the time."

"You're just saying that because I said the other guy turned around and looked at you when you went by."

"Well, was that a lie?"

"No," she says.

"Well, if it wasn't a lie when you said it to me, why is it a lie when I say it to you?"

"Because it is," she says simply.

She's right, it's a lie.

"What's his name again?" she asks.

"Jeff Nelson," I tell her. "He's in Dunk's math class. I guess he's smart but the teacher hates him because he'll yell out the answer while she's still writing the problem on the board."

"Does Dunk like him?" Felicia asks.

"She doesn't like any guys," I remind her. "But if she did, she probably would because she said he was funny."

"*I* like funny guys," Felicia says, perking up. "Although not too funny."

"Too funny stops being funny," I agree, running a damp rag along the light fixture over the medicine cabinet.

"He isn't *that* funny," she says. "He's not a clown. Stop dusting the lightbulbs."

"Stop getting them dirty," I say, looking around for the next thing.

"We didn't get them dirty, it's dust," she says.

"That's why I'm dusting," I say. Next: desliming the bar of soap.

"Mom," Felicia hollers. "She's washing *soap*, tell her to stop."

"Stop, honey," her mom calls.

By early evening, I'm sick in love and Felicia isn't far behind me. She's on the floor with her feet up the wall and I'm slowly sliding upside down off the bed, inch by inch.

"I just remember that time he said, 'God,' and the monitor gave us all another detention," Felicia reminisces. "He goes, 'God,' and she goes, 'That's another one for all of you,' or something like that."

"That was funny. Remember that time mine tried to run out at exactly four o'clock and the door was locked and he goes, 'Everybody! Out the window!' or something like that."

"That was funny. I like mine's hair," she says.

"It's shiny. Mine's might be a bit girlish," I say modestly.

"Not to me it isn't," she says. "So what're we going to get caught for?"

Before we can review our options, the phone, which is resting on her stomach, rings. It's my sister. I roll the rest of the way off the bed and take the receiver. I feel light headed from being upside down for so long.

"Get home," Meg says in a not-unfriendly voice.

"I'm staying over," I tell her.

"You can't."

"Did Mom say?"

"Yeah, she said to call and tell you to get home," Meg explains.

"But why?"

"Hmm, let me think. How about because she said?" Meg says patiently.

"But *why* is she saying?"

"The end," Meg says, hanging up.

*　　*　　*

Everyone's yard light is on but ours, and next door, Curly is sitting very close to his apple tree. As soon as I hit the back walk, I can hear it: ranting coming from our kitchen.

"I'll say *this* about *that!*" my dad shouts.

Curly's chain is wrapped tightly around the base of the tree; that's why he's huddled like that. He looks miserable and harmless.

"I'll say *this* about *that!*" my dad shouts again. It's one of his famous drunk sayings, and he will repeat it anywhere from twenty to fifty-five times before my mother makes him stop.

Even though I've been told over and over not under any circumstances to get near Curly, I take a step into the dirt circle and look around. No human but Old Milly has ever seen the neighborhood from this perspective. There's a root poking out of the soil that's been gnawed on like a bone.

"I'll say *this* about *that!*"

Curly looks at me entreatingly. His battered old face and his bowlegs, the thick, stubby tail: all he wants is a human to pat his head, to lead him around until he has all his dirt back again.

"I'll say *this* about *that!*"

Suddenly Curly snarls and jumps at me, an orange blur brought up short by the chain. He twists and turns, trying to get out of his collar, wildly biting the trunk of the apple tree in frustration. By that time I'm all the way up the back steps and inside the porch, panting and trembling.

Now he's snubbed even tighter, because of me.

"I'll say *this* about *that!*" my father booms.

"Shut up!" I cry, slamming into the kitchen. My father is

sitting slumped in a kitchen chair, baiting my mother, who is standing at the stove, pretending to ignore him.

"Hey," she says sharply. "Who are you talking to?"

"Why did you make me come home when he won't *shut up?*"

"That's enough," she says, handing me a spoon and putting me in front of the stove. "Stir."

I stir while my dad stares at me dully, trying to figure out who I am. "Well," he says quietly to himself. He's in an undershirt, and she has somehow gotten his shoes away from him, which means he can't go anywhere until he sobers up at least enough to tie a lace. It'll be a while.

He opens his hands in a gesture of defeat and licks his lips clumsily. He recognizes me. "Honey," he says in a pleading, blurry voice.

The thing I'm stirring is a dark broth with something very large bumping around in it. I try to bring whatever it is to the surface.

"Honey..." And he begins to cry in a soft, hopeless way. "Honey, I'll...I'll..."

The thing keeps getting away from me. "You'll what?" I say finally, trapping it against the side of the pot and bringing it to the surface. It's thick and gray, with bumps on the top. Slightly furled on the end. It looks familiar but I can't quite place it.

"I'll say *thiiis* about *thaaat,*" he brays, right at the moment I realize I'm stirring a tongue.

"She says one more outburst like that and we're sending you to the mental home," Meg tells me. She's brought a plate with Jell-O, peas, and a warmed-up sweet roll for my dinner.

I can't talk yet.

"It wasn't *human*," Meg says.

What around here is. I roll over and look out the window: Curly has been unwound from the tree and is staring mildly around. Down in Old Milly's kitchen the Chinese checkers board is set up on the table, ready to go, all the marbles in the starting gates.

"She'll probably let you out of here if you go down and say you're sorry," Meg tells me, stuffing a wad of clothes under her bed and shaking out the bedspread to cover them. Mister Ed is picking her up to go to a double feature at the drive-in movie with a bunch of other girls. It would be good, clean fun except that the drive-in movie theater is closed for the season, which none of the parents have figured out.

A car honks in the alley.

"She'll probably let you out anyway," Meg says, pausing in the doorway. She looks pretty in her navy peacoat and eye shadow.

Alone, I read for a while, a fat paperback I got out of the free box at the library. *The Carpetbaggers,* a book so squalid and overblown that it wouldn't even stay bound: all the pages in the center have come loose and are out of order, so it's slow going. When the phone rings I have to trace the cord from the wall to under Meg's bed.

"Why did you have to go home?" Felicia asks.

"Family dinner," I say.

"What did you have?"

"Jell-O," I tell her.

"I know, but what did they have?"

"Some kind of Transylvanian meat," I say. My grandmother's second husband is a butcher, as crabby as he is bald. A tongue isn't even the worst thing he's given us.

"Lucky," she says. "We had pork and beans and green beans. I said to my mother, 'These are both beans,' but she didn't care."

"What are you eating right now?"

"Girl Scout cookies," she says.

"What kind?"

"A whole thing of Savannahs."

"I hate Savannahs," I say. Anything with peanut butter, actually. My mother told me that once when I was a baby, she opened a jar of peanut butter at the table, and when she looked over, I was gagging in my high chair.

"So," Felicia says, crunching, "I can't wait to get in trouble."

The one-person fight takes off again downstairs ("I'll tell you another goddamned thing! You better watch out!") and I hang up just as there's a knock at my door.

It's Ray. He's got two bottles of Pepsi and two glasses of ice that he's managed to carry upstairs.

"I brung us pop," he says.

We end up skipping medicine ball and not getting caught for it. We walk by the office, we walk by the hall monitor, we sit on the front steps of the school without our coats, we go back in and make the rounds of classrooms where we have friends and stand outside the closed doors, waving at them through the portholes. Nothing.

"We're like ghosts who don't yet know they're dead," I say to Felicia.

"Ha, ha, nobody can see us." She pantomimes pulling her shirt up. "Waaah! Get a load of this!"

In the last five minutes of the hour we position ourselves down the hall from our friend Dunk's math class. She said

Felicia's blurter, Jeff Nelson, turns to the right when exiting, so we will start walking toward the classroom from that direction when the bell rings. As the clock hops its last seconds before the bell, Felicia places her three-ring binder against her chest, folds her shoulders around it, and rests her chin along its top edge. It's like watching time-lapse photography of a plant wilting.

"No, go like this!" I hiss, standing up straight, thrusting my chest forward. Her eyes bug out, but she does it, just as the bell goes off above our heads, a bone-rattling blast. When the door springs open he's the second one out, muttering to himself and tossing his head sideways. Blue stretched-out sweater, a textbook stuffed with papers, and a knock-kneed walk that I never noticed before.

I veer ever so slightly, herding Felicia into his line of vision. He's still talking to himself, but then — he looks at her. For an instant, nothing, then there's a faint pursing of the lips, a narrowing of the eyes, and a subtle but deliberate tipping of the head backwards.

"How far backwards?" Dunk asks. She has short, wild red hair and wears little round glasses.

"Three inches or so?" I say, and then demonstrate. When you do it yourself, it definitely feels like something. Perhaps not an actual nod, but an acknowledgment. I open the bun they just gave me in the lunch line and remove the brown flap of hamburger.

"Really?" Felicia says dreamily, adding the flap to her own sandwich and handing over her spare pickles.

"Weren't you there?" I ask her. Now I have chocolate milk, a bun filled with pickles, and a jelly-flavored long john.

"I thought he more or less just went like this." She narrows her eyes and purses her lips.

"He did. And then like this." I tip my head back about three inches. "Sort of mocking."

"Like this?" Dunk asks, squinting, pursing her lips, and tugging her chin forward. I know Dunk from when I used to go to church; she's the one who talked me out of believing in God, pointing out that he was basically a ghost and they even call him one.

"Not like trying to loosen a necktie," Felicia says, finishing her last bite of hamburger, "but more of a lolling of the head. It was a mocking loll."

The cafeteria is almost empty of kids. The famously testy à la carte lady is closing her counter, lifting a tray of buns and using her hip to push open the bumpered door into the kitchen.

"Good luck," Dunk says, and then vacates the table.

Felicia wads up the paper her sandwich came in.

I wad up my paper too.

When the à la carte lady walks back through the swinging door, we stand and throw. One wad hits her smack in the chest and the other lands in the hot dog vat.

"Launching of projectile?" my mother exclaims. "You have got to be kidding me. Sit the hell down right there."

They made me bring a note home this time, to be signed and returned. It's a form with a space for the number of detentions given (five), a list of crime categories with boxes next to them, and then a space at the bottom where Mr. Jaggermeyer, the corrections officer who also poses as a civics teacher, has scrawled a message: "Your daughter seems to be at a crossroads: This is her *2nd* infraction in under *3* weeks—after what we consider nearly excellent comportment. Perhaps undo influence of another is partly to blame."

I sit down at the kitchen table.

She fumes, smoke trailing from her nostrils, while my dad is summoned from the bathroom. He comes to the table in his undershirt; it's Monday night and he's as sober as he gets. My mother hands him the form to read, and lights another cigarette off the burner.

She can't believe it! They are heartsick over this, they don't know what is happening to me. They could understand if I were deprived, or if I were some kind of mental case. But I've had every opportunity, every benefit of every doubt whenever it was called for, every type of discipline and support parents could reasonably be expected to give their kid. I ask for a dress, somebody sits her ass down and makes me one. I ask for a nightstand to keep my books on, somebody hauls one down out of the attic and puts a coat of paint on it. I want to spend every goddamned minute over at some house six blocks away, hanging around with a girl who won't open her mouth when you talk to her, but then suddenly this same girl who can't say boo is willing to behave like an idiot "launching projectiles." Whatever the hell that means, and it better not mean what she thinks it does. Talk.

"I..."

"Shut up for a minute. What do you think?" she asks my father, who has placed the form facedown on the table and is shaking his head at the floor.

"I don't know until she tells us what happened," he says sadly. "I do know they misspelled *undue,* not that it makes a difference, but they did."

"Let me see that," my mother says. She reads the form and then puts it, faceup, in front of me. "I don't care what they spelled how, you better talk."

I clear my throat.

"Well," I say, "first of all, this whole day started out bad. I had a history test that I studied and studied for, and I was terrified I wasn't going to pass it—and it was really hard!—but then it turned out that I not only passed, I did perfect! And then I was at lunch right after, in such a good mood, and then Debbie Duncan got up and was carrying her tray to the belt, and I said, 'Hey, Dunk, throw my stuff away,' and so did Felicia, and I was in such a good mood—over the history test— and Flea was too, because she had a test *she* did well on (we studied together over the weekend!) and so we threw our hamburger papers, trying to land them on Dunk's tray, and we went overboard, is all. And mine didn't hit the lunch lady, it went in the hot dogs."

"That's what they mean? You threw trash at a cafeteria worker?" She stares at me in disbelief, and then at my dad, who is starting to look like he could use a drink.

"Mom! If I threw a feather, it would count as launching a projectile—you can't go by the categories!"

My mother looks pointedly at my father.

"Honey," he says, staring at his hands. "Those people really work hard in there, cooking and cleaning up and I don't know what all, for you kids." He sighs and shakes his head. "Boy, oh boy. Something like that is really, really..." He trails off.

The stove clock ticks. Tammy sidles into the room, checks

her dish, takes one piece of kibble, and tiptoes out with it. I wait for a second, then get up to follow her.

"By the way," my mother says, "you can forget seeing any more of Flea."

"I'm grounded from you," I tell her when she picks up the phone.

"Yeah, I'm grounded from you too," she says. "Mick Jaggermeyer told my mother you were a bad influence. We have to meet on the corner because I'm not even allowed to walk by your house."

"I have to bring the à la carte lady a plate of fudge tomorrow."

"Who's making it?"

"She is." Even with my door closed, I can hear the sound of angry candy making going on downstairs.

"What're you wearing?" she asks.

"I thought maybe culottes and my blue vest."

"With what?"

"White shirt?"

"Too plain."

"I know. What about you?"

"That spongy dress with nylons."

"I never know which one is spongy."

"Green with gray stripes that have triangles inside them; you think the neck is funny."

"Oh, right. Listen. No matter what, we have got to talk to those boys *tomorrow*. Otherwise, we were mean for nothing."

Instead of yelling at us, the cafeteria lady had stood there stunned, paper hat askew, cheeks aflame.

"It made her feel terrible," Felicia says in a hushed voice. I can't bear to think about it. She somehow thought we were making fun of her. All the fudge in the world isn't going to fix that.

Next day, three o'clock, we linger in the detention doorway, sizing things up. I went against the culottes at the last minute and am wearing a short wool wraparound skirt instead. While the monitor checks the paperwork of some new recruits, a hoodlum plays with the science skeleton, which has been left out by accident. He puts his hand through the pelvis from behind and turns it back and forth, like a periscope. The boys we're in love with sit up front on opposite sides of the room, while our table is at the back, in the center. Right before the buzzer, Felicia heads down one aisle and I head down the other.

Just when you depend on time to do its job and keep things moving, it slows down completely.

Mr. Prentiss, hunched over a drawing he's working on. Glances up. Looks right at me. His eyes are brown and narrow, friendly. There is a small indentation next to his eyebrow, like someone has pressed a star into his temple. He's wearing some kind of leather string around his neck, inside his shirt, which is not flannel today but corduroy. Green. The drawing is of a lion's face. It's good but the nose is like a beagle nose. Lion noses are wider than that. His hand holding the pen is grubby.

"Hi," I say.

Silence. The wind blows across the barren landscape of my chest. Time reverts to normal and I make my way to our table in the back, hands trembling, and sit.

Well, that's it, then; all is lost. Why would someone in such a beautiful, soft shirt, with those narrow, clear eyes, ever want to speak to me, with my doughy face and fishing-pole legs? My wraparound skirt is held together with a big, decorative safety pin. I unfasten it and refasten it, taking a moment to stab myself in the thumb.

Hers said hi back; I can tell and I'm not even looking at her. She's looking at me, though. I dig around in my purse until I locate a nail file, and then in small, jagged letters I carve a thought into the table. When I take my hand away she leans over to read it.

SHITE.

She slumps back in her chair.

A canyon yawns between us now. She has leaped across it, hollering hi and having her hi come back to her. I'm thrilled for her, she deserves it, but I'm alone over here and it's making me feel wavery and unsound, like I should be home in bed waiting to die.

Instead I do algebra, which I've recently started working up to capability in. Poor old Mr. Lepkis, with his speckled head and spidery equations, put a couple of things on the board one day that were first of all readable and that second of all made sense to me. It was like getting the key word in a crossword puzzle, the word that releases all the other words from where they're hiding in your brain. I would just stare at the board until suddenly I got the key thing, and then the rest of it was easy and satisfying, like tidying up a house — put this over here, put that over there, go like this and you get this, then go like this to get this. I could do the staring part from my seat but had to go to the board in front of everyone for the tidying up. We always thought he was using faulty, squeaking chalk, but I've had no trouble with it. And x always ends up equaling something simple, like n to the second, or even one.

It's a burden, actually, because poor old Lepkis now keeps saying, "Let's ask hherr," whenever there's an uncomfortable pause; so it means not only that I have to pay attention in class but that class pays attention to me. I've had to stop repeating certain clothes; everything has gone into regular rotation.

My favorite clothes are a white shirt with extralong, hand-hiding sleeves, a charcoal gray dickey that I can thrust my whole face into, and two things given to me by a slightly older cousin: a tartan plaid skirt with fringe along the bottom and a long black crocheted vest. That cousin may live in the country and have to take a bus to school, but nobody can fault her taste in clothes. Her dolls even had better clothes than mine, although mine were professionally made by my mother on a sewing machine, while hers were constructed by her, using household materials and a stapler. While my Barbie was wearing a shirtwaist housedress with piping and roomy pockets, hers would be tightly bound into a Japanese kimono made from an old satin negligee and belted with a strip of flocked wallpaper. She once made both of our Barbies reversible rain capes from a plastic tablecloth. The rain side had a latticework theme, with sprigs of cherries; the other side was the white flannel backing, which we thought looked like a fur stole.

Anyway, I have favorite clothes that I like to repeat.

"If I am forced to respond, Mr. Prentiss, you will receive the first of *next* year's detentions," the monitor says without looking up. She now has something angora blooming in her lap, a rainbow-colored scarf with frilled edges. Very pretty, although people don't actually wear things like that.

He's waving his arm around.

If x equals zero, then n and p equal zero too. It's a trick question. You hardly ever see a trick question in a textbook, although it does happen. I check my work, but it appears to be correct.

"Mr. Prentiss, what can I do for you?" she says wearily.

"Thank you! This has to do with homework, which Mr. Bingham—gym—kept us too late last period for me to get to my locker, which I had planned on doing to get homework for in here. We were climbing the ropes and nobody could do it, we were all just hanging there, so Bingham took off his whistle and started showing us!" He pauses to look around. "The Buffalo climbed the rope."

This causes a stir among the male detainees. When the monitor starts to set her needles aside, Mr. Prentiss hurries on.

"Anyway, can I borrow an algebra book from this person so I can copy down today's problems? Otherwise I'll just be sitting here for an hour, wasting time and probably who knows what."

She squints at him, considering all the angles. "And who has the book?"

"That girl at the last table, with brown hair. I don't even know her name."

She looks back at me. "Do you have what he's talking about?"

I nod.

He starts to get up.

"Oh no, you don't." She points at me. "You. I don't want him walking around."

I collect my math book and walk up the aisle. He doesn't look at me and I don't look at him. I return to my seat and a minute later his hand waves and she nods at me. I go up the aisle, take the book, and return again.

Inside the front cover is a sheet of notebook paper, folded twice. I open it under the table, where Felicia can see. It's his drawing of the beagle-nosed lion. Below it, floating, is one word in tiny cursive: *Hi.*

The next couple of days are a whirlwind of speculation and advice, impromptu conventions around my locker, home of the dwindling plate of fudge. The à la carte lady had been gone the day I brought it, and by the time she returned, I wasn't too sure about taking food to someone who spends all day up to her neck in it. Instead, we ironed our sewing projects and gave them to her, a ruffled pillow sham and a smocked apron, both orange and white gingham.

"Well," she said. "I don't know what to say."

We didn't either.

Mr. Prentiss says hi to me twice more on my way to the back of the room, each time widening his narrow eyes as though he is about to say something else. I can't stay for it, whatever it is, because I've begun to feel weightless and slightly faint. Now that I'm over here on this side of the canyon, everything seems so intensified—his long, expressive feet in their ripped sneakers, hooked abstractly around the rungs of his chair, the way he bounces a pencil, so lightly, against his temple while he reads, the way he raises his head when someone walks past but doesn't raise his jaw, so his mouth drops open a little bit. Not in a way that makes him seem impaired, but in a way that makes the looking up seem uncalculated. He's just looking up, is all, because he wants to see who is walking past. He isn't thinking about his mouth! That's what's so overwhelming.

"She has to calm down," Dunk advises Felicia.

"I know, but she can't," Felicia replies.

This delirious, buzzing feeling is neither unpleasant nor unfamiliar—I used to get it lying in the mildewed hammock in my grandmother's backyard, utterly relaxed in body if not in mind, the tops of the trees moving back and forth across the sky, the rope creaking, the peeling paint on the garage coming into view and then leaving again, slower, slower, slower, until I had to reach out with my stick and give another push. I do miss childhood: one long trance state, broken only by bouts of sickening family discord.

What if this guy actually wants to talk to me?

"Don't worry," Felicia says soothingly. "He won't."

"This is clinically depressing me," Gina Maroni, Duncan's best friend, says. She's a tall, graceful girl with a large nose and silky black hair who used to be a figure skater until her butt grew—as she puts it—and threw everything off. She's outgoing, which means she doesn't really belong with us, but we like having her. "Not talking to someone is snotty. Why would you want to be snotty to him?"

This kind of psychology never works on me.

"You ought to give him a piece of this fudge," Dunk suggests. "Just go, 'Want some fudge?' and then hold out a little piece of this."

"What if he says no and I'm just standing there with fudge in my hand? Or what if he asks where I got it?"

"Then you tell him. Go, 'I brought it from home.'"

"Then he'll think I'm someone who's making fudge and bringing it to school. He'll think I'm Amish."

"No!" Felicia says. "Say you made it in home ec. Go, 'I made this in home ec.' This shows you're being nice, yes, but it doesn't look like you're offering him *fudge*. It just looks like 'I have to get rid of this fudge I made in home ec; I'll give some to a kid in my detention.' "

"How can she be giving him fudge when she can't even look at him?" says Jan Larson. Her parents call her Yawn. White blond hair and a round face, braces, also has a bird, but hers talks. After it bites you, it says it's sorry in a flat Norwegian accent. "Too complicated. Why not just have her go—" and she shrugs, does a Mona Lisa, braces-hiding smile.

"She needs to do both," Maroni says definitively. "Fudge, then smile. Or maybe smile, then fudge. And while he's eating it, ask him if he's going to the game."

They're giving me a drowsy, moth-headed feeling, as though I'm in a beauty parlor, being turned this way and that, a plastic sheet snapped around my neck, under which my hands are nicely folded in case it's whipped off unexpectedly. Snip, snip.

"Look, she can't even listen to this," Felicia says.

"So do it with yours," Maroni says. Felicia's hasn't been saying hi to her, but he's been veering into her when they pass in the halls. "Smile, fudge, game."

"Okay," Felicia says agreeably.

This kind of psychology does work with me.

"Wait," I say.

"Don't try to tell me you're going to a football game and it isn't with Flea, because I know better," my mother says. "You are not to be seeing her whatsoever."

"I'm going to a football game with Dunk and Maroni," I say patiently. "And maybe Yawn and maybe Luekenfelter, if her mom says."

"Why *wouldn't* her mom say? Is there something I don't know about these football games?"

"No. *God*. It's a game, people throw a ball around; it's exciting. If I can't go, just tell me, and I'll get someone else to use my ticket."

"You have a ticket?"

"You can't go to a game without a ticket! God!"

There's a long wait as she reads her newspaper and smokes.

"Be home by nine," she says.

"The game begins at eight! God!"

"Be home by ten," she amends it. "And if I hear the word *God* again, you won't know what hit you."

"There's pizza afterward!" *God.*

She reads and smokes, turns a page. "Eleven," she says finally.

Friday afternoon detention. Smile, fudge, game. Smile, fudge, game. I tried to do it yesterday but couldn't get started. Now the fudge is on its last legs when I carry it in and hand it to him, frozen faced.

He looks at me first, then at the fudge, resting on a brown paper towel. The buzzer goes off and I make my way back to my seat. When Felicia asked hers if he was going to the game, he pointed at her and then mimed laughing, holding his stomach. For some reason, we've taken this as a positive sign.

After class, Mr. Prentiss waits instead of racing out. I collect my things slowly and then walk up the aisle.

"That was good," he says.

I nod.

"You got any more?"

I shake my head.

We walk out together and stand waiting to see which way the other will turn. His green army jacket is slung over his shoulder, held by one crooked finger.

"Game?" I say.

"What?" he asks.

"Tomorrow night's game," I say.

"Oh," he answers, nodding.

We look down the hall in opposite directions. In my direction, Felicia stands at a respectful distance, staring at the floor. In his direction is the door whose crash bar he likes to kick.

"Yeah," he says, stepping on his own sneaker, where a piece of rubber is coming loose. He pulls the stepped-on shoe out from under the other shoe, thereby tearing off the strip of loose rubber. He kicks it thoughtfully into the center of the clean, empty hall. "I'm usually either sitting in C or standing under it."

"Oh," I say.

"Yep," he answers, looking at the crash bar.

"Well," I say, looking at Felicia.

"Finally get to go home," he says.

"Yep," I say.

He shifts his jacket to the other finger and I shift my books to the other arm. His free hand is six inches away from my free hand. I feel breathless and unstable, like we're standing on the wing of an airplane.

Felicia clears her throat, still staring at the floor.

"She's waiting for me," I say.

"See you, then," he says.

Once outside, he jumps all the way down the steps, landing

in a crouch. We watch him through the door as he lopes across the lawn, dodges a car, waves at the driver, and disappears down the street.

We're speechless.

"That was a million times better than somebody holding their stomach and laughing," Felicia says finally.

My sister will let me wear her peacoat to the game only if I tell her what's going on. After an hour or so, I give in.

"There's a guy I might talk to," I tell her. She stares at me for a full minute. I try to stare back but I can't.

"And are we thinking our sister's peacoat will make him fall in love with us?" she asks gently.

"No," I say miserably. Why did I even start this? "I like it, is all. And I get so cold, I'm just sitting there shivering."

"And what about our CPO jacket that we thought was the way to go?"

During our family coat-buying expedition, instead of a peacoat, I asked for what is known as a CPO jacket, which is styled like a shirt and made of heavy plaid wool, to be worn over a hooded sweatshirt. I have no idea what CPO stands for, but cold has to be the first word. My mother let me get it because I already had the sweatshirt and she was broke, walking around the store staring at price tags and getting more and more upset.

"I'm sick over this!" she said at one point, looking at Raymond in a warm zip-up jacket with padding and attached mittens. She took it off him and hung it back up. "Half the price of this is the mittens, and we don't even want them."

"I want them," Ray admitted.

"You do?" she cried. She stood there in the little-kid aisle and we stood there with her.

"No," Ray said.

"He doesn't," I said.

"He liked the other one," Meg said.

"He did?" my mother asked.

"I did," Raymond agreed. "Which one?"

"That one," Meg said, pointing at a jacket with an emblem on the arm.

"That has that goddamned emblem," my mother said.

"I like an emblem," Ray said. "What is it?"

"It's just a thing," I told him.

So, that was coat shopping. Every month we have less and less money. My mother made all three of us kids go to the bank with her last Saturday, to sit quietly in chairs while she spoke with a woman about the house payment. The woman had a large, friendly face and short, iron gray hair with a fringe of bangs, like Captain Kangaroo. She fiddled with her wristwatch the entire time she was listening to my mother, winding it on her wrist, lifting it to her ear, winding it again.

"You are not the kind of person we worry about," she said reassuringly as they walked over to where we were sitting. "It's the *others* that we worry about—things you would not believe."

"I'll bet," my mother agreed vaguely.

The woman went behind the counter where the tellers were and came back with an all-day sucker for Ray, a set of knives for Meg, and a manicure kit for me.

"Free gifts," she told my mother. "For when they open a checking account some day."

While Meg considers the peacoat request, I clean her half

of the room, hauling clothes out from under the bed and folding them. It's incredible what's under there, stuff from summer, plates my mother has been looking for, makeup, curlers, and way in the back a really cute shirt all balled up with the tags still on it.

"That's for you," she says quickly.

It's a dark, rich burgundy, fitted at the top and loose at the bottom, gathered right under the bodice with a narrow black ribbon. Meg jumps up from her bed, yanks off the tags, and puts them in her pocket.

"It looks big but it isn't," she explains, holding it up to me. "See?"

It's true, and when I try it on, something amazing happens — boobs appear out of nowhere, nestled right above the black ribbon. No matter which way I turn, they're still there. It's a dazzling, expensive shirt, given to me by my sister for unknown reasons. I yawn casually, take it off, and stow it in my dresser.

Once her side of the room is as clean as mine, she lets me try on her peacoat, which doesn't fit. At all.

This puts her in a genial mood. "So, what's that kid's name?" she asks.

"Prentiss," I tell her after a long pause.

"What's his first name?"

"Kevin," I say after a longer pause.

"And what do we like about Kevin Prentiss? Is he cute?"

I try staring at her the way she stares at me. Both of us have brown eyes. Brown eyes staring at brown eyes. Still staring. Brown eyes like pools of muddy water, seeping toward one another. Still staring. Water, seeping toward other water, getting ready to merge. I blink.

"He's okay," I say.

*   *   *

Once Whinny collects my sister, I put a mud mask on my face and talk on the phone to Felicia while it dries. Then I scrub it off and get out my manicure kit and use all the tools in order, even the one I don't know what to do with, which looks like a miniature shovel. Then I get the shirt out and try it on again, with various pants. Then I look at the CPO jacket and try to figure out how to make it warmer. Then I go downstairs in my nightgown and make popcorn.

Everybody is gone but me.

The dog and I go back up and get in bed to read with our bowl of popcorn. We've got two books going at once—*David Copperfield*, which we know by heart, and *Look Homeward, Angel*, which we don't altogether understand. A stone, a leaf, an unfound door... that's the underlying theme. My mother got it at a yard sale.

I read a few random chapters about David C., just for the simplicity of it—"I Am Born," "I Fall into Disgrace," "I Have a Memorable Birthday," et cetera—and then switch for a while to reading about Eugene, the fellow in the other book. Tammy curls up beside my knees and stares at me for popcorn, which she doesn't like. I hand her several pieces, which she takes and then sets down on the bedspread.

"No, eat them," I urge her, and my voice sounds really, really loud and strange. What size stone? What kind of leaf? What color door? Usually I see the stone as smooth and weighty, like a river rock; the leaf slender and serrated, like an elm leaf; and the door as the door to the old chicken shed behind my grandmother's house, dark flaking green with a rusted latch. Right outside that chicken shed was a thick stump with two nails pounded into it about an inch and a half apart. My cousins and

I used to climb a trellis onto the roof of the chicken shed and then jump from the peak onto a pile of loose dirt. I liked the old stump and would lean on it, touching the nail heads lightly, while I waited for my turn to climb, until one of my cousins told me that between those nails was where the chickens' necks were laid while they were getting their heads chopped off.

I suddenly don't feel that well.

My book is full of long, bulbous passages describing things I don't want to know about Eugene and his demented, vain family. The whole thing is florid and thick, too heavy to rest on my chest without hurting.

I feel like I might throw up.

One of Eugene's older brothers, the sweet, melancholy one, dies of typhoid and they put his body on something called a cooling board. Eugene has managed to forget this brother during the short course of his illness, but it all comes back to him—the soft eyes, the strange, delicate demeanor, the birthmark—when he sees the brother laid out on his cooling board. He misses him suddenly with the kind of terrible intensity people in his family are known for: "O lost, and by the wind grieved, ghost, come back again!"

I sob, ill.

Tammy hops down off my bed and walks over to Meg's bed, jumps up, scratches the bedspread into a heap, and settles down again, black nose nestled into her side.

There might have been something wrong with the popcorn.

My own brother is at a Cub Scout sleepover in his school's gymnasium; the last time I saw him he had on his dark blue Cub Scout shirt and a bright yellow neckerchief, held in place with a Webelo clasp. I creep over to the desk and upend the plastic wastebasket to dump out its contents, then carry it back to my bed. After a few minutes I retch into it, and a lava flow of dinner comes up, with kernels of popcorn here and there. The dog jumps down and leaves the room.

Help, I'm sick.

My mother is over at Tuck's, the neighborhood tavern. "I guess I'll go have one," she said after the dinner dishes were done. "I'm too tired to do anything else."

On nights like this, when my dad is missing, she sits with other couples and with her best friend, Kay, a small woman with a gravelly voice and a similarly drunk husband. It's a mysterious, damp cave over there at Tuck's. No kids are allowed, but they can peer in from the propped-open door during daylight hours and see the dark wood, a glimpse of mirror, and every kind of liquor possible, lined up on shelves behind the bar, like a library, only booze. There are usually one or two people sitting on stools with an ashtray and a glass in front of them. You can order cheese sandwiches there; I've had them brought home to me.

More retching, more molten lava.

I grab the phone cord and reel it in from my bed, dial the number to Tuck's and Tuck answers. Ten minutes later she's coming up the stairs. I feel better, but not that much. I can't stop shivering.

"I-I-I-I c-c-c-c-can't st-st-st-stop sh-shiv-shiv-shivering," I tell her.

She peers into the wastebasket. "Oh boy," she says. "I thought you looked funny all week."

Her cure for everything is to grind up a bitter white aspirin and have us drink it in a tablespoon of water.

"No," I croak.

"You've got to," she tells me firmly. It's the middle of the night and I'm in her bed, throwing up over the side into a series of wastebaskets that she's collected and washed out. I keep falling asleep and imagining things. Hands, inflated like rubber gloves, a kitten in a T-shirt. Once, Kevin Prentiss jumps down a set of stairs and bounces back up in the air like he has giant springs on his feet, arms pinwheeling. Bounce, bounce, across the landscape and gone. Raymond in his Cub Scout kerchief, taking miniature cars out of his pocket and setting them loose on the floor, where they race toward me across the bedcovers.

"Get them off," I holler, and they are swept away by Mr. Dreil, the custodian at my old grade school. He steers a long red dust mop down a hallway and into the detention room, where Felicia is bent over a biology tray, poking a scalpel at a fetal pig. My mother takes the biology tray away from Felicia and puts it in the oven, twists the knob on the timer.

"It's formaldehyded!" I cry, waking myself up.

"What? What did you say?" my mother mumbles, dozing beside me.

"Nothing," I murmur, embarrassed, and slide backwards into it again. Poor old Lepkis sweeps equations off the board with a whisk broom, into a spoon that my mother puts against my lips.

"No!" I say.

"Yes," she tells me. "You have to, you're burning up."

She needs to put me on a cooling board. Eugene's sister carried him in to show him the wasted husk in the bed—soft, willing Grover, dead at twelve. I see an ironing board balanced on its thin heron's legs, a dead boy stretched out on it. My mother approaches with a steam iron in one hand. The boy is Prentiss, in a burgundy shirt with the tags still on it.

"No!" I cry.

"Yes," she says. "Now here."

I drink the spoonful of chalk, and by morning I'm sitting up, eating toast.

She's got me in the living room with sheets and pillows on the couch and cartoons on the TV, while she's in the kitchen, cleaning cupboards, talking on the phone, and every once in a while stretching the cord around the corner to check on me. Trying to radiate a sense of health and well-being, I ignore her. When she snaps her fingers, I nod without taking my eyes off the TV.

These cartoons are nothing like during my era. The drawings aren't that good, if you compare Mighty Mouse or Donald Duck, say, to the Archies or Scooby-Doo. If I want to know about Archie and his friends, I'll read one of the three thousand *Archie* comic books that we have in our attic—in the comics, the characters are dark and ridiculous, that's the joke, that's why it's a comic. In the cartoon, they aren't meant to be ridiculous at all but are members of a rock band. Scooby-Doo is also depressing, if you think about it—the dog is a Great Dane, and they don't live very long, maybe seven or eight years at the most.

"How long has this show been on?" I ask Ray. He's back from his sleepover, eating bowl after bowl of cereal.

"An hour?" he says.

"No," I say patiently. "It's been on a *few minutes*. I mean how many years."

"Ten?" he says.

"No," I sigh, rolling over on the couch. I'm sweating again.

My mother hangs up, comes in, and feels my forehead.

"Your hand is cold," I say without opening my eyes.

"I'm defrosting the freezer," she explains.

My plan is to get gradually better and better all day until game time, at which point there's nothing she can do but let me go.

"Your sister isn't going anywhere," she says to Ray, preemptively.

"I know," he agrees. "She's sick. Last night Kippy Cappert threw up macaroni on a Tonka truck."

"Can you tell him to shut up?" I say nervously. It's not the macaroni; it's the thought of Kippy Cappert, who has been in our house before and who walked around with a thick green caterpillar under his nose all afternoon.

"It wasn't a dump truck," Ray continues. "It was one of them with wheels like this." He makes an inexplicable jabbing motion with his hands. "A whatchacall, and he threw up macaroni on it."

"That's enough," my mother tells him. "She's right on the verge."

Too late.

After that, I retire to my parents' bedroom for a few more hours of festering sleep, and wake completely renewed. My mother is sitting on the edge of the bed with a thermometer, smoking a cigarette.

"I'm not sick anymore," I say, sitting up.

"Good," she says, poking the thermometer under my tongue. It's strange how when you're telling the truth, they know it.

"I'm hungry," I tell her.

"Quiet for three minutes," she says, raising the shade to stare out the window, smoking and frowning, gray eyes pale behind her glasses. She's waiting for my father. Every once in a while a car door will slam and voices are heard, but it's just neighbors leaving and returning from their Saturday errands. If he shows up at Tuck's, someone will call her—either Tuck himself or one of her friends, whoever happens to be over there having one.

"I'm here to tell you, not to sell you" is the motto of the company my dad works for—Best Home Improvements, supposedly run by Dick Best, a man who shouts the motto on late-night television commercials. In fact, the man is an actor; there is no Dick Best. That's the thing about being an independent door-to-door salesman: you are the one sending yourself out there each day, so hating the boss means hating yourself. Which is why a lot of them work in twos and threes— not only does it help with the loneliness and inertia, but it gives them somebody different to hate.

The way it usually goes when my dad works with a partner is that the partner shows up sometime midmorning and drives the two of them to a shabby neighborhood where they knock on doors, showing poor people their sample cases until they get one or two to sign up for siding or a new roof. Then they drive to the nearest bar and sit drinking for the rest of the day, and sometimes one or two days after that. After a few weeks of this, when the partner slides up and honks, my dad won't go out. Eventually the partner drives away, and my dad stays home for a few days or a week, petting the dog and drinking in the garage; then he disappears completely, which is the phase we're in right now.

The thin afternoon light reveals dog hairs on the rug, the covers thrashed into a snarl, and two wastebaskets sitting on the other side of the bed, damp washrags draped over their edges. On the night table, along with a full ashtray, is a bottle of Pepto-Bismol, a sticky spoon, and a glass of water with an expanded crumb floating in it. As soon as I get the thermometer out of my mouth, I'm going to put everything back where it goes, strip the bed, remake it with clean sheets and pillowcases, sweep the rug, call Felicia, take a bath, wash my hair, put on my new shirt, go to the game.

"Normal," she reads. "But we'll wait to feed you. I just made Jell-O; when it's set up, you can have a little bowl."

"What kind?"

"All I had was orange," she says.

"*Orange?*"

She flinches at this and looks out the window again, her lips bunched up in the way she does when she's getting ready to cry. She thinks better of it. "You're welcome to starve," she says, standing up.

On her way downstairs, she pounds on the door to Meg's and my bedroom. "It's almost three," she says. "And I won't tell you again."

From somewhere inside the room comes a dull thud.

"What?" Meg cries, voice muffled.

"Listen," my mother says through the door, her voice now

tearful, wavering. "I've got your dad drunk, one kid sick, one kid exhausted, and one kid who better get her ass out of bed *now*."

Another thump.

"What?" Meg cries.

"You've had about forty calls this afternoon," my mother tells me when I pass through the kitchen carrying laundry to the basement. "I told them all you were in bed with the flu."

"I'm going to the game," I inform her. She'll just have to get used to it.

"Forget it. You're not going anywhere sick."

"I ate bad popcorn!" I say.

"There's no such thing as bad popcorn," she says.

Tammy follows me down to the basement and stands outside the coal cellar, a room nobody ever ventures into, staring at the door intently.

There's a Ping-Pong table next to the washer, which we use for folding things that come out of the dryer and, on the far end, for stacking the things that migrate out of the laundry—some ancient and war-torn underwear, a dense, miniaturized sweater that should have been dry-cleaned, a melted shower cap, the usual limp, disoriented socks—and all household flotsam not suitable for the attic. Once, I came down and there was a mouse on the Ping-Pong table, nibbling on the green foam block from the bottom of a florist's arrangement. Because the block was perforated with holes, the mouse might have thought it was cheese.

"Come here, girl," I coax Tammy.

She glances over once and then looks back at the door,

steadily. Waiting. What does she think is in the coal cellar? I crouch down.

"Come here, Tammo…come here, Tam o' Shanter…come here, Tam o' Shay." Nothing.

An ancient wringer washing machine stands under the open-riser steps, thick rubber lips pressed together. No matter what you do with its cracked black hose—coil it inside the tub, hang it over the edge, or lay it on the cobwebby floor—you'll always have to look twice to make sure it isn't what you just thought it was. An old buffet with chipped veneer stands along the wall, filled with cupcake tins, cookie sheets, and stacks of empty Cool Whip containers and their lids. Jumbled along the top are various canning supplies and implements, a box of shotgun shells, a paper bag stuffed with other paper bags, some plastic rope, and a ceramic Easter bunny for the center of the dining room table.

Across from the buffet is the furnace, tentacled and wheezing. Behind the furnace on the left is the door to the coal cellar, where Tammy is stationed, gazing with pricked ears at the doorknob.

Something feels wrong. I stand for a moment, listening to the washer fill. When it stops, there's a pause before it clunks into the next cycle. It's during the silence that I figure out what's wrong.

There shouldn't be shotgun shells down here.

"Now what?" my mother says as I run up the basement steps and through the kitchen.

"Nothing," I say, panting. In the upstairs hallway, I pause at the door leading to the attic. Up there is where the shotgun is kept, zippered into a case that hangs way in the back, behind a beam, invisible from most angles. The front of the beam has two hooks from which a wide, obscuring clothing bag hangs; next to the bag is a stack of hatboxes. In the third one down, underneath a man's gray hat, the shotgun shells are kept.

"Meg!" my mother calls up. "Help your sister!"

Our bedroom door flies open and Meg stares at me. She's still in her pajamas, holding a book. "What?" she asks me.

"She thinks I'm throwing up," I tell her. I yell back down the stairs. "I'm not *sick,* I told you."

"You're not going anywhere either," my mother replies.

"I am too!"

"How big do you think you are? Because if I call you down here, you'll find out who's bigger."

The thing is, now that I've hesitated, I'm scared to go up to the attic. For a few months, in fifth grade, I used to sneak up there every morning and every evening, taking the gun down from its case and hiding it in a box of quilts before school, and then putting it back later. In those days I couldn't go into the house alone after school but would sit on the front steps, waiting for Meg, who got home a half hour later. My dad was usually inside, sitting at the kitchen table watching the backyard, making notes on which birds were visiting the feeders. I knew that, but I also had it in my head that whoever went in first might find him dead by his own hand.

Once, on a day so cold that the fronts of my legs were burning from walking the six blocks from school, I was huddled on the steps, breathing into my mittens, when Meg got there.

"Why don't you go in?" she asked.

"I didn't want to," I said. "I just felt like sitting out here."

"Look," she said, sighing, and sat down on the step, took

her pencil box out of her coat pocket, and opened it for me. Inside, along with pencils and pens, were the razor blades usually kept in the bathroom cabinet.

If I go up in the attic and there's no shotgun, I will have no choice but to go back down to the basement, move the dog aside, and see what's in the coal cellar. I lean against the wall and look at my sister, but what I see is the door to the coal cellar, which is slumped on its hinges and has to be lifted slightly or it won't open. During the summertime, worms are kept in there: two large Styrofoam coolers filled with soggy shredded newspaper and fat night crawlers, which my brother sells by the dozen. Once a week he and my dad run the hose under the tree in the backyard and pick up what pops out on the grass. I happen to have a morbid fear of worms, which is one reason they're kept in the coal cellar. The other reason is that it's cool in there, like a tomb, with a dirt floor and damp walls.

Meg stares at me curiously. "Maybe go take a bath or something," she suggests, not unkindly. "You look like shit on toast, which is why she thinks you're still sick."

"I'm not sick, I'm nervous," I say.

We call them dew worms. In the mornings when the grass is wet, my dad will open the back door and say, "Get the dews, Tammo," and the dog will hop all over the yard, chasing worms.

Along one wall of the coal cellar are rough shelves that hold jars of preserves: tomatoes, corn, beans, beets, pickles packed in brine, fruit floating in syrup, jelly in juice glasses, grape and currant, each sealed with a disk of paraffin. Eventually she'll send one of us down there while she's cooking.

"Everyone is nervous when they're meeting a boy," Meg assures me.

Meeting a boy? Oh, right.

The bathtub is long and claw footed, with a wire soap dish that hangs over the side and an old-fashioned curved faucet that I can get my head under. My meditative bath activity is to lay a washcloth flat on top of the water, poke the center of it from underneath to make an air bubble, gather the sinking ends so it looks like an air-bubble bouquet, and then pull it down into the water, forcing the air through the terry-cloth holes to make an explosion of tiny, fizzing bubbles. I do this over and over and over, without thinking of anything but the air-bubble bouquet and its offspring. By the time I get out, I'm clean and calm.

Meg has gone downstairs, leaving her book facedown on the bed: *A Tale of Two Cities,* which I haven't read yet. She says it's good, even though it was assigned for school. The cover is a black-and-white drawing of an angry woman knitting, with a guillotine in the background. The guillotine is one thing, but I don't know if I'll be able to read a whole book about a woman knitting. The detention monitor with her long tubular scarves; my mother, making a pink mohair turtleneck for my Barbie; me, knitting a famous pot holder that actually conducted heat instead of absorbing it. It was white with a blue edge and had a wooden ring crocheted to a corner, made at Bible school one summer, back when I was religious.

Being able to conveniently remove Barbie's head while changing her clothes is what made the pink turtleneck possible. The book's guillotine is crudely drawn, a slanted blade in a wood frame. The notch at the bottom of the frame serves the same purpose as the two nails in the stump outside the chicken shed: it holds the neck in place.

If only I were still religious. If something has happened already and you just don't know about it yet, God would be the only one who could turn it around. Not that he would—he being the creator of the guillotine, the chicken stump, the shotgun, and several other devices that make it clear why people are always begging him for mercy.

Drying my hair makes me dizzy for a minute and I have to lie down again. Old Milly is getting supper in her kitchen, moving back and forth between the counter and the table, carrying things and setting them down: a plastic butter dish, a bowl of bright orange carrots, a container of cottage cheese, a white plate with flowers around the rim and a pork chop in the center. Nothing to drink. After she sits down, she gets back up for the salt and pepper. Then she sets her elbows on the table, folds her hands, puts her forehead against them, and stays like that for twenty seconds or so.

Dear God, please make my dad be out drinking right now.

Jesus I never really minded because of the way he appeared in Sunday school books, in a belted frock with a pleasant, beaten-down expression on his face, surrounded by either sheep or children—not a person you'd think would invent a guillotine or a gun, although he did turn one fish into a thousand, just to eat them. That's not that holy, but those were different times, and look who his father was.

My dad, on our family's fishing trips, every Saturday during the summer, would prop his own rod and reel on a forked stick, then work his way up and down the bank, baiting hooks with my brother's worms, taking the fish off the line and releasing them if they were small, putting them on a stringer if they weren't, tossing them back up into the weeds if they were bluegills.

Sunfish were what everyone caught a lot of, shiny and flat, like big coins; less common were the bass, with wide translucent mouths, or the catfish, with long whiskers. The whole thing made me feel desperate, from the squeaking Styrofoam cooler of worms in the backseat, to the lawn chairs that stuck to the backs of your legs, to the clouds of gnats, to the fishing hat my mother wore, to the pair of needle-nose pliers my father kept on his belt and would use, turning away so we couldn't see, to get the hook back when a fish swallowed it. The little bluegills in the weeds would lie there forever, staring blankly up at the sun until you were sure they were dead, and then they would flop again. What was it about bluegills that made everyone hate them so? They were small, the size of my hand, not even blue.

Dear God, please. If you make my dad be drunk right now, I'll do whatever you say.

I go back downstairs at some point and sit in the kitchen while she cooks dinner.

"You always think you're getting the raw end of the stick," she says to me, tenderizing a piece of meat with a pronged hammer. "Half the time when I look at you, you're pouting."

"Short end of the stick," I say.

"What did I say?" she asks.

"Raw end."

"I meant short end. And why? Because you aren't getting

what you want, is all. And that's the action of someone spoiled. Do I like to tell you no? Do I like to tell any of my kids no?"

"You never tell them no," I say automatically. I don't even care about this. I thought maybe when I came down here the dog would be next to her bowl, waiting for supper, but she isn't. "Where's Tammy?"

"I do tell them no, not that it's any of your goddamned business either way." She slaps the meat into a skillet and puts a lid on it. "She better not be upstairs. If she's on my bedspread, I'll kill her."

A terrier is utterly loyal to its master, although it's true the master is sometimes a tennis ball. My dad bought our terrier for a dollar at a body shop in a little town north of Zanesville. She's never gotten over it—even as a tiny white puppy that he'd carried home in his pocket, she used to stand on his shoe and stare devotedly up at his knees. Eight years later, she still tags him everywhere, and when he isn't around, she waits by the door with a pair of his old socks, knotted together. If something has happened to my father, I don't know what Tammy will do.

"I think she might be in the basement," I say tentatively, heart pounding. What am I saying? "Sitting outside the coal cellar."

"Doing what?" my mother asks. She's got a cigarette going and is staring into the cupboards.

"Just waiting at the door," I say.

My mother whirls around, stricken.

"This is what I need now?" she cries, yanking the lid off the skillet and pressing her spatula into the meat. A cloud of sizzling rises and is muffled by the lid, clattering back into place. "Another goddamned *mouse?*"

She hands me a stack of plates and I put them around the table without getting up. My heart feels like the meat. She goes back to staring into the cupboards.

Silence.

"I don't think it's a mouse," I say finally.

"Well, you're going to find out, because I need a jar of green beans, if there's a small one, which I don't think there is. Otherwise, yams."

"I-I-I," I say, "can't."

"Now you're afraid of a mouse? You who tripped the traps?"

"I don't know what yams even are!"

"They're along the bottom shelf, dark orange colored but in chunks, not slices. The sliced ones are carrots."

"I don't like yams," I say. "Why can't we have something from up here?"

"I don't have anything up here!" she says, her voice rising. "How am I supposed to go to the goddamned store with you sick, your father drunk, and now *mice?*"

"I'm not sick," I say.

She calls into the living room. "Who'll run to the cellar for me?"

Raymond appears instantly, something all down the front of his shirt.

"What's that?" she says, scratching at it with a fingernail.

"Not him," I say. "I'll get them."

"My thing went upside down," he explains.

"You sit right there," she tells me.

I sit back down. "But not him," I say.

She turns to Ray. "Can you get me a small jar of beans, and if there aren't any, then yams?"

"Okay," he says.

"Do you know what yams are?" she asks.

He nods.

"What are they?"

"They're little yams, in the jars," he explains, curling his fingers.

"Okay," she says, sighing. "Help your sister set the table."

She's going down herself! Never in the history of needing preserves has she ever gone down there herself.

"Mom, wait!" I say quickly. "Just let me — I have to change the laundry." And I push past her into the stairway and pull the door closed.

On the landing is a case of pop and two cases of empty beer bottles, other trash, a broken yardstick. In the gloom at the bottom of the stairs I can just make out the white dog, waiting.

A stone, a leaf, an unfound door.

Dear God, please. Give me courage to go in there after changing the laundry.

All the bedding is wadded together against the side of the washer. I peel it out and stuff it into the dryer, clean the filter and add it to the giant ball of lint I've been making, twirl the knob, push the start button, and then fold some stray things on the Ping-Pong table. The phone rings and I hear Meg call for my mother.

Dear God, please. Now is the time to give me courage.

A river rock, an elm leaf, the door to the chicken shed.

The coal cellar will have one bare bulb hanging in the center, with a dusty string you have to pull. There will be the empty worm coolers, nestled into one another, there will be the antique wicker basket with leather straps that the fish are carried home in, there will be the shelves of jars with their murky floating contents. In the corner, under the black grate where the coal used to be funneled down, there will be the shotgun and what it has shot.

Dear God, please. If you change what has happened, I will give you anything.

Why would God want anything of mine? He wouldn't, and that isn't how it works anyway—a bully only takes what someone else wants. All I've wanted recently is Mr. Prentiss.

Dear God, if you make my dad be all right, I will give up Kevin Prentiss, the guy I was going to see at the game tonight.

The door at the top of the stairs opens and my mother's feet appear on the landing. She crouches down so I can see her face, excited and pale.

"Where are my beans?" she demands. "That was Kay on the phone and I have to go to Tuck's. She said your dad just walked in without a coat, not a dime on him, and they're buying him drinks to keep him there."

If there is a God and he truly is all-powerful, then he's the one who arranged to get me off on a technicality—the call from Kay actually coming in moments before I made my deal, thereby annulling it. While getting dressed I thought about it and thought about it, coming to the conclusion that there's a limit to what people can be expected to believe, which is why I'm at the Grassy Knoll at the appointed hour, waiting for my friends.

Down below, the crowd shuffles along Elm Ave on their way to the stadium gates. Above, the sky is cold and sparkling, although I'm not cold at all. Just the opposite, in fact.

All the boosters come out for the last game of the season, parent-aged people wearing white carnations tipped with magenta, capping and uncapping flasks. Tonight the Zanesville Zephyrs are playing the Central Valley Voles, who always win, insulting everyone in Zanesville's idea of proper conduct for a school that is both poor and rural. They have rawboned, implacable players who trudge out on the field like coal miners going to work, and solid, unlovely cheerleaders who wear pants. Their mascot is technically not a vole but another tiny-eared mammal, the badger. I have no idea what to do if nobody shows up. Obviously, I can't go in there and be walking around alone; I'm supposed to be a sidekick.

How does my dad do it, going off by himself for a week, two weeks? The days, I can imagine—small-town bars where no one can find him, dark clinking places lit by Old Milwaukee signs and jukeboxes—but the nights I can't picture at all. Eventually the bars close, don't they? And then there's just the big black Illinois sky stretching overhead.

Dear God, if you make my dad be all right, I will give up Kevin Prentiss, the guy I was going to see at the game tonight.

It's like a tree falling in the forest with no one there to hear—it makes a sound wave, but not a sound. If there's no one to hear a promise, it can't possibly count, can it?

Trees and stars, stars and trees. My feet might be getting a little bit cold in their sneakers, but in a pleasurable way, like sticking them out of the covers on a winter night. I like sitting here on this grass, even if nobody ever shows up.

A stone, a leaf, an unfound girl.

"Hello?"

She came up the side way, past the Fertilizer Home and over the big hill, so she's breathless, appearing out of the dark in a plaid car coat and mittens. It's like being trapped down a well and having a familiar face appear at the top. I haven't seen any real people at all for twenty-seven hours, ever since detention let out, and now here is my friend. Tears of relief burn behind my nose. Hers is running and she swipes at it in her old, familiar way, then pushes her glasses up.

"We heard you were sick, so everybody just decided to meet at the gate," Felicia explains. "But then at the last minute I thought, what if you really were up here?"

"Never listen to my mother," I say.

"That's what I told them," she replies.

She pulls me to my feet and we head out, through the trees and down the back way. It's so beautiful tonight, everything washed in stadium light, casting inky black shadows. Up ahead is the gravel path that leads to the side gates.

"How come you're wearing glasses?" I ask.

"Stephanie kicked me, and my contact popped out of my head," she explains. "It's somewhere in that rug in front of the TV—blue and green shag and it's a green contact! Forget it."

"Did she get killed?"

"She got taken after with a wooden spoon, but my mother never hits, she just brandishes."

Her mother, my mother, her sister, my sister, her, me. You can see why somebody might go into a coal cellar and never come back out.

"So, do they look stupid?" she asks, glancing over at me. Her hair is freshly washed and tied back with a ribbon, like clean, baled straw. Cheeks pink, eyes watery and magnified.

"Nobody notices glasses except the person who's wearing them," I remind her.

Single file along the path, which is covered with leaves. Just before we join the crowd stuffing itself through the gates, she unties her ribbon and shakes the straw loose. Suddenly I feel flushed and uncertain, coat open, hair sticking to my neck.

Mr. Prentiss is in there, somewhere in the vicinity of section C.

"I-I-I c-c-c-c...," I say.

"You have to," she replies smoothly, slipping her glasses into her pocket and blindly grabbing my sleeve. As the crowd surges around us, I pull her along, trying to lead and follow at the same time.

We meet up with everyone—Dunk, Maroni, Yawn, Luekenfelter, a tall, brown-haired girl who is Yawn's best friend, and Luekenfelter's cousin Jane—at the snack hut located at one end of the bleachers. Inside the hut, two very wide men try to work around each other, passing popcorn and hot dogs over the counter to grown-ups. It's considered weird for kids to eat this food, although Maroni is holding a raspberry Sno-Kone in a gloved hand. I love raspberry.

"Don't even ask," she warns me. "You've got the flu."

"Please?"

"Okay," she says.

The bite is blue and icy, so refreshing that I suddenly like everything: the night, the weather, the crowd, my girlfriends. I like Luekenfelter's cousin, a pretty girl who is sent to stay with Luek on the weekends because of a sick mother.

"How's your mother?" I ask her.

She shrugs. "Sick but not too sick—she sits up during the days. They're thinking about doing one other surgery, which we hope they will. It all depends on certain things, but we think they'll go ahead. If she continues to sit up on her own . . . that's what will tell."

Silence. Maroni chews ice; everyone else nods thoughtfully.

The cousin clears her throat. "I could have stayed back there this weekend but I heard you guys were meeting up with boys."

"These are the two who are," Luek explains, pointing to me and then Felicia, who puts on her glasses so we can see her.

Suddenly a wave of Kevin Prentiss washes over me. Detention hallway, his hand, warm and golden looking, with a pencil wart on one finger, hanging there next to my hand.

"I-I-I," I say.

"It's just sitting with a guy, it's not marrying him," Felicia says nervously.

"Who are you — Maroni?" I ask her.

Maroni laughs.

The only way to get to section C is to walk the narrow gauntlet down in front, between the first row of packed, people-watching bleachers and the cinder track where the cheerleaders perform. We'll have to enter at G, walk along the chain link past F, E, and D, then head up into the stands at C, climbing until we get to the empty seats. At which point we can finally sit and survey the situation without the situation surveying us.

"I can't do it unless I'm holding on to her," Felicia says, taking off her glasses and gripping my sleeve.

I can't have anyone holding on to me; I'm too tense.

"You're not the only one!" Felicia hisses. "I'm supposed to

be meeting up with what's his name." She looks around blindly. "What's his name?"

"Jeff Nelson," Dunk says patiently.

"You're *Flea*," Maroni adds.

Duncan leads, with Felicia attached to her sleeve, then Yawn, then me, then Maroni, then Luek, then Luek's cousin.

When walking in front of fifteen hundred spectators, it's best not to do it in one's normal hunching and scuttling style, but instead to think of the shoulders as a coat hanger and the body as a chiffon dress hanging from it. Unfortunately, the gauntlet is narrow and people in the front row aren't good about retracting their feet, so right out of the gate we have a stumble and a pileup. I get a mouthful of Yawn's platinum hair, and Maroni walks up my ankle.

People are really getting on my nerves.

Single file, past sections F, E, and D, then up into the stands at C. It's hard to be chiffon climbing bleachers, but I do all right until Maroni yanks at the hem of my jacket, holding me fast. Foot groping for the next bleacher, I see him, amid the undulating ocean of faces and Windbreakers. Out here in the great, dark night, Mr. Prentiss looks more like a hoodlum than he ever has before, dark bangs falling across his eyes, coat open, no gloves. He raises one hand and cups it against his mouth and yells something at someone behind me, people's knees turn sideways like pinball flippers, and I'm shoved down the row of seats toward him.

I'm the person he was yelling at behind me.

"I saw you down there," he says by way of greeting, nodding at the gauntlet below. At the bottom of the sloping bank of bleachers, a steady current of kids moves past, like a river. There are spots where if you step into the Mississippi it will pull you away from the bank before your feet even touch. You have to think of yourself as a bottle, inanimate and buoyant, and simply bob on the current. Don't open your mouth or water will get in and the bottle will sink.

"Mm-hmm," I murmur.

Below, the two teams move across the field a yard at a time, arranging and rearranging themselves kaleidoscopically. Who knows what they're doing down there—it seems remarkable that they can do anything at all, given the circumstances up here in the stands. Eventually, a lone Central Valley Vole breaks loose from the pack and runs, his white jersey and helmet bobbing above the churning orange of his legs. The crowd roars to its feet. Mr. Prentiss squints at the running Vole and then swears self-consciously. I squint too and sit back down when everyone else does. On the cinder track, a teetering hive of Zanesville cheerleaders forms—*Hey, hey, that's okay, we're gonna beat 'em anyway*—and then collapses. One girl takes a running start and does a series of increasingly sagging backflips, spelling out Z-e-p-h-y-r-s. By the end she is nearly landing on her head.

"Ha, that's sick," Mr. Prentiss says to the field.

The side of his face is soft and faintly fuzzed. Not like one of the man-boys with their strange sad sproutings of facial hair, and not like one of the maiden-boys with the opposite problem, but somewhere in between. Broad shouldered and mysterious, wearing desert boots instead of his bandaged sneakers; they look new, but his jeans are very old, with a series of overlapping patches on one knee and a fringed rip on the other, through which I can see long underwear.

Right while I'm looking, the ripped knee moves about an inch in the direction of my knee but then shifts back to where it was. He was just stretching.

I shiver involuntarily.

He glances over at me and then back at the game. "Your lips are sort of blue," he says.

What?

"Oh," I say. "Sno-Kone."

"Yeah?" he says lightly, leaning forward to look back over his shoulder at me, tucking a strand of hair behind his ear the way he does when hassling the detention monitor. His eyes at close range are brown green hazel, and not all that narrow. "You like *blue* Sno-Kones?"

The sly, teasing grin, the shaking of the hair back over the ears, and the clear-eyed gaze, all directed at me—it's as disconcerting as having my name suddenly announced over the loudspeaker. A guy who isn't one of my uncles is teasing me, and it calls for something other than sidling out of the room backward—it calls for a teasing answer. *You like blue Sno-Kones?*

"They're raspberry," I say eventually.

Silence. We watch the field, where nothing is happening.

Raspberry. Raspberry. Razz-beery. A word designed to make you feel like an idiot. His leg is closer to mine now, and his hand rests on his knee, just above where the fringed rip and the slice of long underwear are.

A blast of wind hits the bleachers, and people put their mittens to their faces.

My teeth make a chattering noise.

"I was boiling," I explain. "That's why I'm only wearing this coat."

"I'm always boiling," he says. "Here." And he takes off his green army jacket and puts it over my shoulders. It's heavy, heavier than a girl's coat, and it has a frayed, body-heated aspect to it that makes me feel relaxed and sleepy. When I was very little, I used to curl up on the coat bed at family gatherings, wind someone's satin lining around my thumb, and suck on it until I fell asleep. Something about the strange, borrowed fabric enhancing my old familiar thumb, and about burrowing into the lumpy mound of coats, knowing that my parents couldn't get out of there without running across me — that's the feeling I have now, resting against Mr. Prentiss's arm, which is behind me.

A Vole takes off running, darting in and out of confused Zephyrs, and the crowd rises to its feet again. We don't move, but continue staring ahead, into the matching Windbreakers of the couple in front of us. When they sit back down, it looks like the green board has been tipped and all the players have slid down to one end.

"Ha," Mr. Prentiss says. "They're smoking us."

"Yep," I say.

His hand is on my waist now, resting lightly against the fabric of my shirt. It's the same hand, the left one, that I always stared at in detention, the nervous-energy one that drummed his hip, felt around on his head, pulled the leather string out of his shirt, and then dropped it back in. That hand.

"Yep," I say again, sitting up straighter.

The girl cousins I played with at those long-ago family gatherings all turned out boy crazy, and I see now why, leaning against this kid while he slowly bunches my shirt up, an eighth of an inch at a time. There's something delirious and drowsy about the whole endeavor—the term *sleeping together* is starting to make more sense, because that's what I feel like doing. Just curling up on the coat bed and taking a nap.

My father would never make me wake up and walk, but

would carry me to the car for the ride home. Borne aloft by my tall dad through whoever's house it was, aunts reaching out to shake my foot as they said their good-byes, the night feeling of the family in the car on the highway. It's night right now, vast and beautiful, and the boy I nearly traded for my father's life has his fingers hooked in my belt loop while the thumb moves back and forth along a shoreline of skin.

Dear God, I give up Kevin Prentiss.

Back and forth.

Forth and back.

I don't believe, even if there is a God, that he could have saved someone retroactively; and yet what if there is one, and he did? This is what's so confusing about religion—it's all based on trying to make you believe in ghosts. If you accept that idea, then anything is possible.

My father, rising from the coal cellar to walk into Tuck's five minutes before.

O lost, and by the wind grieved, ghost, come back again.

I shrug off the coat and the hand, standing up.

"I have to go," I say.

On my way out, I get momentarily hung up on the gauntlet while the junior all-city marching band passes through on its way to the halftime show, a plumed and confused caterpillar running into itself. The flute is a tall, slouching girl who is fingering the keys with her head angled so her flute points to the ground, the way I used to do it.

Come on, come on.

Then they're gone and the current surges forward again, carrying me along until I cut behind the hot dog hut and pass through the side gates, where a man sits on a stool with a hole puncher and a transistor radio.

"You don't want to watch them lose, do you?" he says to me.

"Nope," I answer.

"He better wake 'em up when they're in that locker room!" he calls.

"Yep," I call back, over my shoulder.

I'm warm again, and my head is throbbing. The gravel path is still washed with stadium light, but now the inky shadows are as scary as they are beautiful, like a black-and-white movie where somebody is going to get killed. At the end of the path, I take the dark way, over the Knoll.

Once, I watched a movie on TV after everyone else had gone to bed, an old western where a group of men are discovered by another group of men, and the second group decides to hang the first group, unless they can talk their way out of it. I was falling asleep the whole time but couldn't go to bed without seeing how the first group, who were innocent, talked their way out of getting hanged.

Running footsteps. Coming up behind me. My heart begins galloping around in circles. I have no idea what to do. There's nothing up here but trees.

Help.

"God!" Felicia says, panting. "I was yelling, 'Wait up,' and you just kept going."

Anyway, the movie has a surprise ending: they hang them.

"We were watching you from the top, with that kid's arm around you," she says, falling into step, "and then all of a sudden you got up and left. I thought you might be going to the bathroom, so I decided to go to the bathroom too, and then when you didn't, I just kept following you."

"Where was yours?"

"Sitting four rows down and about ten seats over with some blond-headed girl. I had a perfect view of him."

We drop down and circle behind the Fertilizer Home, where we can see into a rec room of sorts, lighted but empty, with folding chairs set in a circle. That old cotton-haired woman who once came to our door is probably dead by now; if she isn't, I don't want to think about it. Years now, that she would have been in there, thinking they're trying to kill her.

"Did you ever see that movie, *The Something-Something Incident*, where they thought those guys had stolen the horses?"

"I saw it with *you*, and we fell asleep," she says.

"I woke up just when they were hanging them," I say.

"I know," she says.

I've got my coat unbuttoned and my hands in the pockets, fanning myself. There's going to be a certain amount of yelling when I get home, but it's dark and quiet out here, under the winter stars. The air feels metallic.

Up close, Mr. Prentiss had seemed so real he was almost surreal—like having a character in your dream show up when you aren't asleep and suddenly put their hand in your shirt.

A boy put his hand in my shirt! I feel strangely elated, even though it didn't work out.

"We thought that guy was going to kiss you," Felicia says. "Right there in the bleachers, in front of God and everyone."

"There is no everyone," I tell her.

We are required to take a shop class instead of home ec the second half of the year, starting right after Christmas. I get metal shop, where I'm making a tackle box for my dad, and Felicia gets wood shop, where she's burning a design into a step stool with a branding iron. You get a choice of two patterns; one is foliage with your father's name in the center, and the other is a farm scene.

I used to love the farms where all my relatives lived, big dark ramshackle houses with boot scrapers set into their stoops. I could make our family a boot scraper, if we wanted one, now that I'm in metal shop. I've never used a blowtorch before, but I see why people like it—it cuts metal. I've taken to talking about it at the dinner table, which I wouldn't normally do about anything else, but this is different.

"You can cut *steel?*" Raymond asks me, raising his head from a bowl of cornflakes, chewing and dripping on the tablecloth.

At that exact moment, I remember a dream I had from the night before, where I was at my uncle's pond watching everyone fish and suddenly there was a moose standing knee deep in the water, moss dripping from its chin. Why was I dreaming about a moose?

Ray uses both shoulders of his shirt to dry his face and then goes in again. "How can she cut *steel?*"

"Close your mouth," I tell him.

"You let me be in charge of table manners," my mother says.

"It melts the molecules," I tell him.

"It *melts* them?" Ray says incredulously.

"I wonder if it melts them," my dad says. "I'm not sure if that's what a cutting torch does."

"That's what it does," I say.

"You're liable to melt your own molecules," my mother says, "if you don't watch what you're doing. And I'm tired of seeing a book at the table."

"We never had shop," Meg says, closing her book. "We learned how to sew your fingers together and how to make cinnamon toast."

"This is what they're burning their bras for over in Washington," my mother says. "So these girls can end up in the hospital if they aren't careful."

"Boy, be careful," my dad says to me.

"I am," I tell him.

I wish my mother wouldn't mention bras in front of my father; I don't know how much he knows or doesn't know about certain matters. My mother's own bras are large quilted things that I used to think were funny. Now when I see them on the laundry table, one cup folded into the other, I have a sense of impending doom. It's like being on your way to the Alps and knowing that when you get there you'll have to wear lederhosen.

Upstairs right now is another gloomy contraption that was recently bestowed on me — the sanitary belt. This is a piece of elastic that goes around the waist with garters in the front and back, used to strap on a sanitary rag. No matter how much you scrub it, the belt keeps its pale pink stains from month to month. I wonder what my father thinks of that thing when he sees it hanging from the bathtub faucet.

My mother serves up bread pudding for dessert, a dish nobody likes. We sort through it with our spoons while she smokes and my dad looks over our heads. He's been sober now for several weeks, ever since New Year's, but it's coming to an end. His resolve cracking is nearly audible in the silence.

"Why can't this just be pudding?" Meg asks finally. "Why does there have to be wet bread in it?"

The best thing about shop isn't actually the cutting steel, but the fact that all anyone has to do is ask to use the bathroom and Mr. Rangel, the teacher, lets them leave. He's never taught girls before and it's making him frantic — the first mistake he made was putting us in pairs on the torch. Within five minutes somebody created a column of fire in the middle of the room, brief but riveting, and Rangel locked the door afterward and explained for about an hour how it happened (lack of safety) and why it would never happen again (he would personally supervise every instance of acetylene use from there on out) and the reason it was never to be discussed outside the classroom (shop would be permanently closed to girls, regardless of women's lib).

There's always somebody you know in the bathroom. This

time it's Luekenfelter, so we sit on sinks and talk for a while about our current topics—what if she tries out for chorus and ends up making a screeching sound instead of singing, and what if my only chance to have a boyfriend has already happened and I ruined it. At this point, all that's left of Mr. Prentiss is a piece of rubber off his shoe that I've been using for a bookmark. He either got sent away or moved away.

Lately Luek and I have been trying to help each other be more confident but it isn't working; we're actually making ourselves more nervous. We joke around about that for a while before we realize Patti Michaels is standing on a toilet, blowing smoke into the ceiling fan and listening to us over the top of the stall. This girl has the distinction of being the only cheerleader who is also a hood—she transferred from another school, and the tryouts took place before anyone knew anything about her, beyond the fact that she looked like Gidget and could do a no-handed backflip from a standing position.

"I'm dead if that door opens," she says.

"We'll cover you," I tell her.

"If that kinky-haired bitch walks in here, stab her," she answers.

That gets a moment of respectful silence, and then we hop down and address the mirror. One of my ears constantly pokes through my hair, possibly because it's bigger than the other, just like one of my eyes is slightly higher than the other. No matter how I tilt my head, everything is off-kilter.

"I look like modern art," I say.

Patti snorts.

"Girls, I'm going back," Luek says. She scans the corridor on her way out, looking for whoever is in pursuit of Patti. "Empty," she reports.

"Don't leave yet," Patti says to me. "What do you have?"

"Shop." I need to go back and finish my hinges, but this girl has a certain authority, being a cheerleader standing on a toilet.

"Rangel or Dim-dick?" she asks. Mr. Dimmek is the wood-shop teacher.

"Rangel," I say. I show her the hall pass, a flat piece of metal with a room number painted on it. "This is the plate out of his head."

Patti snorts again, dropping her cigarette in the toilet and giving it a flush.

"You hang around with that girl Flea, right?" she says. "You and her should come to my slumber party this Saturday. It'll be Cindy, Gretchen, Kathy, Cathy, Deb, and then three friends from my old school. My grandmother said I could have ten."

Crap! The problem with Patti Michaels is that she not only doesn't know she isn't cheerleader material, but she doesn't know who should and shouldn't be invited to one of their parties. This is a disaster.

"Well, what do you think?" she demands.

"Fun," I say.

We open the door and peer up and down the hall, which is empty except for a desk that has been pulled out of the sewing classroom. In it, a banished kid is bent over a needlework project. He has Mr. Prentiss's same hair.

"So come to my locker after school," Patti says, and sashays past the boy, who looks up from his tea towel to watch.

"Wait—how many cheerleaders?" Felicia asks suspiciously.

"A lot," I tell her.

"Yeah, but how many?"

"All of them," I confess, "and a couple people from another school."

"And this is Patti Michaels, right? Not Patty Jackson and not Patty what's her name?"

"I know those Pattys—this is Michaels. She was in the third-floor bathroom when I went in there, and she invited us to her slumber party."

"And did she say me, or did she say you, and you said me?"

"She said, 'Flea.' 'You hang around with that girl Flea,' or something like that," I tell her. "You're actually in this more than I am. She never called *me* by my name."

"Does she know she looks like Gidget?" Felicia asks.

"Probably. So, do you think we should go?"

"I agree with you about Shakespeare," she says suddenly, as the shadow of a teacher looms over us, listening. This is gifted English, which means we work at our own pace, learning about literature through interaction with our peers. "The *tempest* he's referring to is actually a storm. At sea, it looks like."

"It's where the old saying of a *tempest in a teapot* comes from," I tell her.

"We have to think about how the ship is like a teapot," Felicia suggests.

"Don't worry about that now, okay?" Miss Van Leuven interjects. "I'm asking people to read this with the idea that they're listening to the *music* of Shakespeare. Think of it— and hear it, if you can—as mellifluous. It will help if you read passages aloud to one another. Try closing your eyes while you listen!" She pauses, chewing on a hangnail. "Or, I don't know...does that seem silly?"

"No," I say.

"It's a good idea," Felicia says.

Van Leuven continues on her lonely way, drifting and prodding. She is the youngest of all the teachers and somewhat of an outcast. She showed up this year from Minneapolis, bringing the gifted program with her. This happened to occur at the same time the Annex arrived—a trailerlike structure pulled up and parked behind the real school, containing three new classrooms, a science lab, and a closet filled with vented plastic boxes full of rodents and frogs—and the same time the mandate came down about girls in shop and boys in home ec. So poor Van Leuven is forever linked with progress, and when you see her with the other teachers, no one is ever talking to her.

The first day we had her, she wore a windowpane-patterned dress with a vinyl Carnaby Street hat, the second day she wore a denim jumper over a black leotard, the third day she wore a Mexican dress with a rope belt, the fourth day she wore a granny dress and granny glasses, and the fifth day she wore a pink suit with a too-short skirt and got sent home, like a student. When she came back, it was in a dirndl skirt and a white blouse, which she has worn some variation on ever since.

Felicia thumbs through her book. "Close your eyes," she says, and recites:

> *O wonder!*
> *How many goodly creatures are there here!*
> *How beauteous mankind is! O brave new world*
> *That has such people in't!*
> *'Tis new to thee.*
> *What is this maid with whom thou wast at play?*

Van Leuven is right: when you close your eyes, certain words bloom out. Hollyhocks in a field of soybeans: *goodly, beauteous, wast at play.* The simplest, most unadorned words—'tis, new, to, and thee—become *'Tis new to thee,* a perfect little phrase.

'Tis + new + to + thee = *'Tis new to thee.* I've been put in gifted math too.

"You can open your eyes," Felicia says.

When I do, we're still in the Annex. Across the hall is the closet where the rodents and frogs are being held, waiting to take part in experiments. "So, what about the party?" I ask.

"I think we should just go and see," she says, handing me the book and closing her eyes.

She wants to go! I was afraid of that.

"Me too," I say, turning pages. "Listen to this. Trinculo: *I shall not fear fly-blowing.*"

"What's fly-blowing?" she asks.

"Self-explanatory," I say. "Listen to this, it's about your sister: *I am not Stephano, but a cramp.*"

"Ha, she *is* a cramp," Felicia says, eyes still closed. "Are the friends from the other school cheerleaders too?"

"Probably," I tell her, turning pages. "Listen: *Monster, I do smell all horse-piss, at which my nose is in great indignation.*"

"Ha, *horse-piss!*" Felicia says, this time too loudly, her voice carrying across the room.

Van Leuven makes her way toward us through the tangle of displaced desks and chairs, drawing nigh just as the bell tolls. She stands aside then, a pale, pretty woman in a Dacron blouse, as students scramble over one another to get out of her classroom.

As we pass her, she says, hopefully, "He's funny, isn't he, girls? Shakespeare."

*   *   *

Patti Michaels is standing at her locker, waiting, at three o'clock.

"Hi," she says to Felicia.

"Hi," Felicia answers.

She hands over two invitations with our names scrawled on them.

"Where do you live?" I ask.

"You know that house that looks like a plantation, on Twelfth?" Patti asks. "That's my grandma's house, where I now live. We get the whole basement and she's ordering us pizzas delivered. All anyone needs to bring is a sleeping bag — it's my birthday but I'm not asking for presents."

The plantation house! A wide, sloping terrace, lions on either side of the front door, a circular drive with a stone arch, a carriage house. We stand for a moment, uncertain what to say next. Halfway down the hall, three boys are horsing around, two of them swinging notebooks at each other's heads while the third tries to trip them.

"We might have to do something else that night," Felicia barely audibly tells Patti. "We aren't sure."

"This party is better," Patti says definitively. "Ask anyone who ever knew me before I lived here: you'll have fun."

Suddenly one of the notebook boys hits the other one broadside in the head, causing him to stop for a moment in astonishment before swinging back, very hard and wide, missing the first kid, who ducks, but slamming the notebook into the metal lockers. The first kid then uses his notebook like a shield, forcing the second kid into walking backward, red faced and laughing. The third kid follows them around in circles, putting his foot out to trip whomever he can.

The detention buzzer goes off and they light out down the hall. That's where I remember the second kid from.

"Hey, why did you say you look like modern art?" Patti asks me.

"My features are asymmetrical," I explain.

She looks at me keenly. "They are?"

"She *thinks* they are," Felicia says.

"Do you think they are?" Patti asks Felicia.

"If you measure them, yes," Felicia admits, "but if you just look at her, no."

"She thinks *she* has a bubble butt," I tell Patti.

"Turn around," Patti says.

"No," Felicia says.

"Don't worry," Patti says. "I wouldn't have invited you if you did."

Sometime midweek, while the rest of us were bending steel and taking math tests, Luekenfelter's cousin's mother died. It happened during the afternoon, while the cousin was at school and one of the neighbors was over, keeping an eye on things. The mother and the neighbor were watching a series of soap operas over the course of the day, the mother taking one pain pill after another, trying to get some relief, until the whole bottle was gone and the neighbor was watching the soap operas alone, without knowing it.

For some reason, instead of going to glee club after school, the cousin got on the early bus and went home, where the neighbor lady was upstairs running the sweeper. She actually sat in the chair next to the sofa where her mother was and ate a Pop-Tart before figuring it out.

"How could they not know?" I ask.

"I guess the eyes were open," Luekenfelter says, and then starts crying. "This is my aunt we're talking about, and she wasn't supposed to even *have* the bottle of pills, but the neighbor didn't know that."

We're in the cafeteria, but no one is eating. Poor Jane, the cousin.

"She's acting like nothing happened!" Luek says. "We were out there last night, and if I started to cry, Jane would go" — Luek demonstrates, opening her gray eyes wide with a look of annoyed surprise — "and at one point when someone hugged her and then stared at her, like, *Why aren't you crying? Your mother is dead,* she goes, 'I'm not sentimental, I guess.' Her dad sat in an old Firebird the entire time we were there, parked in one of the Quonsets."

"She's probably in shock," Yawn says. "I've seen her cry before — when her mother had surgery and it didn't work, she cried when she told me about it."

"She did?" Luek says.

"Remember when we were at your house and we were watching the show where the woman who wore all the scarves was dying and no one could help her? When you went upstairs to get pillows, your cousin rolled over on the couch and was crying. I asked her if she was okay, and she said that her mother had surgery and it didn't work."

At this, Luekenfelter puts her head in her arms and sobs, right at the lunch table.

Felicia walks up to the counter, gets a handful of napkins, and brings them back.

"You should be able to go home from school," Maroni says.

"Really?" Luekenfelter asks her, pressing the napkins to her face. "If it's my aunt?"

"In this case, yes," Maroni assures her. "Because your cousin is like a sister to you, which means your aunt was like your mother, in a way."

"She looked just like my mother," Luek says, and then stares around at us, red eyed. "I've known her my whole life. She made them get a pony for me when I was six. She *made* them."

Yawn fiddles with her hall pass. She doesn't even have lunch this hour, but Luekenfelter is her best friend.

"I never knew you had a pony," I say.

"It was kept out on their farm but it was mine—I called it Little Brownie and I rode it all during the summers."

"What happened to it?" I ask.

"They had to tear down that barn, and in the new one there were no stalls; it was one long aisle with stanchions for the milk cows," Luek explains, accepting the piece of bubble gum Yawn gives her before heading back to class. "Thanks. Ponies can't be kept outside year-round, so they were sold. Mine went to a man who had a little girl with one leg, but they had rigged up a saddle where she could ride anyway."

"Really?" Felicia says, picking up her hamburger and looking at it but not taking a bite.

"That's a good ending for somebody's pony." I tear the end off my long john and place it on the waxed paper.

"Jane's went to people in their town, so she got to see it whenever she wanted to. And ride it." Luekenfelter shakes her head. Her hair, which is usually bouncy, hangs lankly around her ears, like mine. "To tell you the truth, I never really believed the story of the one-legged girl."

When she picks up her hot dog and takes a bite, the rest of us quickly stuff our food in our mouths and sit chewing.

"But who would lie about something like that?" I say finally.

"A bunch of A-holes, that's who," Luekenfelter snaps. With that, she gets up and walks out of the cafeteria, not taking the side route but going right past the row of boys eating hot dogs and judging girls. Their heads turn as she stomps past, a sturdy, flat-haired girl in a pleated skirt and kneesocks.

We look at one another.

"I'll do her math homework tonight," I say.

"I'll finish her history paper," Maroni says.

Felicia thinks. "I'll take her tray back," she says.

From the dining room table I can see the television in the living room, but I don't even feel like watching it, it's such a relief to be doing regular math again—a whole page of Luek's equations that look difficult but aren't. It's like double-Dutch jump rope: from the outside it looks complicated, but once you're in there it's just basic. Like so many things, it's designed to make people seem more talented than they are, which is how I got into my current gifted-math mess.

I'm working far beyond capability now, in a classroom where they roll maps and screens down over the blackboards so regular people won't have to see what's up there. I haven't known what was going on from the first minute I sat down and saw who I was in there with: Velda Burnett, who carries an enormous plastic pocketbook; two twin boys with butch haircuts who are so smart they come across as retarded; Larue Varrick, first flute; Toby Merkel, a kid with a mustache; and then the usual pack of beautiful ones, known for being good at everything from honor roll to hitting a hole in one during golf week to giving a speech to the principal on Turnaround Day to making a soufflé that stays inflated until the teacher sees it. They're the ones with money, for the most part, the rich cream that rises and is eventually skimmed off and sent somewhere else.

At my house, we're still the opposite of rich—my mother is sick over the fact that right now all of us kids need things and there's no money to buy them. She blames my father, who responds by going out to the garage in the dark and staying there.

Which is fine with her if he wants to walk out in the middle of a conversation. And if he isn't going to work to support this family, then maybe she won't either. She can sit on her ass as well as he can sit on his, instead of every morning of her life getting up and going to that office and listening to people talk about how they're doing this and that to their kitchen, how they're buying a boat for the river, how their kids are going all the way to Spain as part of some school group. She doesn't care about herself, she always expected she'd have to work for a living, but what she would like is for her kids to have the things they need. Apparently too much to ask.

"I can't do homework when people are yelling!" I yell.

Tammy hops up on the dining room chair next to me, puts her chin on the table, and stares at the centerpiece, a long canoe-shaped seedpod filled with plastic fruit. I offer her a tangerine and amazingly she takes it, hops down, and trots away. I have to go after her, right after I finish the problem I'm on.

"That goddamned dog has my fruit!" my mother yells.

"Mom! Shut up a minute, will you?"

This is Meg, trying to watch TV. There's a pause, and then my mother materializes in the doorway between the dining room and living room.

"I didn't mean shut *up*, I mean just be *quiet* for a minute until this show is over," Meg says.

My mother walks over and turns the television off.

"I hate this house!" Meg yells. She looks across at me in the dining room. "And she's laughing at me, the B-hole!"

"I've heard enough. Get to your room," my mother says evenly. She glares at me and I get up and go crawl behind the couch, take the tangerine out of Tammy's mouth, and bring it back to the seedpod. My mother comes over, picks it up, and looks at the bite marks on it.

"This is ruined," she says, but puts it back anyway, alongside a pear that also has bite marks—human ones, but she doesn't know that.

Overhead is the sudden sound of chaos, a shattering noise followed by a series of bellows. Raymond, in the bathtub, has shot at the overhead fixture with his squirt gun until he finally hit the hot lightbulb, causing it to explode, plunging him into darkness and raining slivers of glass down into the bathwater. It's not the first time this has happened, and my mother hollers at him to stay put while she fishes around in the junk drawer for a flashlight.

"You're going to have to go to the garage," she says to me, heading up the stairs. "Tell your dad to give you the flashlight out of the car, if he can put down his drink long enough."

I can't go out there. I don't want to catch him with his brown paper sack.

"I'm in my socks!" I call up the stairs.

She comes back down to the landing. "I have a boy sitting in a bathtub full of glass," she tells me icily. "If you can't go out there, then why don't you yell from the back door—you're good at that."

He appears in the dark garage doorway but can't hear what I'm saying, or won't, and I have to hop down the sidewalk in twelve-degree cold. "She needs a flashlight for Ray," I tell him, and hop back to the door.

Nothing.

Then he appears again, weaving slowly down the sidewalk, shining the beam on the snowbanks and the bird feeders. This is how he picks fights—by driving the other person mad with his palpable, infuriating reluctance.

"I held off on filling the big feeder because the raccoons empty it during the night," he says.

"We have a boy sitting in a bathtub full of glass," I tell him icily, taking the flashlight out of his hand.

"What?" he replies placidly.

I push the back door shut in his face.

I have terrible dreams all night—a professor in a black coat with numbers all over it lecturing me with a piece of chalk, a raccoon riding in a bicycle basket, my mother staring down into a crystal ball that explodes in her face, flying monkeys wearing clothes that I currently have on layaway. I feel like dog crap at school the next day.

"Why would I have *Wizard of Oz* dreams when I haven't been thinking about *The Wizard of Oz*?" I ask Maroni, whose locker is two down from mine.

She thinks about it for a moment. "It's a menstruation dream," she says, slamming the door shut and twirling the knob.

That's why I feel like shit! I can't believe she knows that. How could she know that?

"It's the ruby slippers," she explains.

I always loved the ruby slippers, although I didn't care for the little blue ankle socks she wore with them.

"Do you need anything from my locker?" Maroni asks pointedly. She offers tampons to people the way missionaries hand out Bibles. She believes in them.

"I have the other kind in my gym locker," I tell her. Our last box of napkins had in it a soft vinyl napkin-carrying case, lavender with an embossed girl holding a finger over her lips— *Sssh, don't tell anyone there are two giant napkins in this lavender thing.*

"Good luck, Lena Gibb," Maroni says.

Lena Gibb is a girl who had to be called out of class by the nurse after walking around half the day with a growing stain on the back of her dress. Nobody told her before that because her personality was such that everyone was afraid to. She thought of herself as a witch and put elaborate hexes on people—nobody believed in the hexes, but it was embarrassing anyway.

My first class is art, where I share a table with a boy named Steve who thinks I'm funny and nice. I think he's funny and nice too, although not as funny and nice as he thinks I am. In fact, our whole friendship is based on him telling me what he and his friends have been up to and showing me the drawings he does of race cars with rats driving them, and on me responding with funny comments about the escapades and nice comments about the drawings. He may not even know my name; he may think it's Joan.

Today we're continuing to work on our papier-mâché sculptures. Mine started out as a giant chicken, but I couldn't get it to stand on its legs, and so I'm giving it human hands for feet. I used Steve's hands and wrists to model them, and now he's in love with the chicken, as is the teacher, even though it still won't stand up.

"Ever heard of surrealism?" Mr. Ringgold asks the class, which hasn't. "A guy named Salvador Dalí? Your minds would be blown instantly! I mean, this guy turned it around, in terms of how he saw time—his specialty was the melted clock, but it didn't end there by a long shot." Ringgold usually seems depressed, but the chicken has livened him up. "Another guy, Magritte, turned it around in terms of space—ever see a painting of very ominous-looking silver spheres floating over a landscape?" No one has. "Again, blown minds everywhere. Time, space, and here with this chicken we see incongruity."

Suddenly I feel the warm, creeping sensation that means I need to get to my gym locker. Weird, because usually I have about five hours of warning, starting with a sense of doom and ending with spine-crushing cramps. *The Wizard of Oz* has done me different this time, sending it without warning, like a tornado, when I'm wearing light blue. I lean slightly to the left, rolling onto my hip, and casually tug my skirt away.

Ringgold won't shut up, and now he's calling us people, which means we've got a ways to go. "Get yourselves over to Chicago, but forget the galleries—go straight to the Art Institute and stand there for five minutes in front of a Chagall, that's all I ask. If I could get you people over there I would, if for no other reason than to shake up your ideas of who's important and who isn't, in terms of these current guys who just try to follow the fads. Yeah, there are fads in art just like there are fads in everything else — hairstyles, what have you. This is what you find out when you're in that world, and that's partly why I'm here, trying to direct people toward what's real, at least to some extent." He pauses, pressing on his mustache, thinking. He's forgotten my project, which I'm grateful for, since the hands weren't my idea anyway; they were based on a childhood hallucination of Dunk's, where she was riding in a car and thought birds were waving at her from the side of the road.

Oh God! There it goes again. I roll off my left hip and rearrange myself, elbows on the table and one knee tucked under, so I'm half sitting, half kneeling, on my bench.

"It wouldn't be a time to horse around, but if I could swing it, how many of you people would want to go to Chicago to see some of these things?" Mr. Ringgold asks suddenly. Everyone raises their hand.

"If it worked at all — and who knows if it's even possible — this would be a trip reserved for serious artists, the people who are able to grasp the difference between a museum and a gymnasium..."

Right at the end of this hall is the girls' locker room, where everyone goes when this happens; it's like a menstrual bomb shelter. There's always somebody on guard in there, folding towels or reading a book, sitting out gym class because of cramps. Whoever that person is would help me. Steve pushes a drawing over to me: one of his veiny-eyed, whiskered rats sitting in a fire truck.

I look down and nod: cute.

"One minute," he whispers.

I nod. One minute you're invited to a cheerleader party and the next minute you're Lena Gibb.

Without warning, another creeping trickle of warmth. Why, oh why didn't I wear plaid? Thirty-one minutes to the bell—what if Ringgold talks that entire time? By then it'll be long past too late; I'll be leaving here in a boat. I stand partway up again to switch knees, and as I do, there's a surge. It's got a life of its own now.

"Joan!" Steve whispers.

I tip my head in his direction. I wish all men would shut up.

"Half a minute," he whispers.

"Half a minute what?" I whisper, eyes on Ringgold, who is now sitting on the edge of his desk, swinging one leg and pressing his mustache, describing I have no idea what. Some art assignment where he had to drop an egg off a roof.

Steve leans over and whispers: "Five…four…three…two…one…"

The fire alarm goes off.

Ringgold jumps to his feet, startled, and then stretches. "Okay, people," he says, raising his voice over the intermittent blatting sound. "Nothing to hustle for, but let's hustle anyway. Let's be the first ones out so we can be the first ones back in."

I fiddle with my chicken while they file out, and then I sprint for the locker room. The girl who's guarding has a cast on her leg.

"There's no fire, right?" she asks me, propping the door with her crutch.

"Nope," I say, ducking in.

"Good, because I'm not going anywhere," she says, hobbling back to the bench, where she's been coloring on her cast with a set of markers. She's wearing a peasant skirt and a blouse with big, billowy sleeves. "These fucking crutches are killing my armpits."

"I need my locker," I explain. I'm shaking now, out of breath from sprinting and humiliation.

"Why?"

"I started," I tell her. "In art class, and then couldn't get out. It's everywhere, I'm destroyed."

"Oh you poor pale thing," she says kindly. "Let me see."

I turn around and stare into the green bank of lockers.

"Nothing," she says, going back to her coloring.

Nothing?

"You're fine," she says.

I am?

I spin open my gym locker, retrieve the lavender carrying case, and head back to the stalls.

Once there, I discover she was right. False alarm.

"Stop giving me subliminal suggestions," I tell Maroni that afternoon.

"You're the one who had the dream, not me," she says.

We're sitting out gym class, waiting for Felicia to join us — she gets off early on Fridays for School Beautification. This is a program run by the health teacher that mainly involves picking up candy wrappers outside, scraping gum off the pile of desks under the stage, and taping up holiday decorations. You have to be on the honor roll to do it, because it only takes about twenty minutes and then you get to go home.

"Guess the candy bar most eaten at this school," Felicia says on arrival. "Then guess the gum."

"The gum is Bazooka and the candy bar is Hershey's," I answer.

"Wrong."

"The gum is Juicy Fruit and the candy bar is Clark," I try.

"Right," Felicia says.

"How can you know the actual flavor of the gum?" Maroni asks her.

"Because when you have about sixty petrified pieces in a bucket and you add hot water, it turns into a giant vat of Juicy Fruit again."

"Ha—who did that?" I ask.

"Peter Sheldon and Don West. They used the hot-tea water in the teachers' lounge."

"Why do you get to go in the teachers' lounge?" Maroni asks, suddenly interested. "What's it look like?"

"We went in there to staple president heads to the bulletin board. All their stuff was everywhere—knitting, newspapers, crap like that. A bunch of Tupperware with people's names on it. Ashtrays every two feet."

"Was Mr. Carlisle's toupee anywhere?" Maroni asks.

"That's his *hair*, Maroni," Felicia says.

"People don't have hair like that," she insists.

"People don't buy *toupees* like that," Felicia argues. "Plus, who cares what his toupee looks like when he wears his pants up around his neck?"

"They do something weird in the back," I add. I'm somewhat of an expert on Mr. Carlisle because he was my homeroom teacher and my history teacher in seventh grade. He was in the war and cries during the Pledge of Allegiance. Everyone talks about his pants, but nobody talks about that.

"Can we blow up balls, please?" Maroni says. We have several cages of gym balls—basketballs, soccer balls, volleyballs, kickballs—that need to be checked for softness and then affixed to an air hose and pumped back up by stepping on a pedal. Since I actually do have cramps—Maroni is faking—I'm doing the checking and affixing, and she's doing the stepping.

"Here, I'll do one," Felicia offers. "That'll get the old butt smaller."

It seems like the entire fleet of volleyballs is flat; it's going to take forever, and the whole point of Maroni sitting out class and Felicia sneaking into the locker room was to do something besides jamming air into gym balls—we're supposed to be getting me started on tampons so that when I go to the cheerleader party tomorrow night I won't seem like some demented pioneer girl who's out there scrubbing her rags on a washboard and hanging them on a line.

If only I hadn't left metal shop to meet Luek and talk about boys, none of this would be happening. No Patti Michaels, no angry cheerleaders at a ruinous party where we don't belong, no possibility of bleeding all over somebody's rich grandmother's possibly white furniture. It's all my fault, I freely admit it, picking up one of the sinking volleyballs and kicking it down toward the shower area as hard as I can. It hits the wall halfway there and rolls to a flaccid stop.

"Here, now calm down," Felicia says, opening her locker and rooting around in it. "You need to relax the muscles in your hooey. *Flehhhh*...just let her go." She hands me a box of plugs and sends me into a stall.

"Do everything I say," she says through the door. "Even if it seems wrong."

"I'm not listening to you, because you think this is funny," I say. "I'm only listening to Maroni."

"She's busy," Felicia says briskly. "First of all, sit down."

"I'm no busier than anyone else," Maroni protests.

When my mother demonstrated how to fasten the rag to the sanitary belt, she tried to actually put it on me while I was standing there. She pulled the same trick when she took me shopping for a bra too, right in the middle of the store, and then laughed about it later on the telephone. Say what you will about Maroni, but she doesn't laugh at anything, even jokes, which is why she comes in handy at times like these.

"Help, Maroni."

"Okay," Maroni says calmly. "Are you looking at the picture?"

I look at the insert that comes in the box, showing an outline of a girl seated on a toilet and another outline of a girl standing with one foot on the edge of a bathtub. In both cases, the girl is placing what looks like a firecracker in the outline of her uterus.

"Not a uterus, a vagina," Maroni says. She pronounces it like her own first name — Gina — shaking my confidence.

"Felicia?" I call out.

"Right here," Felicia replies smoothly. "Just do what it says, and tell me what happens."

"Nothing is happening. There's nowhere for it to go."

"Yes, there is. Keep at it," Felicia says.

"It's right there," Maroni says encouragingly.

"It doesn't fit where they're showing," I tell them.

"I hate to tell you this, but you have to make it fit," Felicia says.

The girl in the drawing looks like she could be related to the girl embossed into the lavender carrying case; they're cut from the same calm cloth. They should show one of them screaming.

"Goddamn it to hell," I say through my teeth.

"This is why they call it the curse," Felicia replies.

That night, Felicia and I have to go to Heyworth, a little town thirty miles from Zanesville, to attend the visitation for Luekenfelter's cousin's mother. This is an idea dreamed up by our own mothers, but since it's Friday night—a big euchre night for my parents and a big jigsaw puzzle night for Felicia's—Meg has been enlisted to drive us out there in the family car.

My parents, who will walk to Tuck's instead of driving, laid a lecture on us, with information about how to behave in the backseat of a car being driven by one's older sister, and how to behave if one is the older driving sister with two girls in the backseat, and why Whinny is not allowed to come along for the ride this time—too distracting—but if everything goes well, and people behave like adults, she can most likely be included next time. We ought to remember the way because Aunt Else and Uncle Jimmy live out in that direction, but just in case, we are to take Minonk Road, follow it down to the one way, go left past the bowling alley, the liquor store, the bait shop billboard, and the house with all the wrought iron, then over a bridge into Plain Acres, where we bear right at the root beer stand, onto Highway 9, past the movie theater on the right and a roadhouse on the left, and then straight out into the country.

"Woo-hah," Meg yells, pushing it up to seventy.

Whinny lights a cigarette and rolls her window down halfway, blasting us in the face with country air. We yell at her until she gives in.

"You girls owe me," she says in the new silence.

"You owe us," I say automatically.

"For *what?*" Meg asks the rearview mirror.

I have no idea. Felicia is wearing a dress that her mother got at a yard sale and I'm wearing a gray jumper with a white blouse; we better hope nobody from our school is at this visitation besides us.

"*For what,* I asked you," Meg says, swerving the car back and forth. Far up ahead are taillights and far behind are headlights.

"For not telling that she's here, for not telling that she's smoking, and for not telling that you're swerving," I answer.

"I'm swerving?" she asks, veering suddenly from one edge of the highway to the other.

"Ha-ha," Whinny says worriedly. "Ha-ha, you're scaring them."

"Ha-ha, she is not," I say from the backseat. "Do it some more, you ass-H."

She does it a couple more times and then returns to regular driving and her cryptic, blacked-out conversation with Whinny.

"She goes, 'I'm going to *ahem*,' and then Vicky goes, 'You better not because blah-blah,' the usual, and then she starts screaming, 'If you let Jeff *ahem*, then I will personally take this'—she was holding some kind of thingamajig out of her father's *ahem* cabinet—"

"Liquor cabinet?" I interject. "Probably a corkscrew."

"—'and I will jam it where the sun don't shine...'"

"Where's that? Finland? She'll jam it into Finland?" I ask helplessly.

"Yeah," Felicia snorts quietly to me. "Right in the old Finland."

"What, Flea?" Meg asks suddenly, groping around in the rearview mirror to find Felicia, who is slouched down out of view. "What was that?"

"Nothing," Felicia says.

"But wait," Whinny says to Meg. "I don't know which *ahem* you were talking about when you said Jeff."

"The Sara kind," Meg says, giving her a long glance while the highway scrolls by underneath us.

Whinny exhales, and they stare out the windshield in scandalized wonder.

"You talking about Sara Barton, battlefield nurse?" I ask.

Whinny turns around. "Where did you learn that—Finland?"

"I read books, that's where I learned it."

"Next time, turn a light on," Whinny says, looking at my sister, who barks out a laugh.

Unlike Felicia, I don't mind dead bodies. Our relatives extend backward into the last century—we have people who show up at family dinners barely visible inside their rusty black farm clothes, people who can't walk or talk but still need to work so get carried in and set in front of a bowl of potatoes and a paring knife, people who ignore real kids but shout, "Whose are you?" to our parents. Because the versions that appear in the caskets don't look that different from the versions we've been seeing all along, it takes a lot of the fear out.

Luekenfelter's cousin's mother is different. She's young, wearing a wig that makes her look like Sandra Dee.

"I can't be here," Felicia whispers. "I'm getting faint headed."

I know what she means. We're off to the side, with a perfect view of everything, waiting to say hi to Luek and her cousin Jane, who are standing together, greeting people as they file past. They're wearing clingy dresses, nylons, and pumps, like Avon ladies.

A group of Jane's friends goes past, all of them in Capezio saddle shoes, a fashion at her school. When they're gone, Luek catches sight of us and brings Jane over.

"God," Luek says, by way of greeting.

"God," I say in agreement.

"How are you doing?" Felicia asks Jane.

Jane pulls at her dress, looking around. "We're having to hug half these people."

"Sorry," Felicia says. "Your dress is cute, though."

"Yours too," Jane says.

A long pause while we watch mourners shuffle past, whispering. It seems like everyone is staring down at the carpeting, which is rich looking, a dark green patterned with gray and gold paisleys.

"Want to go up there?" Jane says suddenly, nodding toward the casket.

"Okay," I tell her.

Felicia looks wild eyed. "That's all right, I already saw," she says.

The crowd parts to let us in, and for a moment it's as though

Jane is introducing me to her mother: "This is my mom," she whispers, staring at her, and I nod. The face is flushed and claylike with makeup, but she was pretty like her daughter, you can tell. Around her neck is a thin gold necklace, its heart-shaped locket opened to show two tiny pictures: young Jane, with bangs, and a small grinning boy.

We keep standing there as people file past. After a couple of minutes, a man comes up, takes hold of Jane's arm, and starts crying. She looks at me and rolls her eyes.

Felicia and Luek are nowhere to be found. I put my jacket on and make my way outside, and they're there, sitting on the cold steps.

"Your aunt looked nice," I say to Luek.

"Is Jane still acting like nothing is happening?" Felicia asks.

"When we first came in and saw her mom in the coffin, she acted a little bit like something was happening," Luek says. "But otherwise, no. She just keeps saying these things to me to make fun of people, which is more like my other cousins, not like Jane at all. She just said to me about this person, this huge guy who I guess used to work on their farm...I can't even repeat it, it was so awful, and he could have heard. At her mother's visitation!"

I think I saw that man in there, enormous and strange, with a little bow tie and a broad sweating forehead.

"What if this turns her mean?" Luek goes on. "And she's an alternate cheerleader, which she never would let me tell people before, but now she's telling everyone. How they might use her at some stupid parent-teacher exhibition game, they might use her for some swim meet, they might put her in for basketball if it turns out this girl is pregnant..."

"A cheerleader is pregnant?" I ask.

"Who *cares* about cheerleaders, I told her," Luek says pointedly, "when someone's *mother* is dead."

"Yeah," Felicia agrees, and we stare out at the small-town street, which doesn't look any different from a street in Zanesville, really, except that it's about all they've got: two blocks over is a cornfield. People are still coming in, although there isn't a line like before.

"I wasn't trying to say anything about your cheerleader party," Luek says apologetically.

"We know," I say.

Two blocks in the other direction is the town square, where there's a dark dime store and a tiny park with a bench and a war memorial. Teenagers were sitting on the cannon when we drove through, which is why it's taking forever for Meg and Whinny to come back for us. Eventually Jane walks outside, and then Jane's younger brother, and then Luek's mother comes out too. She looks eerily like the body in the casket, only heavier, and for one disorienting second it's like Jane's mother has gotten up and thrown on a coat to come to find her children.

"You girls tell your mothers thank you, from me," Mrs. Luekenfelter says, lighting a cigarette.

"We will," Felicia says.

"Not just for getting you out here, but for the desserts they sent over last night," she goes on, exhaling into the cold night. She fastens her red eyes on me. "I've got to meet your mom one of these days—she knows my friend Edna, and Edna just loves her."

"Oh yeah," I say. "Edna."

"I do know your mom, though," she says to Felicia. "She works for the glasses doctor I go to."

"Yeah," Felicia says.

"Get your paws off me," Jane says to her brother.

Glaring at Jane, Luek tries to pull the boy to her side, but he squirms away and goes back to his sister, pushing against her more insistently. He's about Raymond's age, and embarrassed.

"Paws *off*," Jane says, shoving him.

"Janie," Mrs. Luekenfelter says quietly, then puts out her cigarette on the steps and kicks the butt into the bushes. "Don't tell anyone I did that," she says.

"We won't," Felicia and I say.

When Luek's mom takes the brother inside, the four of us stand on the steps, shivering and watching people leave.

"Well, bye," I say finally.

"Don't worry about being with a group of cheerleaders," Jane says suddenly. Luek must have told her about the party. "They're probably really nice. It's just that they're popular, and that makes people hate them."

"It's not that," I say.

"We don't hate them," Felicia explains. "We think they hate us."

"Well, they don't," Jane says, then turns and runs up the steps, where she stands waiting with her back to us while Luek shrugs and then follows, using the railing to pull herself along. Like a weary married couple, they link arms and go back inside.

There are still teenage silhouettes hanging around the cannon when we get to the square, but it's hard to tell whether they're the right ones or not. We wander along the storefronts for a few minutes, waiting to see if they'll spot us.

"What if you had to get your hair cut at a place like this?" Felicia says, staring into a beauty shop where the window display is pink and black combs arranged in a sunburst pattern around a houseplant.

"What if you had to go here to mail your letter?" I say, staring into the bleak little post office, where there is nothing but a clerk's window, a wall of brass mailboxes, and a wastebasket. The whole place is the size of my family's kitchen.

"What if this was where you lived and all you could do was sit around a cannon for fun?" Felicia says. The teenagers have melded into one dark shape in the town square, a big restless creature with cigarette coals for eyes. A few feet beyond, in the moonlight, is a little pyramid of cannonballs, like something the creature left behind.

Suddenly our Oldsmobile roars around the corner, races past us, and jolts to a stop. We walk the half block, then another half block after she pulls away again. When we are finally in the backseat, Meg says, "Where were you?" accusingly.

We gaze out our respective windows.

Whinny turns her long face in our direction and asks, "So, was it icky?"

"Not really," I say after a moment.

"Was the girl you knew crying and everything?" she asks.

Pretty Jane, with her thin dress and her rural-looking charm bracelet, had said something else while we were standing at the coffin. "This is Ellen's friend," she had whispered, staring down at her mother. Ellen is Luekenfelter.

"Not really," I say.

Whinny turns back around, pushes in the lighter, and waits with an unlit cigarette in her mouth.

"It was a lot of fun driving all over looking for you," Meg says.

There's nothing out the window; all I can see is my own face, made haunted by the black glass.

"I may have to tell Mother that you took off and were running around Heyworth," Meg tries again, "if she wonders where we've been."

Instead of slapping the back of her head, I do what they tell you to do: count to ten. Only I do it the gifted way: 123 + 456 + 789 + 10. When your sister has hurtled you swerving into the darkness, stranded you at a funeral home, and threatens to get you in trouble, just stop and count to 1,378 before you respond.

"Did you hear me?" Meg asks. "I may have to tell her."

"Try it, duck lips, and see what happens," I say calmly.

"Maybe I better pull over and dump you out so you can walk home," she says, yawning.

"Maybe you better not," Felicia says in a low voice.

"What's that, Flea?" Meg starts slowing the car down.

"Maybe you better not," Felicia repeats, her voice dangerously quiet now.

"*What's* that?" Swerving onto the shoulder, gravel hitting the bottom of the car.

I'm not sure I've ever been in a winter cornfield before. The furrows are farther apart than they look from a distance, and this one doesn't seem very well plowed—there are clods the size of our feet, making it hard to walk, and if you veer the wrong way, your ankles are stabbed by corn stubble. We walk down the frozen rows, through patches of old snow gleaming in the moonlight.

"Where are we going?" I ask Felicia.

"Away from those two," she says.

I wonder what lives in a fallow field at night. Coons and possums; maybe coyotes run through.

"My aunt Else and uncle Jimmy live around here somewhere," I tell her. "This could even be their field." I doubt it, though. This field is the opposite of them.

"Could we go there if we have to?"

"They aren't exactly old, but they don't really have any kids."

"Oh," she says.

They do have a one-eyed cocker spaniel named Jiffy, though, who wipes his feet before stepping into the kitchen. It's less impressive than it seems—you can say, "Jiffy, feet!" anywhere, even outside, and he will stop, look blindly around, and then shuffle his paws before continuing on.

"Ow!" Felicia yells. She tripped and was stabbed by cornstalks. "I'd like to shove this corn up your sister's ass!"

We move a few rows over to see if it's any easier, but it isn't. It's the same.

"Sorry," Felicia says.

"It's Whinny making her act like that," I say.

"Maybe," Felicia says after a moment. "But it actually seems like Whinny is nice, compared to her. Just seems."

I'm getting slightly tired of walking in a frozen cornfield.

"I guess she's a little like your sister, in a way," I comment.

"Step On Me? She's a bug," Felicia answers. "Know what I do to her?"

I stop, balancing myself on two clods, and put my head back so I can see the whole sky overhead, black and cold, just the way I like it. We're on the moon out here, except the moon is up there.

"I step on her!" Felicia yells, her voice instantly sucked into the night. There's nothing for the sound to bounce off of, just miles of bald prairie and leaning fence posts. It's like shouting into a wadded-up quilt.

"Feck!" I yell.

"Shite!" she yells, flinging her arms out and turning in bumpy circles, her face to the sky.

Suddenly, fifty feet away, car lights go on.

"They were lurking!" Felicia says. "The crap faces."

We crouch for a while, until our knees give out, and then we sit down on the frozen dirt. My dad should have been a farmer, everyone knows that—he spends half the year with a spade in his hand, chopping up the ground and then pushing various things into it. Nobody knows why he ended up coming to Zanesville, moving my mother thirty miles away from her family, and spending the other half of his time in the tavern, but I do know one thing: that if he hadn't, I'd be living in the country instead of the city, I wouldn't go to John Deere, I wouldn't know Felicia or any of my other friends, I wouldn't be sitting out here so far away from home, because I'd actually *be* home. I'd be living in the middle of an ocean of dirt.

"If we lived out here, at least we wouldn't have to worry about the cheerleaders," Felicia says. "Because we'd basically *be* the cheerleaders."

Another thing that's impossible to imagine when you don't have the clothes for it.

"But if we lived out here and we still couldn't do any better than we do now?"

"The only thing is at least we'd still be weird together," she says. "What if I lived out here alone?"

"I guess you could hang around with Jane," I tell her.

"Maybe," she says.

I can't believe that tomorrow night I'm going to be sitting around in my peach-colored pajamas in Patti Michaels's grandmother's house. Are we supposed to bring slippers, or what? As it is, I'm having to use Stephanie's sleeping bag, which means keeping my legs bent. I don't mind that, but I do mind everyone else in a nightgown when I'm in pajamas; I can't bring a nightgown because the only one I have is hot pink and electric yellow, with flower-power flowers all over it, made by my mother, and now too short.

The car lights flash on and off, and a minute later Whinny comes stumbling partway into the field. We can't really see her, but we can hear her, and then the horn honks and she screams, and then we hear her scrambling back to the car again, both of them laughing like monkeys.

"Ally ally in free!" Them, in unison.

Once, when I was a kid, I played hide-and-seek in a cornfield where the stalks were taller than we were. My cousins knew what they were doing: while somebody counted, they scattered, crouching and running down one row and then jumping through to the next, until they were deep inside the field, hiding motionless in the stalks. I couldn't stand it—the corn seemed like people to me, touching my face and legs—so while they were dodging and catching each other, I swung on the swing set, high enough to get a view of the whole green enterprise, a trembling tassel here and there the only sign that anything was going on. How will Jane endure it, the thought of them closing the lid on her mother's face?

"Get...in...here!" Meg shouts.

The horn honks again, a bright splash of sound, and then silence.

"Please!"

We stand up from the frozen ground. Getting out of the field proves a lot more efficient than getting in: we find a furrow and keep to it, back toward the car lights, straight across the shining patches of snow. We emerge behind them, sneak up, and throw open the back doors, causing the driver and her idiot friend to shriek and claw at each other, Whinny losing her cigarette somewhere on the floor and the two of them diving for it, bumping heads with an audible crack.

Felicia and I crawl into the dark backseat as they clutch their foreheads and moan. The heat is blasting, which feels good.

I spend the next afternoon mentally preparing for the party by hiding out behind the green velvet chair in the corner of the living room. When I was younger and shorter, I made a reading nest for myself by stuffing a couch pillow back here and an old afghan and then crawling in with my book, staying all day if they let me, creeping out only to get provisions. Now I have to fold myself in sideways, with the register jabbing into me and my feet sticking out. Tammy waits until I've got it all arranged and am still before she gingerly climbs in and over, to settle behind my knees.

I still like it back here—the familiar scuffs and scribbles above the baseboard, the bright, unfaded back of the green chair, the headless carpet tack you have to watch out for. This is where the pivotal events of my childhood unfolded, while I ate banana and root beer Popsicles, two by two, tucking the sticks neatly under the skirt of the chair. It's where Sunnybank Lad met Lady, Ken met his friend Flicka, Atlanta burned,

Manderley burned, Lassie came home, Jim ran away, Alice got small, Wilbur got big, David Copperfield was born, Beth died, and, on an endless, gloomy winter afternoon, Jody shot his yearling. The pretty little deer named Flag, staggering and bloodied, doomed from his romp through the tender shoots of corn and the mother's bad aim, pursued by the desperate, crazed boy who had to put him out of his suffering. All the fault of mothers and corn. My own mother had had to come in and pull the chair out in order to see what was going on that day. She was sympathetic until she saw the Popsicle sticks.

"That's a bit ridiculous, isn't it?" she says now, passing by on her way somewhere and seeing me crammed into my old space.

"What's ridiculous is that there's nowhere in this house to do homework," I reply.

"What do you call that big table in the dining room?"

"What do you call the crap all over it that I'm sick of cleaning up?"

She peers over the top of the chair at me. I open *The Tempest* and stare into it.

"Listen, smart-ass. If this is how you talk to your family, you'll stay home tonight."

"How I talk? You just called me ridiculous!" I say to my book.

"I did not," she answers. "Look at me."

I look up at her. She has rollers in her hair.

"I did not. I said it might be a *bit* ridiculous to be jammed in there like that when there are plenty of other places you could read in this house."

"That's not what I heard."

"I actually don't give a shit what you heard, and I'm not going to stand here arguing with a teenager about what I did or didn't say." And with that, she wanders away, because she knows she's in the wrong.

I'm sick of being a teenager. Being a teenager so far hasn't gotten me anything beyond period cramps and nameless yearning, which I had as a kid too, but this is a new kind of nameless yearning that has boys attached to it. And one thing is for sure: there are boys close behind wherever cheerleaders are, like wolves following the campfires. What if they show up at Patti Michaels's grandmother's house tonight, what will I do then? What if there are popular boys there, ones who aren't used to being around uncute girls? I think about getting up to call Felicia to see how nervous she is, but the register is pouring out heat, and the dog and I have melted together.

"Ray?" I call.

No answer. Everyone is somewhere else.

"Raymond!" I call again.

A moment later his face appears over the top of the chair. "I found a harpoon in the alley," he says.

"What?" I ask. "Would you get me the phone?"

"Okay," he says. "It's a harpoon, for whales, that I found in the alley."

He stretches the phone from the hall as far as its cord will allow and then brings me the receiver.

"How will I dial?" I ask him.

"I can," he offers.

I tell him the number and he dials. Stephanie answers.

"Flea is not allowed to talk on the telephone for more than two minutes," Stephanie says severely. "My mother asked her to do things that have to be done by the time she gets home from work, and she's getting home in" — she leaves the phone and comes back — "forty-seven minutes."

"I doubt if you know the exact minute she's walking in the house," I say.

She drops the phone.

"Hi," Felicia says.

"How does thy bounteous sister?" I say in a British accent.

"Hey, that's what I'm reading too—a tempest in a pee-pot," Felicia says. "How're the tampons working out?"

"Fine, if you don't mind sitting on a spatula."

"It means you're doing it wrong, but I know," she says, sighing. "So, are you getting nervous about tonight?"

"Are you?" I ask. "I mean, it was your idea to go, so I think you probably know it will be okay."

"No! Are you kidding—I just said to go see what it was like, but it wasn't my idea. You're the one who brought the whole thing up. If it was anyone's idea, it was yours!"

"Really, it was her idea. Patti Michaels."

"Patti Michaels," Felicia repeats.

We think for a minute.

"I have to clean my stuff and Stephanie's before my mother gets home, otherwise the little skrizz is gonna tell on me," she says finally. "And I washed my hair at eight A.M. and it still looks like a wad of hay."

"Your hair is pretty," I say.

"Yours is," she says, yawning.

"What's Stephanie telling on?"

"We were fighting and I threw a bowl of macaroni out the upstairs window."

"Ha."

"My mom wouldn't care about the macaroni, but the bowl went too."

"Don't let her tell," I say nervously.

"Okay, I'm hanging up."

Now I have the phone receiver and no brother. When I yell for him, Tammy's eyes fly open for a second, and then she burrows deeper.

"Let me see your harpoon," I say, handing Raymond the receiver. He disappears and reappears a moment later with a rusted fireplace poker.

"This is it," he says.

One of the more memorable things I ever read back here were the Cliff's Notes for *Moby-Dick*, which I found in a box of old comic books my mother brought home. It was a gripping story, but also sickening. Mostly what I took from it was that nobody on a whaling ship has much sympathy for a whale.

"Don't let Mom see it," I say.

"Why not?"

"Because it actually is a harpoon. I thought it wasn't."

"It is?" he asks incredulously. "It's a har*poon*?"

"Hey," I ask him, "how do you think I look?"

"Okay," he says uneasily, looking not at me but around. "I don't know. I have to go hide this harpoon."

Then again, who really cares? Somebody has to be the sidekick. Somebody has to be Ringo. Without him, no Beatles, and I hope these people know that.

"I wish I had this house and they had a better one," my mother says, taking a right turn into the circular drive at Patti Michaels's grandmother's house. There are lights shining from under the bushes, lanterns hanging on the carriage house, and a stone bench and table with a spotlight on them. She drives up to the stone archway and stops.

"Don't stop here!" I say. "This isn't where you stop!"

In the backseat, Felicia peers out, chewing the inside of her lip.

"Yes, it is," my mother says, leaning over me to look at the front door. Actually two doors, painted dark green, with a brass knocker and a medieval-looking latch. On either side of the steps are the cement lions, who tonight have birthday hats on, set at a rakish angle. "Ooh, those are cute."

"This isn't where you stop," I insist.

"You better notice everything they've got," she says. "Because your mother is going to want to hear about it. Now get out, because somebody's coming up behind me."

We crawl out with our gear and stand there between the lions. As my mother pulls away and the other car pulls up, the green doors open and there's Patti and several girls. Behind them is a large space with black-and-white flooring at the bottom and a huge chandelier at the top. Somewhere in the middle is a blur of curving staircase and gold railing. The girls with Patti we've never seen before; the girls coming up behind us are our own cheerleaders.

Help.

I step back, pressed against a lion, while everyone surges together, sleeping bags are being dropped, people are saying things, somehow Felicia is standing on the black-and-white floor with the rest of them, but I'm still out here with the lion, whose back I've momentarily sat down on. Directly below the sparkling chandelier is a round, marble-topped table, in the center of which sits a big silver bowl filled with malted milk balls. Hundreds of them. The grandmother walks into the room, tall, with a cloud of white hair and high cheekbones: a wealthy person who has somehow gotten old.

"Come in, come in!" she calls gaily. "Don't be a stranger, my dear."

Everyone turns to peer out the door. Oh. They mean me. There's nothing to do but go inside with my stuff, letting them close the door.

"Lovely, girls!" the grandmother cries, clapping her hands and looking around animatedly. "You're all just the loveliest things!" And with that, she walks suddenly out of the room, as though summoned.

Patti must have just taken her curlers out—her hair is so soft and bouncy, making her more like Gidget than ever. There's a girl who looks vaguely like Hayley Mills as well—she's not one of ours, but a small, doll-like girl with a thick cap of yellow hair—and one that looks like Patty Duke, only slightly chubbier. The Patty Duke one seems like the ring-leader of the other girls, while the ringleader of our girls is and always has been tall, black-haired Cindy Falk, who looks like an unsmiling version of That Girl. She stands now, staring around at the room thoughtfully. Finally she glances at me.

"I knew somebody who had a house like this," she says. "Only it was bigger."

"Really?" I answer, flooded with gratitude. Everyone says Cindy Falk is a huge stuck-up snot, but here she is, talking to me right off the bat.

"Mm-hmm," she says, looking over my head.

After a moment I slide my sleeping bag across the gleaming floor until it's next to Felicia's. "Hi," I say.

"Hi," she says back.

"This house is just like one Cindy Falk's friend or somebody used to have," I say so it looks like we're talking.

"Really?" she says.

"Only bigger, I guess. The friend's house was."

"Really?" she says, her eyes swiveling.

"Yeah."

"Really?" she says, still not looking at me.

"Why do you keep saying 'really'?" I ask her.

She blinks. "Because I'm just trying to keep talking here."

"Oh. Yes, we're talking away. Talking, talking."

"Happy and laughing," she murmurs, "because what we're saying is really good."

"What you're saying is *so* funny," I tell her, and then laugh.

She laughs too. "I'm saying something very true and funny and then I'm listening to the funny, true things you say back."

"And yes, blah-blah, what do we do if someone wants to know what's so funny and true?"

"Then we're up shit creek, so disperse," she says, turning away to look at a painting on the wall. The painting is a mishmash of blue, green, and yellow blobs connected up with spidery black lines. Here and there, little crimson worms inch their way across the blobs. It might be something Ringgold would like.

I slide my sleeping bag over to the pile of other sleeping bags and stand there with an interested look on my face until Patti notices me.

"Hey, what were you laughing about?" she asks.

"Not really anything," I tell her.

"But you were laughing with Flea," she insists.

"Oh, that was about something from earlier."

"But what?" Patti says.

"Just something she did today, that was earlier," I say. "Not about anything here." The black-and-white tile is creating some kind of optical illusion that's making me feel like my legs are too short.

"But what?" Patti persists. Everyone now seems to be listening. Dizzy from the fun-house floor, I put my hand on the marble table beside me. It feels like a cemetery monument, not the sort of thing you want to fall and crack your head on.

"Uh, she threw a bowl of macaroni out the window," I say.

Everyone stares at Felicia as she stares at the blobs. For a few seconds there is a flush-faced silence and then Patti guffaws.

"I threw half a bag of marshmallows out my bedroom window the other night," she says. "They were making me sick."

Felicia turns from the painting to look at me, swinging her hair back from her face, which is bright with courage. "Now we know why it was taking *you* so long to come inside."

There's a pause as everyone pictures me out there scrounging marshmallows off the cold ground. I laugh and then everyone laughs.

Felicia and I don't look at each other.

"'Za, girls! The 'za has arrived!" the grandmother says, sweeping in to lead us from the hallway, past a living room filled with couches, trees and a grand piano, down a carpeted corridor, into a dining room with a long, quiet table surrounded by upholstered chairs, through a swinging door, and into a big, bright kitchen. A wagon-wheel chandelier with false candles hangs over a long, ranch-style table with benches. On one wall is a display of shining copper pans, and on another wall is a large painting of fruit, a pheasant, and a deceased rabbit.

The appliances are avocado and the floor is brown-speckled tile, shining with wax. The pizzas are served on pedestals, three of them, and there are eleven places set around the table, each with two forks and two glasses. I have no idea what two forks could mean in terms of pizza. Everyone crowds around the table, with me on the end of the bench. The napkins match the tablecloth — green, orange, and turquoise plaid — and have been rolled and stuffed into wooden napkin rings carved to look like zoo animals. Mine is a monkey.

"Do you all love pizza?" the grandmother asks.

I usually don't, although I've only had the kind my mother makes, which she crumbles hamburger on top of, making it impossible to eat around, and by the time you pick it off, it looks like you're eating something from out of the trash. The closest thing here to one without meat looks like the pepperoni. Across from me is the Hayley Mills girl, also on an end; we smile at each other.

"Hi," she says, rolling her eyes. "God."

"Hi," I say, rolling mine in agreement. We're referring to how crowded we are on the bench.

Suddenly the grandmother appears next to me, holding a large wooden bowl in her arms. The bowl is filled with lettuce, and the grandmother just stands there holding it. I look up at her and she nods encouragingly.

I don't know what she means. *Just set it down.*

"Darling, I'm serving you," she says gaily. "Take some delicious greens!"

In the bowl is a large plastic scissorlike utensil that I've never seen before. On one side is a big spoon and on the other side is a big fork, hinged in the middle. I don't know how to use it. *Start somewhere else, why don't you.*

"Don't you love salad?" she asks, still gay. "I insist!"

It appears to be a difficult tool, the scissor fork/spoon, and I don't want to try it—what if it has some other purpose I'm not even aware of, like it's something that her grandmother has to carry around everywhere for some condition, and I suddenly start trying to use it to serve myself salad?

I shake my head.

"None?" she cries. "Even just a tiny taste of something so lovely?"

She won't move on; she's stuck there, cradling the bowl like it's a dear thing, staring around the kitchen, speaking over our heads to an unseen audience of parents and local officials. "It's a new era! Let them eat 'za and cake...only!" And with that, she moves on to Cathy Olessen, sitting next to me, who expertly tongs herself out a few leaves, a radish flower, and a slice of cucumber.

Eventually they all have salad and are eating. The grandmother starts pouring water from a silver pitcher into one of everyone's two glasses.

My little gray monkey has his arms clutched around the cloth napkin; I take it away from him, place it on my lap, and stand the monkey up near one of my drinking glasses. He has a white face, pink lips, and brown eyes, each with a tiny fleck of white paint in the center. I turn him so he's looking at Cathy Olessen's tiger, painted in brown and yellow. Again, pink lips and the eye flecks.

"Can I enlist you, darling nonsalad child?" the grandmother asks me as she refills her pitcher with ice and water. She gestures to the counter, where there are five bottles of pop waiting. I get up but I don't know what to do with my napkin. I could leave it on the bench or put it next to my plate, but either place, it would look just dumped there. Instead, I slip it into the waistband of my pants.

The pop is Pepsi, Teem, and Dr Pepper. Two, two, and one. With an opener sitting there. Am I supposed to open them all and leave them there for her to pour, or am I supposed to carry them over to the table and hand them out, one to each two girls? Am I supposed to ask people which they want? If I do that, everyone will say Pepsi and nobody will say Teem, let alone Dr Pepper. Why didn't I just take salad?

She's pouring more water and they're all eating away. I look at Felicia, who looks back at me, coolly, chewing. I point to my chin, and her eyes bug out in alarm. She takes her napkin and saws away at her own chin, eyes grateful. I give her a slight nod— *Yes, you got it*—and then glance questioningly at the pop on the counter. She discreetly mimes opening a bottle and then looks back to her plate.

I open the bottles, put the tops in a little pile, and then stand there until the grandmother says, "Would you be so kind as to serve? And Patti, darling, you help. Pour some icy cold drinks for your friends!"

"Who wants what?" Patti says, getting up and throwing her napkin down on the bench.

I take one of the Pepsis and pour half in my glass and then walk down the table, squinting to see who might want it, and pour the rest in Felicia's. Then I wander around with the last Dr Pepper until somebody accepts it; then I sit back down. Getting up like that really makes you appreciate your spot on the bench. I turn the monkey so he doesn't have to look at the tiger anymore, and try to figure out how to get the last slice of pepperoni. How are people doing it? It's too far down for me to reach. I could just ask someone sitting near it, but then they would have to hand this big, limp thing along from person to person. I could send my plate down, but nobody is doing that. Or I could just eat the one I can reach, but pepperoni can be taken off and stacked like tiddlywinks on the edge of the plate, whereas the closest other pizza seems to have sausage on it, which would have to be picked off bit by bit.

I feel like I might start crying. Not out of hunger but out of sheer exhaustion. The clock says only seven thirty. Seven thirty! Whoever the guy is who Ringgold says turned it around in terms of time should be here for this extravaganza. If I do start crying, I'm ruined unless I can come up with a reason. It would need to be good —like my mother just died. But she dropped us off here! My grandmother then. But how would Patti's grandmother feel, knowing that another grandmother had just died?

"Could I have a piece of the pepperoni, please?" I say suddenly, startling myself.

Cathy Olessen takes my plate and passes it down the table, and the last piece is lifted from its pedestal, slid onto the plate, and sent back to me.

"Thank you," I say distinctly. I feel a strange surge of confidence—here I am with pizza and pop, just like everyone else.

Wait! Where's my napkin?

It's in your pants, the monkey whispers.

The clock starts moving faster. Cake from a bakery, decorated with white icing and a megaphone that says *Zanesville* on it in cursive; ice cream; little favors handed out from a basket the grandmother carries around the table—lip gloss and Bonne

Bell face soaps; and then adjournment to the basement, a long, open pine-paneled space with green shag and modern furniture. In fact, it looks like my old Barbie Dream House, everything sleek, low, and built in—low plastic chairs around a low glass coffee table, vinyl beanbags slumped here and there, a long hi-fi and TV console in blond wood, two barstools and a bar. The ceiling is low too, and the only lights are a fizzing fluorescent over the bar, a blue green Lava lamp, an array of hanging globes over the coffee table, and, in one dim corner, glowing eerily, an aquarium with a ceramic diver releasing bubbles, some suckerfish, and one lone molly with diaphanous trailing fins.

Patti locks the door so the grandmother can't come down.

"Shitfitteroony," she bursts out, and then does a series of controlled and graceful cartwheels across the long room, narrowly and expertly avoiding ceiling, coffee table, beanbags, and lamps. The other cheerleaders follow, with mixed results: Cindy Falk perfect, Kathy Liddelmeyer comes perilously close to the hanging globes, Gretchen Quist perfect, Deb Patterson dislodges a ceiling tile, and Cathy Olessen goes off course and lands so close to the fish tank that the molly rushes forward and hangs there, billowing.

While all this is happening with our girls, one of the ones from the other school walks up to the wall and presses the pine paneling, which pops open to reveal a cunning cupboard, stacked with games.

"A secret compartment," I say.

"We were coming here before this was even a finished basement," the girl who pushed on the wall informs me. "Her grandmother had the whole thing designed by a man from Chicago. A lot of it is just for Patti, like these games."

"Wow, lucky you, lucky her," Deb Patterson says lightly,

flushed from her encounter with the ceiling. Her cartwheels are wooden, windmillish, and she knows it. I personally can't stand her because she once cried, "No boys allowed!" when Dunk walked into the locker room after gym class. We all thought it was embarrassing and out of line, but everyone was forced to laugh, including Dunk.

The girl stares at Patterson for a moment, red faced, and Patterson stares back.

"What are you going to play?" I say finally, and the girl digs around in the cabinet and pulls forth a Ouija board.

"Want to?" she asks me politely as she and her two friends gather around a low white ottoman. At first I thought they were plain, all wearing a variation on the same mix-and-match Bobbie Brooks wool outfits, all with their hair curled like Patti's, but now I see: they're really cute.

"I'll go later," I say.

Felicia is sitting atop a red beanbag chair, shoulders hunched, pretending to be lost in thought. I feel better now that we're down here, but I can tell she feels worse. I want to get a beanbag too, but then it'll be the two of us sitting together like outcasts, so I just stand there.

"Why not *grab a beanbag* and sit down?" Felicia asks, her face expressionless.

"Okay," I say, and pull the orange one over. It's very comfortable, even being vinyl, although you feel a little like your head is sticking up strangely and maybe there's nowhere for your feet to go.

"Want to get a game and start playing it?" I ask her.

"No," she says quietly.

"Want to do anything?" I ask her gently. Her weakness is giving me strength.

"*No.*"

The Bobbie Brooks crew is hunched over their Ouija board—two of them with their eyes closed and the tips of their fingers on the planchette, while the third waits with a pad and pencil in her hand to write down the message. Our girls are in a clump as well, on the other side of the basement, watching one another do splits and backbends while talking in low voices.

Patti is behind the bar, setting out Dixie cups on the counter, eleven of them. She then ducks down and comes back up with three bottles of Coca-Cola, which she opens and then pours into the cups. After this, she comes around from behind the bar, pushes on the paneling, disappears into what turns out to be a bathroom, and reappears with a bottle of aspirin. She opens it with her front teeth, shakes some out onto the bar, and then drops one aspirin into each Dixie cup.

"Want a turn?" one of the Ouija girls asks us.

"Not yet," I say warmly.

"I will," Felicia says, crawling out of the beanbag and walking on her knees over to the ottoman. I tug the orange one a few inches over in their direction. There's silence on the other side of the room as our cheerleaders watch us possibly being absorbed by the other group.

"Are you asking Ouija or calling up spirits?" Felicia asks the girl.

"Right now, spirits. Either this girl's neighbor lady," she says, indicating her friend, "or Lee Harvey Oswald."

"To ask what?" Felicia says.

"The neighbor lady was found in front of her washing machine, just dead, with no warning," the girl explains. "And so there's a question of what really happened to her—was it a heart attack or could it have been foul play?"

"She was really old," the girl whose neighbor it was says, "and I don't even want to call her up—what would I say? Remember me from when you were alive?"

"You ask her what happened in her last moments. Say that you're trying to get at the truth."

"She's going to know this is a slumber party!"

"I heard they can't see anything," Felicia offers. "They can only hear."

"How can you hear if you're invisible?" I ask, just for the sake of argument. "If you don't have an ear bone to pick up the sound waves?"

"Um, I don't think an ear is a *bone*," the Hayley Mills girl says.

"Here," Patti says, sitting down. "Shut up and ask it a question."

She and Felicia put their fingers on the planchette and close their eyes. Felicia intones, "Is there such a thing as the curse of the mummy?"

Mummies again! Everybody has had something traumatic happen on a grade school field trip, but she's never gotten over hers. Patti steers the planchette expertly over the board, visiting several spots before coming to rest over the NO. They open their eyes.

"Whew," Felicia says.

"You," Patti says to me.

Felicia gets up and I sit down, place my fingers on the planchette with Patti's.

The cheerleaders are creeping closer without seeming to do

so, still practicing acrobatics but somehow more over here than over there, like the squirrels my father feeds by hand: one minute they're under the tree, refusing to notice you, and the next minute they're eating a peanut off your shoe.

We close our eyes. Silence in the room.

"Are boys showing up at this party?" Cindy Falk asks.

The planchette pulls away from the curb and arrives at its destination without me. My fingers are left hovering in midair. I open my eyes.

YES.

Patti gets up from the Ouija board and goes over to the bar. "Everybody drink this pop," Patti says. "If the aspirin isn't all the way dissolved, just poke it around until it is. Otherwise you don't get the effect."

I've done this before and nothing happened, although I've heard good rumors about it.

"Eek," Gretchen Quist, the littlest cheerleader, cries. She's fluffy and pink cheeked, known for being scatterbrained. She's always squealing and running behind people for protection. The other cheerleaders, with the possible exception of Patti, adore her. "What if it's like LSD?"

"I've heard it is," Cindy Falk says, downing hers in a gulp and then shaking what's left of the aspirin into her mouth. "Some people will probably have a bad trip and some will have a good trip."

"An acid trip!" Gretchen Quist gasps, running behind me and peeking out over my shoulder. I suddenly see why people love her. "What if I think I can fly, and try to jump out the window?"

I realize who she reminds me of—Amy in *Little Women*.

Impetuous, ringletty, and perhaps not too bright, but a relief after the fervency of her sisters. She was the one I most wanted to be, even though I had the same name as another. Little Amy March grew up while no one was looking, wandered away from wherever it was they lived, and became an artist, while the one named after me had to stay and be in a worse book later.

"What if I jump out the window?" Gretchen insists, her little hands on my shoulder.

"You're in a basement, dipshit," Patti answers, crushing her cup.

Deb Patterson and Cathy Olessen go off, whispering, to sort through 45s and put a stack on the record player. First José Feliciano, then Smokey Robinson, then Dusty Spring-field. The cheerleaders look like they're doing cheers when they dance, a lot of straight-armed flailing and kicks, while the girls from Patti's old school have a more plain and studious style, like the glasses-wearing kids sprinkled into the *American Bandstand* crowd. This is where it turns out Felicia and I shine — we have our own version of the twist, which involves keeping the elbows bent, the wrists slack, and staring upward. The key is to think of oneself as a pencil being slowly worn away to a nub, then back up again.

"Being good isn't always easy," Dusty sings.

Maybe it's just the aspirin, but all the girls seem to be doing whatever I do. I twist down to the floor and fall over on my back and keep twisting; they all follow. I twist back up and then go into a funky chicken; so do they. When "Crystal Blue Per-suasion" comes on it sounds more psychedelic than it ever has; waves of music, and we're swimming to it. Kathy Liddelmeyer stops and stares at the Lava lamp, then starts dancing again, then stops and stares at it some more. Soon we all stop and stare at it.

The lava is slow and momentous, bulging up bluely and then breaking apart into pale, stoned globs that slowly find one another again.

"The lava is like a party of people," I say as the song ends.

Everyone nods. I feel even more disoriented now; the most popular kids in my school won't stop following a sidekick. There's a momentary hiss as the needle glides over to the label, a creak, a click, the clatter of the next record dropping, the sudden hiss of the needle again.

"Me shell, ma bell, soan lay moan key bone tray byen on somm, tray byen on somm," Paul sings in a clear, boyish tenor.

What if they were the ones coming over right now, the lads from Liverpool, instead of popular ninth-grade boys? My head feels fizzy and light, in a good way, and I get an insight into how much fun I could be having right now if I were someone else.

Gretchen Quist seems to be running through the basement without her pants. "I'm peed on!" she cries, flapping her hands. It looks like she couldn't get her top unsnapped — a plaid body-suit, fastened in the crotch — and tried to pee around it, but it didn't work. "I'm peed on! I'm Mrs. Piedmont!"

Mrs. Piedmont is a large, torpedo-shaped woman at our school who is referred to, officially and unofficially, as the Roving Sub.

"Help, Cathy!" Gretchen falls on the rug and lifts her legs. The sight of our dumbest cheerleader, half-naked with her feet waving in the air like a baby's, is suddenly, sickeningly hilarious. People are bent over, laughing their guts out.

Cathy Olessen reaches down and unsnaps the bodysuit, gagging with laughter, and then lifts her tainted hand in the air. "Another person's pee!" she cries, and staggers into the bathroom.

Gretchen stumbles after her, first tagging Patti and crying, "Everyone at your party is pantsed!" At which point Patti starts taking off her pants and then her shirt, and then throwing her bra on the hanging lamps. Deb Patterson and Cindy Falk and Kathy Liddelmeyer and the three girls from the other school take off their bras and toss them on the hanging lamps. Suddenly, around us people are stripping all the way down, throwing clothes at one another, launching underpants by their elastic around the room, and crowding into the bathroom, where Gretchen and Cathy are wallowing around in a blue bathtub.

The bathroom is like something out of a magazine, with mirrored tiles, recessed shelves, stacks of blue towels, two toilets, tall jars of bath salts, a macramé hanger holding an air fern. Why two toilets? I wonder. The mirrored tiles make it seem like there are naked cheerleaders everywhere, arranging and rearranging themselves, like living wallpaper. It turns out Deb Patterson is as flat as a boy.

Felicia and I sit side by side on the hamper.

"You have to strip," Patti explains to us.

Mrs. Piedmont, the Roving Sub, one time accused me of spitting on the floor outside the music room, a foaming hocker that I couldn't even look at, let alone produce. She later apologized to me—something a real teacher would never do—when she saw the culprit lay another one on his way out. "I don't know what I was thinking," she said wearily. "You're not the type at all."

But she was wrong, I'm the type to do anything—I've stolen from stores, I've cheated on tests, I've lied, I've punched my sister in the face, and along with Felicia I've vandalized property, most recently the car of a man who called the dog pound on his own dog when it got mange. He lived two doors down from Felicia and actually turned the dog loose and hid its chain and bowl before calling it in as a stray. The dog just stood there at the man's back door, oozing and miserable. Felicia and I told the guy from the pound while he was loading the dog up—using a pole and a muzzle, although the dog was actually friendly—but the guy didn't care.

"I get paid either way," he said.

Felicia spray-painted ASS on the driver's side of the man's pickup truck, and I spray-painted HOLE on the passenger's side. That was in the early fall, back when we did things before thinking about them, but nothing ever happened from it; we never got caught.

So I'll do just about anything, except spit or strip.

"I have my period," I explain.

"Me too," Felicia whispers.

"Hey—how come so many people who invented rag products have names ending in *x*, I wonder," Gretchen muses in her little-girl voice. "Mr. Ko*tex*, Mr. Tam*pax*, like that. All ending in *x*'s." She looks around slyly.

"Why would men be inventing rag products anyway?" Cindy Falk asks, staring into the medicine cabinet mirror, her eyes wide as she examines her chin. "Wouldn't that be so embarrassing—to have a whole factory that just makes *sani-*

tary napkins? What if instead of making tractors, your whole town worked at a giant rag plant?"

That's somewhat of a mindblower. They shift around, thinking.

"What if your own dad was a foreman and brought home all the reject rags for you and your sister to use?" Cathy Olessen says.

"And what about the ob ones, where it's just a bare plug, no tube?" Gretchen pipes up, and they erupt into hysteria, making honking noises, holding on to whatever is nearby — a sink, a faucet, the edge of the tub, a hanging towel.

"It's not *ob*, it's o.b.," someone tells her finally.

She blinks, thinking that over. "What does o.b. stand for?"

Silence. Felicia looks at me. I actually have a lot of tampon jokes, even though I've been on them for only two days.

"Other butt," I say.

"She's funny," Cindy says coolly, still addressing the mirror. "Why didn't we know her before?"

"I think she's in my gym class," Deb Patterson says, sitting on the rim of the tub with her legs crossed, arms folded across her nonexistent chest.

No boys allowed, Patterson.

"At first, people think you're plain," Kathy Liddelmeyer explains to me, "but then they realize you're funny."

"I don't think she's plain," Felicia says.

"Shut up a second," Patti says, listening.

Everyone freezes. When the record ends, there it is: tap, tap, tap on the sliding glass door.

What we've been dreading!

"Go outside and talk to them," Patti tells Felicia and me, pushing us out of the bathroom. "You're wearing clothes."

"But we don't even know them!" I say.

"Yes, you do," Patti answers. "Everybody does."

But they don't know me! I'm making Felicia talk. The door is hidden behind a long drape; we slide behind it and duck out into the night air.

Nothing. Just the quiet backyard of her grandmother's place, a long expanse of grass and patches of snow beyond the brick patio where we're standing, various pieces of canvas-covered lawn furniture huddled here and there. Jed Jergestaad, Tommy Walton, Galen Pierce, and some other dark figures come around from the side of the house.

"Hey," Jed says in a whisper.

"Hi," Felicia answers in a whisper.

"Is Patti here?" he asks.

"Yeah," she says. "They'll be done doing something in a minute."

We all look away from one another. It's glittering cold out here, but nobody's coat is buttoned. Clouds of vapor are silently exhaled as we wait. Somebody stomps a foot, like a horse.

"Cold," Felicia whispers.

Jed Jergestaad smiles down at the ground. He's known for being nice no matter who he's talking to.

"What do you think they're doing?" he whispers finally.

Felicia and I look at each other.

"It's a witch's tit out here," Galen Pierce says in a normal voice, and raps on the glass loudly.

The door slides open and the girls appear, one after another, until there is a big, shadowy group on the patio. It looks like the same number of boys as girls, not counting me. Galen and Patti confer in whispers and then everyone takes off across the lawn, toward the trees that lead to Prospect Point, where there's a fire pit and picnic tables—in the summer the police patrol it, but in the winter there's a chain across the road. As people move out, it seems like they're in pairs already, or maybe I'm just imagining it. Felicia seems to be walking with Jed. It was a game of musical boys and I'm the one left standing.

I don't know what to do.

"Felicia," I whisper.

"What?"

"What are we doing?" I ask.

"Going to Prospect," she whispers impatiently.

"This is hideous!"

"Why?" she whispers, glancing at Jed, who is walking backward, slowly, waiting for her. Jed Jergestaad! The trees are absorbing the rest of them, two by two.

"There are ten guys and eleven girls," I whisper. "I'm the fifth wheel or something."

"Why?"

"Are you listening? *I just said why.*"

"I mean, are you sure?" she whispers vaguely, already moving away, the outline of her head joining the outline of Jed Jergestaad's, and then they're gone, into the trees, and I'm stumbling along behind.

The only thing I'm sure of right now is that I hate Felicia.

Why oh why did I come to this thing? Even in gym class you have the chance of being picked last. It's not perfect, but at least you have a place. Once, in sixth grade, Becky McGill, as thick and squat as a toad, cried, "Her arms are *threads!*" when the teacher made her take me on her team. It was volleyball and had come down to me and Beth Fessler, who chewed her fingertips to the point where she wasn't willing to hit the ball with them. I can still see McGill just standing there on her toad legs, arms folded, jaw set. It wasn't even that she didn't like me; she just liked volleyball better.

Clouds keep going over the moon, making it hard to navigate, and people are stumbling and laughing, boy voices and girl voices, and me way back here, listening to the sound of my own breath as I pant along. As far as I know, it's never happened in the history of gym that someone was just not chosen, left to sit out the game in front of everyone because they had useless fingers or threadlike arms, were plain.

'Tis new to thee.

A cluster of tiny, perfect words, like a little village inside a snow globe.

"Hurry up!" Felicia says, pausing in the dark to whisper-bellow back at me.

Hurry up yourself and plunge down to hell while you're at it.

"I am," I whisper-yell.

'Tis new to thee.

There was something else I heard recently, a word or phrase that I wanted to remember, to think of later. This is later, but I can't think of it. I need something to hold in my mind, like a doll, just for company. How about those desperate kids in Kentucky or wherever who carry around clothespins for dolls, or the ones who dress up a withered apple. How about the UNICEF children with their bare feet, how about people who are hit by cars. How about people who simply disappear, like Kevin Prentiss, leaving everyone wondering what happened to them? The roof of the pavilion comes into view at the top of the hill, silhouetted against the cloudy sky.

Inside the pavilion it's even harder to see. People are sitting on picnic tables or wandering around holding hands. I wander too, through and out again, on the side that overlooks the Mississippi. There is a dark shape at the fire pit, but I ignore it and just stare up at the sky. The clouds shift and the moon pushes forward, the river down below glints into view, and the shape is two people, kissing. After a moment one of them says, "Hi," and I don't know if she means me, or not. I keep looking out at the view.

"Um, *hi*," the guy says pointedly.

Oh. They want me to leave.

I walk around the side of the pavilion and stand where no one can see me. The river has disappeared again but you can sense it down there, black ink rushing along. Above, the sky rushes too, clouds opening and closing the eye of the moon.

Moonflame. That was the name of the imaginary pony I had when I was a girl. All black with a white mane and tail. My friend had one that was all white with a black mane and tail. She called hers Flameglow. That friend copied everything off me, including arithmetic, but I didn't care because I was busy copying everything off another girl. If only Moonflame were here! Luekenfelter actually had a real pony, which I never knew about until she told us at lunch. Kept on Jane's farm until they built a new dairy barn. No stalls, just stanchions.

Stanchion! That was the word I meant to think about later. Until Luekenfelter said it, I had never heard it pronounced. It's *standing at attention,* telescoped into one crisp word, like biting an apple: *stanchion.* A long row of cow haunches, brown and white, as far as the eye can see.

I'm just stanchion here alone.

Two people come around from the side, pushing each other and laughing. The taller one grabs the other from behind, and

I fade out, back down the hill toward the trail. In the woods I stand for a minute, trying to think if there's anything else I can do, and then just walk back to Patti's house, pretty fast because it's weird alone in the woods, just me and the trees.

There's no moon at all now, and from the back, the house looks like a hacienda, rising three stories from the foundation, its stucco smooth and poreless. Far above is a balcony with a black wrought-iron railing.

I've never seen that look on Felicia's face before, like she wished I would disappear. It's like you're a balloon and somebody just lets go.

Inside, the basement is dim and strange without the people, and has sleeping bags and stray clothes kicked everywhere. I tidy it up so it looks more like something out of a magazine again. The only sound is the low fluorescent hum of the aquarium, where the molly swims laps in her hostess pajamas— around the diver and his bubbles, through the ceramic archway, inside the shipwreck and back out, around the diver again. Destined to be lonely, because she eats other fish.

I'm famished all of a sudden. I ravage around the bar and find an unopened can of filberts and an open can of Spanish peanuts. I eat a few of those, but the skins wreck them. What else. A jar of olives, a jar of little white onions. Four cellophane packages of cocktail napkins in geometric patterns. If I thought for one second the grandmother was asleep, I'd creep up the basement stairs and see if there was any cake left.

The stairway is sleek and modern and open, each step individually carpeted, and at the top, the lock is the kind in the doorknob. I turn it and push; all is quiet and dark except for a light on the back of the stove.

The cake plate sits in the dish drainer, washed. In the refrigerator, nothing. Totally empty except for bags of vegetables and things like milk and lunch meat. A package of something that looks promising but turns out to be some kind of foreign cheese. Now what? Hasn't the old girl ever heard of Jell-O? Then suddenly it comes back to me—out there somewhere, in the front hallway, is a big silver bowl filled with malted milk balls, my favorite food.

Surely the grandmother is asleep by now, somewhere up the curving staircase with the gold railing. Though what if she isn't? It wouldn't be like sneaking into somebody's garage or eating grapes off their fence; this I could get caught for, discovered in a rich person's house, trying to steal their candy. But now that I know it's out there, I'm helpless, like Superman in the presence of kryptonite.

The kitchen has a swinging door, which leads into the dining room, still and dark, the white upholstered chairs sitting around the table like a silent committee. At the other end are French doors opening onto a hallway with a thick strip of carpet running down the center. I think at the end of this hallway should be the foyer, with the checkered floor and the marble-topped table and the glowing chandelier, but I'm no longer sure. There was a big tree- and piano-filled room off to the left—which would be the right coming from this end—but instead there is a dark library room, with tall shelves and a built-in ladder, and a little alcove with nothing in it but a stationary bike facing a window.

I can't believe I'm in these people's house in the dark, creeping along their corridor. This is just the kind of ill-advised behavior Nancy Drew was known for—poking around with her flashlight, turning corners, and coming face-to-face with exactly who she was trying to avoid. I could barely breathe while I was reading her books, and now I'm in one: *The Secret of the Cheerleader's Mansion*. The carpeting ends in a right turn, which I take, dumping me out into the living room, with the gleaming black piano, the potted trees, and the couches, one of which has the grandmother on it.

I feel weirdly dreamy all of a sudden, like I've done this before, been caught robbing a house.

"Hello, shiest of the girls," the grandmother says with surprise. "Are you well, darling, or are you in need of something?"

I can't think of what to say. She's reading *The Love Machine*, my second-favorite book. It's embarrassing to think of her, basically an old woman, reading some of the things in there.

"If you're just haunting the halls, I don't mind at all," she says, sipping her drink. She's wearing a dark, silky robe over a dark, silky nightgown, and her voice is slightly thicker, less precise than it was a few hours ago. Bare, bony feet with high arches, like Felicia's.

"They're all asleep," I offer.

"Asleep!" she exclaims. "This is what we can expect from our younger generation? They can't wait out the old dame with the snifter of brandy and the trash novel?"

"I read that book," I tell her.

"No!" she says. "If this is true, I won't be able to read another word, for sheer horror. Darling, trust me—make-believe, all of it!"

"I know," I say.

"Now, you're a friend from the new school?"

I nod. "But not a cheerleader," I clarify.

"There are other things, aren't there?" she asks kindly. "Cheering is one thing, but there are many others. *Many*."

"Yep," I say.

"And may I ask what your father does, my dear?" She sips again, holding the stemmed glass by its bowl, her eyes large and pale above the rim.

What my father does?

I have the prickling, zooming-upward feeling that I get whenever anyone asks me that, like somebody has cut the sandbags loose and I'm no longer Dorothy in the menstrual shoes but the Wizard being yanked out of Oz.

"Hmm?" I ask, squinting into the dark hallway beyond her. He doesn't sit at our kitchen table all day with a bottle of vodka in a paper sack, if that's what you're thinking.

"What your father does," she repeats, setting the glass down again on its coaster. She's barely made any headway on it.

He was sick all week, something with his jaw, the side of his face swollen and tender. He is seeing a dentist now, getting it taken care of. The best lies are as close to the truth as possible, the ones where you only change a word or two. *He's seeing a dentist.*

"He's a dentist," I say.

"Ah!" she says, relieved. "And may I say this? *Such* a brilliant one — allowing his daughter to keep her charming smile! We've straightened our children's teeth into veritable *piano* keys, and it's just terribly, terribly sad. Your father seems to be one of the few who knows that. Your little space, my little overlap, which I've defended bitterly over the years!" She gives me a fixed smile, and there it is. Slight overlap.

"Yep," I say. Help, get me out of here.

"So. Can I send you back down now, or shall I get you something?" She looks exhausted suddenly.

"You can send me back down," I say.

"All right then. But our secret from your wonderful father? Go through that way," she says, pointing behind her, toward the front hall, where the chandelier is glowing faintly. "And take some candy along with you."

They troop back in twos and threes, over the crusted snow and onto the patio, where they slide the door open, the beige curtain billowing out for a second as they disappear inside. *Billow* is to *bellow* as *hiding* is to *hating*. I'm outside, sitting on a brick ledge behind one of the hulking pieces of covered lawn furniture, eating malted milk balls out of my coat pocket. *Pocket* is to *picket* as *hating* is to *hitting*.

Gretchen and Cathy are the first ones back, then Kathy, Cindy, and Deb, then a while later Felicia and the Hayley Mills girl, who is smoking and who takes a last puff before dropping her cigarette on the ground and following Felicia inside. I stand and stretch, pick up the lit cigarette, and hold it for half a minute, until the friends of the Hayley Mills girl come out of the woods, crunch along the strip of snow, and walk across the grass to the patio.

"Hi," I whisper, tapping the cigarette with my index finger, the way my mother does. Off drops the ash, just like that, simple physics.

"Hi," they whisper back.

I like holding the cigarette, but I have no desire to get it near my mouth.

"We have to go in, our feet are freezing," one of the girls whispers.

"Yeah, I just got back and was finishing this," I whisper, flicking the cigarette out into the darkness.

Inside, any pretense of tidiness has gone by the wayside. There are coats and shoes dropped, clothes scattered, and girls sprawled everywhere, Felicia sitting off to the side atop a bean-bag again. I look at her the same way I look at everyone else, and then sit where I'd have to turn my head to see her.

Cathy and Gretchen are in matching nightgowns and knee-socks, Deb Patterson is in a sweatshirt and kneesocks, Kathy Liddelmeyer is kneeling next to her gym bag, changing into a nightgown and crying.

"Poor Liddelmeyer," Cindy Falk says lightly, sorting through records and dropping them on the floor, one by one. She's wearing a hockey jersey as a nightgown, and over-the-knee socks, her black hair in a bun, making her look even taller than she normally does. "She keeps building up, building up, his buttercup, buttercup."

"I do *not*," Liddelmeyer cries. "And you know it!"

"And then he lets her down."

"I do *not*," Liddelmeyer bursts out, and then sobs into the sweater she just took off.

The girls from the other school are over at the bar, whispering and dealing out cards.

Gretchen looks around with wide, worried eyes. "Liddy-biddy cry," she says.

Liddelmeyer laughs, sniffling, and pulls a peasant-style nightgown over her head. Her feet are bare, but she's digging for something, most likely kneesocks. So far nobody is wearing pajamas.

"Hey, I never saw you," Cathy says to me. "Who were you with?"

I shrug.

"Second-to-last one back," she says knowingly.

"Who?" Cindy demands.

Who?

"Horton," I blurt out. "Was that his name? Tall, with sort of long hair?"

I can feel Felicia staring at me keenly from the orange beanbag.

"He could have been the kid who came with Jed, maybe," Cathy Olessen offers.

"Wait—who was with Jed?" Cindy interrupts.

"Just a kid staying with him for the weekend," Cathy says. "He kisses like a sponge."

"No, what *girl* was with Jed?" she asks, looking carefully at everyone but Felicia. "I hope nobody, since he's still technically with Martha Van Dalle."

Jed and Martha were voted king and queen of our homecoming dance and liked each other halfheartedly afterward. Cindy Falk and Tommy Walton came in second. Martha has kinky hair and is slightly tubby, but we all voted for her anyway because she has such a good personality. She's wild, but not like a hood—wild like she doesn't care about public opinion. For a long time everybody thought she had a retarded sister, a girl named Petie, who she tows around everywhere, even to games and parties, but then people found out that Petie was her neighbor, not her sister. That's basically what got her homecoming.

"Did you see she wore her candy-striper uniform to school again yesterday?" Deb Patterson asks.

"I go, 'Martha, why don't you just change on the way?' and she goes, 'Don't worry, Olessen, it doesn't have *bedpan* juice on it,'" Cathy reports.

"Yucky," Gretchen says.

"Wait, look at this doll baby," Cindy interjects, holding up an album cover of a woman in a beehive with a big flat flower behind her ear and a beauty mark. Behind her is a beach and above her are the words *Bossa Nova!* We all watch obediently as Cindy puts the record on the turntable, with the sound low, and sits on the floor to do stretches. Legs apart, eyes closed, she bends her topknot all the way over to one side, gracefully, like a dying, black-haired swan. "Patti's party and where is she?" she says to her knee. "With *Galen Pierce.*"

The thing is, if you didn't know Galen Pierce, you might mistake him for someone cute, with his blond ponytail and sharp, fine features. He's weird, though, and not part of any group, just joining up with whoever will let him, eventually offending people and being driven off again, like a rogue elephant. It's said he carries a steak knife in his sleeve.

"She picks the worst people," Deb Patterson agrees, glancing pointedly in Felicia's direction.

Cindy straightens, reaches her arms as high as they will go, and bends to the other side. "And where's her *mother?*" she asks.

The question hangs in the air for a moment as she straightens again, reaches her arms up, and then stretches forward, somehow flattening her torso until her chin is resting on the carpet. She opens her eyes, looks expectantly at us, and then closes them again.

"Yeah," Deb agrees.

"Yeah," Kathy says. "I wonder that too."

"Where Patti mommy?" Gretchen tries, looking around, but everyone is staring at Cindy, waiting for more.

"Maybe she *died* or something," Cindy says, making it sound faintly disgusting.

"I mean, otherwise, why live with your grandmother?" Deb says.

"Well, I sort of liked her grandmother," Cindy counters. "That's not what I mean."

"No, I know," Deb says quickly. "It's not her *grand*mother."

"It's Patti *I* wonder about," Cindy says, sitting up finally and reworking her topknot.

"I went to a funeral home last night for a girl's mom," I offer.

"Ooh," Kathy says.

Gretchen flaps her hands.

"Whose?" Cindy demands.

"Do you know Ellen Luekenfelter? Her cousin," I say.

"Her cousin's mom," Felicia clarifies.

Everyone turns to look at Felicia and then back to me.

"Ellen Luekenfelter is that girl with red hair?" Cathy Olessen asks.

"No, she has light brown hair. The red-haired one is Dunk Duncan," I say.

"Whose mother died?" Cindy demands.

"This girl named Jane, Ellen Luekenfelter's cousin, who lives out in the country," I say.

"Oh," Cindy says dismissively. "Out in the country."

"She's a cheerleader out there," I add.

"She is? Where?"

I don't know why I even brought this up. "Heyworth," I tell her.

"We killed them last year," Deb says.

"Is Patti mommy dead?" Gretchen asks tremulously.

"Umm," one of the girls from across the room says loudly. We all look over. "Her mother is not dead. She's going through a hard time. In case you're interested."

"We're not," Cindy says lightly, and then gets to her feet, trips over to the hi-fi, and turns up the background music.

Across the room, the other girls stare at one another, flushed.

Kathy Liddelmeyer turns to me. "The thing about Patti is, if you want to be a hood, drop cheerleading; if you want to cheer, drop being a hood."

"You know what we mean?" Cathy Olessen asks.

I nod.

"We mean we don't like her at all," Cindy tells me bluntly.

I nod again, half to Cindy and half to the record, which is cool and tinkling, like listening to a martini. Soon people will shut up and go to sleep.

"I like her," Felicia says suddenly.

Everyone turns.

From my angle, she's foreshortened on the beanbag in a way that makes her socks seem more prominent than her face — pale blue argyle, to go with her sweater. I know the look she has — when her nose turns red like that, she's either getting ready to cry or smack somebody's head off. Her hair looks good in this light, though, hardly frizzed.

"Excuse me?" Deb Patterson asks.

"I like her," Felicia repeats.

The record player lifts its arm and swings it back to the cradle, like somebody putting a hand on their hip. Cindy Falk, our head cheerleader, poses a question.

"Why is your name *Fellatio?*" she asks.

Uh-oh.

"Why is your name Cindy Fuck?" Felicia replies.

In the silence that follows, a scuffling is heard on the patio. Suddenly the door slides open and Patti appears in a swirl of curtain.

"Get me away from Galen Pierce!" she cries. Her coat is unzipped, her shirt is untucked, and when she pulls off the hat she wasn't wearing when she left, there are leaves in her hair. "We just almost got caught by the pigs."

Apparently, some guys from Waynesville climbed the hill and tried to take over the pavilion, throwing a few of our guys down the hill, until finally cops—or somebody—came through the woods with flashlights, causing everyone to scatter.

Cindy and Deb stare at each other without expression.

Kathy Liddelmeyer yawns hugely.

Gretchen puts her head back on the sofa, and her eyes close like a doll's.

I glance sideways at Felicia, who is unrolling her sleeping bag, not looking at anyone. Behind her is the fish tank, but there's no sign of the molly. It must have swum inside the ship-wreck and gone to bed.

"What happened while I was gone?" Patti asks the room.

Nobody says anything.

"This is what happened!" she crows, lifting her chin to show us her neck, ringed with hickeys.

"Good-bye, dentist's daughter!" the grandmother cries gaily, bending to wave at my mom.

"What did she say?" my mother asks, pulling away.

"I don't know. You should see their house."

"But what did she just say about a dentist?" She gropes around in her bag, looking for the cigarettes that are on the seat next to her. I take one out and hold it for a second before handing it over.

"The front hall has a huge chandelier that you can turn down the light on so that in the middle of the night it just glows, like a big glowing ball, up by the ceiling," I say.

"You were up there in the middle of the night?" Felicia says, leaning forward into the front seat, which she would normally never do with my mother right there, but she's trying to get us speaking to each other again.

"I heard her say 'dentist's daughter' or something like that—didn't she?" my mother asks.

I turn around and look meaningfully at Felicia. "Remember how everyone went to sleep so early? I got hungry and I went up there to get malted milk balls."

"Oh, right," she says. "We all fell asleep pretty early."

"Then you all woke up again," I say.

"Yeah," she says, sitting back. "Then there we were, awake."

"Tell me why that woman said that," my mother says, lighting her cigarette and throwing the match out the window.

"Mom, I'm telling you about the house, which you asked me to notice. The kitchen had a wagon-wheel chandelier—did you see that, Flea? It was like a wagon wheel suspended from the ceiling, with all these little candles that had lightbulbs in them shaped like flames."

"No, I never noticed," Felicia says.

"I don't know if I'd care for that," my mother answers, "but I'd take the other one. It's a dimmer switch that lets you turn them up or down. We can't have a crystal chandelier, but we could have a dimmer switch in the dining room if your father had any mechanical ability at all."

There's a silence as we glide up to the stoplight, everyone thinking about all the things my dad can't do.

"I don't know who she called the dentist's daughter," my mother says. "Do you?"

"*Yes,* Mother, and it's sad—why are you making me say this? She was telling me about how candy is bad for you when I was getting the malted milk balls, about cavities and all that, and at some point I go, 'Oh, my dad is seeing a dentist,' just to say something, and she heard it wrong and kept going, 'Your father is a dentist! A dentist!' and I was too embarrassed, so I just went back downstairs."

"Oh," my mom says. "Well, she just heard you wrong; you could have explained what you were saying."

"She was drinking," I say. Nothing more is said as we tick along, heading for Felicia's street.

After Felicia gets out, dragging both her sleeping bag and Stephanie's, my mother lights another cigarette for the three blocks we have to go.

"So she was up having one in the middle of the night?" she asks casually.

"I don't really know, Mother," I say. Everything going by out the window is depressing: houses, people in church clothes getting out of their car, an abandoned yard sale with a sign saying FREE! propped against one of the tables. "I was trying to tell you what their house looked like but you didn't even care."

"Can you see what they've got up there?" my mother asks, slowing.

"We're not stopping! Whatever it is has been rejected by the whole rest of the town!"

"This is what I'm going to get all day now, because you went to a slumber party last night."

"Why can't I do anything fun without being yelled at?" I feel like crying all of a sudden.

"Was it fun?" she asks, pulling into the driveway. "Because I know you were worried about it."

"I wasn't worried about it!" I say, slamming my door.

I read and sleep the rest of the day, first in bed and then crammed behind the green chair with Tammy. I keep *The Tempest* with me because it's homework, but I can't take it, too ornate, so instead I sneak a new paperback book off Meg's stack: *The Red Badge of Courage*, about the Civil War, which I feel a particular affinity for, ever since having to memorize and deliver the Gettysburg Address back in grade school. I still remember what I wore, a velveteen dress made by my mother and ankle boots with white kneesocks, and where I stood, in front of the tall, dusty curtain on the stage in the gymnasium, looking out over a sea of parents. I could say the entire thing right now—that's how well I learned it, sitting doubled over every night on the living room ottoman, faint with gut-cramping dread, while my dad listened to me grunting out the lines.

"You're supposed to call Flea back, Mom says."

Raymond, peering over the top of the chair.

"I'm doing homework, tell her," I say.

He leaves and comes back. "Mom said then call and tell her that—she doesn't want to answer the phone anymore."

"How many times did she call?"

He leaves and comes back. "Three, and Mom said she said she'd have you call, so she wants you to call. Another girl called too, but she didn't say who it was."

"What did she sound like?"

He leaves and comes back. "She doesn't know."

"Did she have a low voice, sort of, or was it high?" Probably Dunk, but possibly Cindy Falk, who had me write my phone number on the back of her hand this morning.

He leaves and comes back. "She said to tell you not to send me back and forth anymore."

"Do you care?" I ask him.

"Not really," he admits. "She's cooking a pie and has crust."

When she makes pies, she always puts an extra crust in the oven, sprinkled with cinnamon and sugar. It's one of my favorite foods.

"Would you bring me some?"

He leaves and comes back, only it isn't him, it's her. "How would you like me to haul you out of there by your scalp?" she asks, peering over the back of the chair.

"I'm doing homework!" I say, holding up *The Tempest*. "This is not easy, Mother—it's Shakespeare."

"I don't care if it's Liberace," she answers. "Your family is not your servant."

"I never said it was! All I wanted was one bite of crust!"

"Well, you're going to have to get up off your ass and walk to the kitchen for it," she replies. "And while you're at it, why don't you go through the dining room and look at what your brother's been doing. Take a minute for him, instead of the other way around."

With that, she leaves, and it's just me and Tammy again, reading *The Red Badge,* which is slow going but good. The boy is joining the army against his mother's wishes. She pleads with him but he won't listen, so she gives up and packs him eight pairs of socks and says to send them back whenever they get holes in them so she 'kin dern 'em.' This makes me feel frantic for a few minutes, the idea of the mother preparing for her own sorrow, filling a cup with blackberry jam and sending it along to the Civil War army.

Me abandoned last night, left to stumble around alone in the woods, like Petie the retarded neighbor. What's a sidekick supposed to do without a side? When the side stares at her with blank unreachable eyes and then fades backward into the dark like a message in a Magic 8 Ball: *Try again later.*

I dislodge the dog and crawl out before panic can overtake me. On my way to get crust, I go through the dining room, where Raymond has draped blankets over the big table and is under there with a desk lamp, several guns, a G.I. Joe, and the harpoon.

"See, this is a trench in a battle," he explains to me, "and we're dug in, watching for the enemy. Don't tell Mom I have this harpoon."

"Who's we?" I ask.

"Uh, nobody," he says, his eyes flickering toward G.I. Joe, who is clinging to one of the table's pedestals with a knife in his hand and bare feet. "I'm all by myself."

"I can play for three minutes," I say.

He hands me a pistol and a kaleidoscope, which he then takes back to demonstrate. "Pretend you're looking through this to see who's coming. Actually you'll see Clyde's scope colors, but don't say that; say you're seeing the enemy."

"It's not *Clyde*," I tell him. "It's like colors *colliding together*, as in *kaleido*scope." I point it at the desk light and turn it a few times. Pattern after pattern, bright flowers of color sliding around in there. "The enemy seems to be wearing an Easter hat, sir."

He stares at me, thinking. "You can just be looking," he suggests. "And then I'll ask you to report."

Suddenly a head appears under the blanket.

"I know you have my book, so where is it?" Meg demands.

"What book?" I ask.

"This book," she says, and reaches out, lightning fast, grabs my wrist, and starts twisting.

"Ow-ow-*ow*," I whimper.

"Ow-ow-*ow*," she mimics.

"Behind the chair," I gasp.

She tosses my wrist back to me, and the blanket flaps shut again.

"Are you going to keep playing?" Raymond asks.

I rub my arm. This is the worst day of my life, unless you count yesterday.

"We can say you're wounded," Ray suggests.

A wound is what the boy at Chancellorsville wanted, a red badge of courage, so he wouldn't have to go on down the road to Gettysburg. Four score and seven years ago, our fathers brought forth to this continent bottles of liquor, which they keep in the garage so they can drink while they putter. Mine has the hood of the car up and can be seen from the kitchen window, looking at the engine with a rag in his hand.

"That's what I'll have next—a broken car," my mother says, peering out.

"Can I have crust or not?" I ask, sitting down at the table.

"Are your legs broken?"

"God, why is everyone attacking me?"

"Who attacked you?" she asked. "Your sister better not have. I told her something I meant to have stick."

"Well, it didn't," I say, rubbing my arm.

The phone rings and my mother takes it off the hook and hands it directly to me.

"Why aren't you calling me back?" Felicia asks.

"Homework," I say.

"For Van Leuven? I already read that thing."

"Lucky you, lucky her," I say lightly, cheerleader style.

Silence.

"Could you believe what happened last night?" she asks finally.

"Sort of."

"Jed Jergestaad? You've got to be kidding me! I got out my yearbook and am just looking at him. I can't believe it."

Silence.

"Why are you acting like this?" she asks.

"I'm not."

Silence.

"Because I don't know what you could be mad about. There wouldn't be any reason."

Silence.

"Nothing I can think of, anyway," she goes on. "Not like somebody called *you* a blow job and I just sat there while it happened."

My mother is smoking and staring at me.

"I still have a lot to read," I say.

Felicia slams the phone down.

"Uh-huh," I say, looking at my mother, who looks back at me. "Yep . . . okay . . . see you tomorrow."

She breaks off a disk of crust, warm from the oven, and hands it to me on a plate. "What's wrong with you and Flea?" she asks.

I take one bite and the whole thing falls apart. "Nothing," I answer. "What's wrong with this crust?"

"I can take it back if you don't like it," she says, peering past me, out the window again. The car hood is closed and my dad has moved out of sight, farther back into the black garage. *Try again later.* The crust is so delicious it's putting me in a good mood.

"I don't know why you wouldn't talk to your friend who called you four times."

"Mother," I say patiently. "I. Have. Homework."

"You can drop that," she advises. "Nobody around here was born yesterday."

"Anyway, I'd think you'd be happy, since you never could stand her."

"What? I never said that!" She returns to the sink, splashes some water around, and then starts attacking the stove with a dishrag. "I said she doesn't *talk;* that was all."

She talks plenty. It's that she doesn't stick by you in emergencies.

"I may have said that you girls seem too thick at times, to the exclusion of others," she goes on primly.

"Well, now other people want to be friends with me, but not with her," I explain. Why am I talking about this? It can only backfire.

"Why not?"

"I don't know. They just don't."

"Well, she must have done something."

"Something about a boy, or something," I say. I must be more tired than I thought, otherwise I'd know better than this. "That she abandons people when a boy comes along."

She stops scrubbing, picks up her cigarette, and points it at me. "I'll hit the roof if I hear there were boys at that party."

"Mother! Are boys going to a *slumber* party? At a *grandmother's* house?"

She takes a drag. "You tell me."

"Okay: no! This is about Flea abandoning people and people not liking it. In a moment of need she'll stare at you like she doesn't know you and just walk away, leaving you standing there like somebody's retarded neighbor."

"When did she do that? And did you tell her you were upset?"

"Not *me*, Mom. Aren't you listening? I'm talking about why the other people don't like her!"

"But you can't let other people influence how you treat someone who has been your friend for years." She sneaks a glance at the garage and then sits down at the table with her ashtray. "That isn't right."

"This isn't *divinity school*, Mother, it's junior high!"

She blinks at that. "How do you even know what divinity school is?" she asks.

"I don't know. Books."

"Well, then you know that divinity school is a place where people go to learn how to treat others," she says, inhaling. "More or less."

"That isn't what it is."

"Of course not," she says, exhaling. "Your mother doesn't know anything, according to you and your sister."

My father is coming up the back walk, carrying something.

"And I said 'more or less,' " she adds as he opens the door, bumping her chair.

The phone rings just as my father is putting what he found on the table—a rusted tobacco tin, full of old-fashioned hand-made nails.

"I found these way back in that white cabinet," he tells me, shaking them out. "And I thought of your metal-shop class— maybe your teacher would want to see them." They are big and rough; each one looks like a rusted lowercase *l*. I can smell something on him, vodka out of a sack.

"Hello," my mother answers.

"Aren't they something?" he asks me.

"Awful sorry, but she's not taking calls this afternoon," she says, hanging the receiver back up.

"Who was that?" I ask her.

"Made by a blacksmith, every one of them a little bit differ-ent. He'll see it, boy, if he likes metal," my father says, holding up one of the *l*'s to show my mother.

"Who was that?" I ask again.

"Get those off my table," she tells him.

The next day, Monday, instead of going to the cafeteria, I go to the art room over lunch to work on my chicken. Ring-gold is excited by this, and even though it's his free period and he's cleaning out the still-life closet, he brings me a stack of books to look at.

"You're going to see some things in here that will blow your mind," he predicts.

The chicken can't be made to stand up straight on its own two hands, because one of its wrists is cocked at a strange angle. I tried to tell Steve this when I was doing the casting, but I couldn't get a word in—he spent the whole time telling me all about how he pretended that he'd severed his index finger once, arranged it in a box with cotton, and thrust it at people. Just as I open one of the books, Maroni pokes her head in; behind her is Felicia.

"Hi," they say from the doorway.

"Hi," I say.

"Aren't you eating?" Maroni asks.

"I needed to finish my project," I say.

"So are you done?" Maroni asks.

"With the chicken, but now I have to go through these books," I say.

Ringgold backs out of the closet, hair astray, lugging a marble bust that he sets on a bench. "Greco-Roman," he says before ducking back in. "Look at the expression."

It has a faraway gaze.

"Well, bye," Maroni says.

"Yeah, bye," Felicia says.

"Bye," I say.

The books are in fact blowing my mind. Everything from a cup, saucer, and spoon covered in some kind of animal fur, like coyote or maybe bobcat—the hairs are tricolored and fairly long, as though whatever it was were shot in the winter— to a big pair of lips floating across a sky, to a train coming through a fireplace, to a red rubber glove nailed to a wall, to a child in a pinafore chasing a hoop with a stick through an abandoned city.

"De Chirico," Ringgold says over my shoulder. "It's that beat of time between postindustrial and pretechnological. Stark and empty, yes, but pulsing with what has been and what is to come, as indicated by the looming shadow, just around the corner. Not true for Magritte—his vision is something else entirely. De Chirico is emotion, Magritte logic; it's like the mother and the father."

I turn back to the cup and saucer. "What kind of fur do you think this is?" I ask Ringgold.

He considers it. "Silver fox maybe?"

He's right, it's the winter coat of a fox. Now I wish I hadn't asked.

"We're starting 2-D next week, but I won't impose that on you, if you want to stay 3-D," Ringgold tells me. He's setting up a still life on a rolling cart, using yards of striped sailcloth which he drapes artfully around and over two blocks of different heights before arranging the objects: a marble bust, a bowling ball, a plastic rose, a brass doorknob, a shard of beveled mirror, and an hourglass. He stands back to look at it, first chewing on his thumb and then holding it straight out in front of him.

"Wait," he says, suddenly going back into the closet.

Why does he think I would want to do a different project than everyone else? In the stack is a big, thin book of paintings, all by the same guy, Max Ernst, each page stranger than the last. In one painting a trick bird figure drawn in chalk presides over a ponytail attached to a hubcap, which is connected in turn by a string to a bottle containing a red blob, and then to an egg. *Loplop Introduces a Young Girl.* What could it mean? Around this tableau are various objects, some painted and some real: a frame, a tree frog, a blue necktie, a cameo, a spidery letter *E*. The hank of hair is real—dark and slightly scraggy, not unlike my own.

"Loplop is the artist's alter ego," Ringgold explains from

atop a ladder above me, where he's tying fishing line to an eye hook in a ceiling tile. It looks like he's going to fall, and his pants have rucked up so that an inch or so of leg is showing above each blue sock. I keep my eyes on the book until he climbs down and gets himself situated. A lot of the pictures have a bird theme of some sort. In one, parts of a cage have been attached to the canvas; in another, a bird in the sky has caused pandemonium among two girls and a man who looks like Mr. Pettle, the gym teacher. Its real objects are an open gate, a little outhouse, a butter knife, and a doorbell. It's called *Two Children Are Threatened by a Nightingale*. I feel uneasy all of a sudden, too aware of the lights buzzing overhead and the sound of Ringgold going about his business. What am I doing, hanging around here with a teacher? I'm supposed to be wherever Felicia is, doing whatever she's doing.

Help. Where am I.

"We're going to add an element of mystery to our setup here," Ringgold calls from the closet.

Please shut up.

He comes out with a large, tarnished skeleton key, which he ties to the fishing line. Then he pushes the still-life cart around until the key is hovering, invisibly suspended, in front of the bowling ball and above the reclining plastic rose. When he switches on the spotlight to the right, stark, purplish shadows leak out from the left of everything. It's beautiful and mysterious, yes, but what will I do if my whole life is like this, watching some adult tie a skeleton key to fishing line while everyone else is having boys like them?

"What do we think?" Ringgold asks, stepping back.

"Good," I say in a tinny, strange voice.

*   *   *

My next class is physics, where the teacher makes me stand up in front of everyone and put my hand on a silver globe to demonstrate static electricity. As soon as I touch it, the globe creates some kind of phenomenon that makes my hair rise up in the air, apparently, all around my head. It causes a sensation, everyone hooting wildly, to the point that the teacher makes me do it again. It feels like when you do a handstand and your hair all falls toward the floor, except you're upright and it's falling toward the ceiling. It's like the paintings I was looking at, surreal, especially if you think about what your face looks like with no hair around it, your ears just sticking out.

Tim Benchfield, my lab partner, blows up a balloon for us to use in our own experiment. "You should have seen your hair, man," he says, pausing to rest. "It made your face look about the size of a nickel or something. Really dinky."

He puts one more deep breath into the balloon and then lets go, sending it fizzling through the air and causing everyone else to do the same thing. In the commotion, I walk out of the room, down the hall, and into the bathroom.

A girl named Jackie Lopez is standing there in a bra, washing something out of her shirt.

"I got thrown a pie at," she explains, "walking out of the cafeteria, and then they just sat there, looking the other way."

"There was pie today?" My hair is still perfectly straight, but lifted off my scalp in a weird way, as though it had been rolled up on soup cans all night. "I missed lunch."

"Blueberry. It wasn't good, though—it was sticky or something—so people were throwing it instead of eating it. Do you know that kid Denny?"

"Denny the Menny, or Denny the one who wears the white shirts?"

"The Jehovah's Witness one! I should throw a pie at him so he can't try to convert people on the way home from school."

"Was that other Denny sitting there, by any chance? Because I don't think Jehovah's Witnesses are allowed to throw things at people."

"Alls I know is one second I had pie on my boob and the next second everyone on the bench was pointing to that kid Denny, who just looked the other way." She puts the shirt back on, flinching at the cold wet fabric.

I'm noticing in the mirror that my face does look a lot dinkier than Jackie Lopez's, which is wide and flat and has a few extra zits, which is probably why she got food thrown on her. Welcome to divinity school.

Felicia is standing outside the physics room when I go back, holding a stack of construction-paper valentines, a tape dispenser, and a chocolate long john in a waxed paper sleeve.

"Thanks," I say.

"I was going to leave it in there, but then I thought that kid Timothy would eat it," she says.

"My money's in my locker," I say.

"It's all right—Step On Me stayed home today, so I got her lunch money."

Normally I would ask whether Stephanie was faking it or truly sick, but somehow I can't. I move so I'm standing just inside the classroom, where there's no teacher, just students milling around, rubbing balloons on one another.

She nods at the long john. "I hope you like it, anyway."

"I will," I say.

"I'm supposed to be putting up hearts," she says. Then, after a moment: "What were you doing?"

"Talking to Jackie Lopez in the bathroom."

"Are you still mad at me?"

"I never said I was."

"You're something."

"Well, so are you."

"No, I'm not," she insists. "I'm being regular and you're being something."

Just then the teacher walks up, Mr. Margolis, waves of cigarette smoke rolling off him. "Where do you belong?" he asks Felicia.

"School Beautification wonders if we could put a valentine on your door," she whispers.

He looks at me.

"I said you'd be right back," I say.

"Are you supposed to have food in here?" he asks.

"No," I say.

"Then deposit that."

I pretend to put the long john in the wastebasket as he bangs the door shut and strides to the front of the room, clapping and coughing, scattering people. During the dismal lecture that follows, I glance back once and see, faintly visible through the frosted glass, a red heart taped to the door.

After school, I find myself unable to go home, and just hang around the building, walking the corridors and stairwells, peering into trophy cases and barren classrooms while the school slowly empties, past miles of lockers, army green and expressionless, like dead, propped-up soldiers. Past detention and then double detention, past the Spanish Club having a long meeting and afterward getting its picture taken while crowded into a stairwell, past an abandoned mural-painting project, with folded drop cloths and sealed jars of tempera, past the special combined Presidents' Day and Valentine's Day bulletin board, where Lincoln stares out, hollow eyed and unsmiling, paper hearts stapled all around him like red badges of courage.

At some point I follow the sound of music—literally—up to the third floor, where a girls' chorus is singing the Raindrops on Roses song. Now for the rest of the night I'll be saying to myself the tedious and compelling line *Brown poop in packages tied up with string.* Back down on second, I nod at the janitor's assistant, a deaf guy who goes to the chiropractic college across the river. From having a deaf girl in my grade school, I actually know how to spell "hi" in sign language, but I'm too embarrassed to try it, so I just wave.

Every once in a while you'll see a locker crammed so full that stray notepaper is coming out the air vents. There are one or two on each floor, and it's somehow disturbing, like seeing pubic hair poking out of a swimsuit. If people can't do any better than that, why even have a locker?

The mural-painting project is by seventh graders and shows Chief Illini and Chief Black Hawk looking out over the river toward Missouri. Both chiefs have miniature hands and feet, and the river is painted a flat, illustrious blue with squiggles of white here and there to show the current. A passerby has penciled in a tiny drowning man, with the usual ripples and a plea for help.

One floor up, I run into the janitor again, who gives me a quizzical smile and then mimes putting a key into a lock and turning it. A pack of cigarettes is just visible in the pocket of his shirt. On the way out, I stop at my locker, and on the shelf, right under the vent, are three notes, shoved in there since sometime after lunch.

Purple felt-tip:

Is this your locker??? Patterson said it was!! I called you yesterday about 3 times—is your mother wierd??? (Mine is!!) Call me tonite and I'll tell ya something!

Signed Cindy, with a flourish ending in a flower, and her number.

P.S. If this isn't you, please ignore!!

Green ink:

Hi! I didn't see you at all today!!!!! But saw Flea and she said she was w/ JED JERGESTAAD!!! No one believes her, but I do, because she's cute!!!!! If you get this call me tonite??? I have to ask you something and your Mom ain't letting calls thru!

Signed Dunk, with a cartoon face wearing granny glasses. The third is in red colored pencil, from Luekenfelter.

Hey Chick!!!! Where are you today Jane might be moving to this school! Next year but wants to come this weekend & there's supposed to be a big party at Prospect. Are you going if there is???? Call me tonite

I have to ask you something about ~~After~~ Algerbra, which we have a test on Wed.!!!!

Signed Ellen, with a banner under it crossed with two lines.

Taking only my jacket and the big thin book of paintings that Ringgold lent me, I head for the side door, where the janitor is waiting, and then I'm out in the February cold. Somehow I only have one mitten. A big party at Prospect? A pitch-black game of musical boys where one lone girl is left standing? This is what I mean by being frightened of the universe: it can do anything, even things you haven't bothered to imagine—like make the worst thing that ever happened to you happen again, one week later.

Around the corner, across a patch of lumpy ice, past the gym, where there are still lights on, over the front steps, along the bike rack and the flagpole, around to the back, through the lighted space between the Annex and building, under the delivery dock and trash area, and then again past the door I left out of. The deaf janitor is halfway down the hall now, following a machine as it glides along, polishing the floor.

Alone in the universe, he is.

A surge of adrenaline propels me out of the school's atmosphere and onto the street. Whatever they did to me in that physics class is still happening—I feel strangely light, but slow, like I'm walking through water, my hair floating around my head. All the houses are black, and then there's one with lights, then another, then another. People eating dinner, watching TV. The Melchers' house, at the end of our street, is getting new siding, sold to them not by my father but by someone else from Dick Best Home Improvement. They've chosen a kind

221

that makes it look like their house is made of piled rocks, like something out of *The Flintstones*. Next door down, the Robileskys are eating dinner on TV trays; I can see Mr. Robilesky's bald dome and all the stuff they have stacked on their dining room table. Old Milly's house is dark because she's in California helping out her sister-in-law, who just had both legs removed below the knee. Our house is going strong, lights upstairs, downstairs, and in the backyard, where Tammy is standing at the end of her chain, waiting for someone to remember her. Next door, the dirt circle is empty, Curly's chain disappearing into the black rectangle of his doghouse.

Through the kitchen window Meg is visible, washing dishes alone, shoulders hunched the way she carries them at home, where she's free to stop being so tall. Through the dining room window my mother is at the sewing machine, guiding fabric along with one hand and smoking with the other. She also seems to be talking. In front the living room drapes are closed on the picture window, but the birdcage is visible on the side, the bird sitting on his perch, head tucked into a wing. *Two Children Are Threatened by a Nightingale*.

At least there were two of them.

Felicia is the only person I never felt nervous around, the only person I could do certain things with—shoplift, look up at the stars without feeling dread—the only person I could go call right now and just start talking like everything was okay and everything would in fact be okay.

Pick up the phone, is all. Go back to being who you were before everything became like this. Nothing happened! You were just at a party and boys chose everyone else, and your best friend stared at you with flat eyes and you walked in the woods and talked to a grandmother. Nothing happened, and yet it feels like something did, because things aren't the way they were before. It's like when you come home and your mother has changed the furniture around, and for one instant it's like you've entered the next dimension over: it's your living room but it's not your living room. That's how this feels, like if you tried to sit down, you might find out that the chair is over there.

I do a few turns around the house, holding the wafer of book with my one mitten. Every corner has a downspout, every downspout has a blob of rutted ice around it, and every time I go around, the ice blobs seem to get bigger. Or else I'm getting smaller. In fact, I've been feeling smaller than usual ever since I left the school, but I thought it was an illusion caused by carrying such a big, thin book. Inside it, the artist's alter ego is introducing a young girl to an egg, a string, and a hubcap with a ponytail coming out of it. My own alter ego is in one of the other books—the girl in a pinafore, chasing a hoop through a city everyone else has moved out of.

I let Tammy off her chain and she runs away from me, to the back door. Inside, the kitchen is clanging with brightness.

"She's grounding you unless it's really good," Meg says, pointing the spray nozzle at me.

I go to the dining room doorway and wait to be yelled at.

"Nobody gives a shit one way or the other what I go through," my mother says, not looking up from her sewing. "Between you and your dad, I'm a wreck."

"I had Yearbook," I say.

"You had what?"

"I'm on Yearbook, and you already knew that. I told you but you didn't listen."

She squints at me, lips pressed together.

"If you don't want me to be on it, that's fine. Just say and I'll be happy to quit."

"I don't care what you're on or not on—I just want to know ahead of time not to sit here worrying about whether you're alive or dead or sitting in a goddamned detention hall for behaving over there the way you do over here." She tugs on a thread, gathering the waistline for a peasant skirt that I had started and abandoned. "What were you doing for the yearbook?"

"Following some kid around while he took pictures, writing down people's names and stuff like that."

"All right," my mother says, holding up the peasant skirt and admiring it. "See? It's just running a seam and then pulling on the thread—not crazy, but carefully—and there you have it."

"I have to call somebody," I say, heading back into the kitchen to the telephone.

Meg has preemptively grabbed the receiver. "First dry the pans," she says.

I dry them while she watches. The towel is wet but neither of us cares.

"Now scrub the floor," she says.

I can either beat her brains in with the black skillet or plead. "Give it," I whimper.

She throws the receiver in my direction but it misses, hits the cupboard, and bounces around on its cord, making a clatter.

"What was that?" my mother calls.

"Meg throwing the phone," I answer.

"You girls have managed to ruin that telephone," she yells, "by stretching the cord and throwing the receiver." *We can't keep anything decent around here.* "We can't keep anything decent around here." *Because of you kids.* "Because of you girls." *Hey, but what about Raymond?* "Your brother is the only one who listens to me." *Is Dad somehow involved?* "And your father doesn't help matters either—he would never have dreamed of correcting you." *Is it all your job?* "I'm the one who's been expected to do everything from discipline to sitting here on a Monday night after working all day, putting a goddamned waistband on a skirt for *someone else*."

"Is she crying?" Meg mouths to me.

"I think so," I mouth back.

We go stand in the doorway. She lights a cigarette and takes an angry puff, looks away from us.

"We're sorry," I say.

"We are," Meg says.

"We weren't fighting, we were having fun," I lie.

"Yeah," Meg says.

"Don't have fun with my telephone," she says wearily. "In fact, stay off it altogether."

"Mom, I have to make a call! Make me stay off it later, but not right now!" I feel weightless all of a sudden, like there's no gravity in the dining room. I grab hold of the doorframe and pull myself, hand over hand, back through into the kitchen side of the doorway.

"What the hell is wrong with you?" my mother asks, narrowing her eyes.

"Nobody will let me call somebody I need to call!"

She turns back to her project. I realize now that the problem with the peasant skirt isn't that the waistband wouldn't gather right; the problem is that I no longer want to be a peasant.

I grope my way across the kitchen to the phone and dial.

Five rings, and then two people answer at the same time. "Hello, is Cindy there?" I ask.

"Hang up," Cindy tells the mother, and the mother hangs up. "God, when I put that note in your locker, these three girls were standing there. Really—do they stare much? That red-haired girl with the little glasses?"

"Debbie Duncan," I say. "Her locker is by mine."

"Well, she should stare less, and so should Gina Maroni and that other one, with the really blond hair."

Dunk, Yawn, and Maroni, all standing at my locker after school when Cindy Falk put a note through the vent. I'm ruined in a thousand different ways now.

"Can you meet us after school tomorrow?" Cindy asks. "We all have to figure out about going to Prospect on Saturday."

"Oh yeah, I heard about that."

"Galen Pierce said he's paying off the cops—he's rich enough to do it, his dad invented some big thing Caterpillar bought off him for their tractors. Rubber or something."

Meg is trying to put Saran Wrap around a plastic bowl half-filled with corn. It won't stick to the bowl at all but sticks to itself completely.

"Wow," I say.

I try to help by holding one corner of the Sarah Wrap, like a bedsheet. Meg peels another corner off itself and we try to stretch it over the top of the bowl.

"So meet us after cheerleading, and you and me and the other people we want to come will talk about it."

Please don't let the other people be Deb Patterson. We try pressing the Saran Wrap edges to themselves, but now they won't stick. Meg yanks the whole thing off there, wads it up into a ball, and throws it at me.

"Come to the gym, but don't let Cling see you—anyone she sees waiting for us she gives detention to. Wait behind the tree."

"What tree?" I grab the Saran Wrap and tear off a piece, which instantly gets tangled. How are we supposed to cover this stupid corn?

"Ha," Meg says.

"I don't know—the *tree* tree. We come out at five. Now I have to go."

I wad up my Saran Wrap and throw it at Meg just as my mother walks into the kitchen. She picks the ball up and patiently unwads it, stretches it over the bowl, tacks the ends down tightly, opens the refrigerator, rearranges, and sets the bowl on a shelf.

"Saran Wrap is expensive," she says.

I need to stay home for part of the next day, just until after Shakespeare class is over. I accomplish this by coming downstairs in my nightgown and standing over the heat vent in the kitchen, next to the refrigerator, while my parents make breakfast.

"I don't feel good," I say, wrinkling my face.

"Uh-oh," my dad says, turning the eggs.

"Don't feel good how?" my mother asks.

"Dizzy," I say. The heat kicks on, inflating my nightgown.

"Come here," she orders me, and I go over briefly so she can feel my forehead and stare penetratingly at me. Then I return to the vent. If she believes me, she'll send me back upstairs to bed; if she doesn't, she'll send me to school; if she isn't sure or if I haven't tried this for a long time, she'll put me on the couch and then go to work. My nightgown flares while she considers.

"All right. Go in on the couch."

Yippee.

I watch *Captain Kangaroo* with Raymond until he has to leave, and then Tammy and I watch *Romper Room,* which seems to have a substitute who is sterner and more teacherlike than the other one. Jack LaLanne comes on next and I fall back to sleep so as not to have to look at what happens to his one-piece body-suit when he does the exercises, and wake up sometime later, when an episode of *Lassie* is on. This is the original version, which didn't have Timmy but had Jeff, a tall, fatherless boy with dark circles under his eyes who called his dog with a shrill bird cry: *Kee-ah-kee.* In the kitchen, my dad clears his throat, stirs his coffee, then gets up and washes the spoon.

In this old version of *Lassie,* the mother had dark, frizzy hair and the crises were wrenching—farm accidents, twisters, copperheads slithering toward babies. *Help, girl,* Jeff would cry, wringing his hands. *Get help!* I close my eyes as my dad goes past me and up the stairs. I hear the attic door open. The old version had a better ending too—instead of lifting her paw and whining at the credits as they roll past, this version shows Lassie bunching up some sheep and moving them down a hill-side. Why would he be going up to the attic?

I tiptoe into the kitchen and grab a sweet roll out of a pack-age on the counter and scamper back just as the next show is coming on—*Password,* which I don't like, too much tension over things that don't matter. No reason for him to be going into the attic when the bottle is down here, standing alongside his chair in the kitchen, a paper bag twisted around it. Although he hasn't hunted for years now, the gun is still up there, hanging on its beam. The shotgun shells that found their way to the cellar are back up there too, hidden under the same gray hat they were always hidden under.

"The password is *dreadful*," the announcer whispers.

"Umm, umm," a man in glasses says to his partner, a woman who used to be famous somehow. "Umm, bad. Filled with"—and he makes a frightened face.

"Horror? Fear? Fright?" she tries. She has on eyeglasses with a chain draping down on either side of her face. I think I remember seeing her in a movie once, where she was blind, trapped in a house.

I can hear thumping around up there. What if the password was *sweet roll* and I was sitting here eating a sweet roll? When I was young, things like that happened to me all the time, or at least I thought they did. One of the things I used to notice was that just as somebody was saying something, I would be thinking the very same thing, word for word. But then I realized that that's what hearing is. Hard to describe now, but it was confusing back when I was really little, before I knew there were some things you just accept without thinking about them, like hearing and seeing. I used to lie in bed at night and stare out at the hallway, closing one eye and then the other and watching how the slightly open door would jump back and forth. It took me a long time to decide I wasn't moving the door with my eyes. No idea what he would be doing up in the attic with me here on the couch.

"The password is *steerage*."

That has something to do with a ship. Or maybe I'm thinking of Steerforth, David Copperfield's best friend, who disappears in the middle of the book and then washes up many chapters later, after a shipwreck, drowned. I hear footsteps on the attic stairs and stuff the rest of the sweet roll into my mouth and chew quickly, eyes closed. He comes downstairs, tiptoes past, and lets himself out the back door. He's carrying something, it sounds like, but I can't tell what.

Steerforth actually wasn't the greatest of guys, but David C. loved him anyway because friends meant everything to him; the chapter where they met was called "I Enlarge My Circle of Acquaintance." Just in terms of coincidences: the chapter where Steerforth dies was called "Tempest," and exactly right now is Van Leuven's class, where *The Tempest* is being acted out by half the class while the other half watches. Felicia and I were chosen for the audience. I'm starting to feel demented again, sick of that giant sweet roll and sick of game shows.

The password is *misery*.

I roll off the couch and follow Tammy, who has jumped up on a chair to watch my dad out the dining room window. It's the bird's window, and he gets excited and starts hopping from pillar to post, sliding down the bars, gnawing his cuttlebone, all the while turning his head back and forth to watch us out of both eyes.

Outside, my father is sitting at our picnic table putting on what he brought down from the attic—trout-fishing boots, hip-high waders made of thick green rubber. As he flips the canvas suspenders over his shoulders and fastens them, he seems to be talking to Curly, who has come out of his doghouse and is listening warily from the end of his chain. My dad has been taking care of him while Milly is in California, filling the cake pan once a day and pushing it into the dirt circle. On the picnic table is a pair of big suede work gloves and Tammy's leash.

He's going to try to walk him.

Forget the gun, this is suicide by dog—I can't think what to do except call my mom and get her to stop him, but before I can move, he steps into range and Curly's face retracts, leaving nothing but teeth. Tammy stands up on the chair and then sits down again, whining. *Help, girl!*

Where my dad grew up, nobody ever kept a dog chained. It was on a highway that now extends forever across the state but back then only went as far as their town, and people from the city would drive out to the end of the road to dump their animals. Old blind collie dogs, puppies, cats with whole litters of kittens, mongrels that had stood barking at the ends of chains all their lives and that suddenly were free to run loose with their own kind. People didn't make a big deal of it—they put out scraps from their tables, tucked straw under their porches for them, and shot them when they thought they needed to be shot. Spud, Bud, Bingo, Old Crip, Big Gyp, Little Kip—I know their names and their personalities as well as I know my uncles from that side of the family. My dad basically grew up like Huck Finn; although not that close to the Mississippi, not that far from it either. Fifteen miles or so.

He takes a step, and Curly attacks him at the ankles and calves. Amazingly, the boots withstand it, and after a moment the dog retreats, head down, hackles up. Another step and it happens again, attack and retreat. At the next step, there's a lunge but no bite. At the next step, nothing. Just standing there on his bowlegs, chest heaving. Still talking, my dad tosses Tammy's leash back into our yard, then slowly reaches down, unclips the heavy chain from the tree, and winds it around his gloved hand as Curly backs up, pressing his thick haunches into the doorway of his house and crouching there, half in and half out.

It's like pulling a car, getting him out of the dirt circle. It's been twelve years since he went beyond the two feet between where his chain reaches and the slanted doors to Milly's cellar. To him, it's probably like being dragged through the TV into the actual show—ears pitched far back on his head in a way I've never seen them, legs braced as my father tugs him along, inch by inch. As they cross the yard, the bird gets more and more excited, swinging energetically back and forth. Tammy whines as they pass out of sight and races into the living room, where she jumps up on the back of the couch to watch out the front window for them.

When they appear again, Curly is out ahead, hauling a tall man in hip waders through a shrub and down a terrace. The man has a look on his face I've never seen before, one that makes him seem like someone else's father altogether. He looks happy, leaning backward as the dog strains forward, into the world.

From the dining room comes the sound of the bird singing.

An hour later, I call my mom. "I'm better and I came to school," I say. "Can you tell them?"

"Put them on," she says. "But tell me first—when did your dad leave?"

"I don't know, just sometime," I say. "Here."

Mrs. Knorr, the school secretary, takes the phone and listens for a moment. "If you could follow up with a note tomorrow, we'd appreciate it," she says, leaning on the counter, pausing to listen. "Oh, you wouldn't believe the stuff that gets pulled." Another pause. "If there weren't ears standing right next to me, I'd tell you one from just this morning," she says, eyeing me. The principal walks in and Mrs. Knorr straightens up. "We do appreciate your cooperation," she says politely, and then hangs up.

The principal is a small man who walks the halls at least once every day, greeting kids with his suit coat off. "Mrs. Knorr," he says now, "what can we do for this young lady?"

"She's coming late," she answers. "I just spoke with the mother."

"Well, let's get her on her way," he urges with a wide smile.

Turning a furious pink, she yanks open a drawer, pulls out a tablet of already signed permission slips, scrawls "Late arrival— please accept student," tears it off, slaps it down on the counter in front of me, and turns on her heel.

"Mrs. Knorr does just about everything around here," the principal says nervously, picking up the slip and reading it with a nod of approval before handing it over.

"Thank you," I say, hightailing it out of there before one of them realizes she didn't put a name, date, or time on it.

I skulk around for fifteen minutes, walking the same halls I walked last night, past the same sullen lockers, past the music room, where now a whole class is standing on risers singing "Up, Up and Away." I go to my locker and collect my health book and a note folded into a triangle, then hide in an alcove to wait for the bell. The note is on graph paper and is from Gretchen Quist. It is a bunch of random dots placed here and there with "See you after cheerleading!" and "Connect these dots while your waiting!" written at the bottom, along with her name and a collection of circles and oblongs arranged to look like a bunny.

When the bell goes off, I stay in my alcove and watch people pass by for three and a half minutes. There they all go,
male, female, large, small, cute, uncute, from the popular to
the shunned, all animals in the same circus, trooping back
to their cages. The warning bell is a brief blast, people scurry,
at the last moment a straggler runs by, losing his books and
papers, and I slip around the corner into health class.

Being more or less meaningless, this class is taught by a
student teacher, Miss Nagy, who talks about hygiene in a force-
ful way to prove that we shouldn't be nervous about it. At the
last class she showed a filmstrip about why people sweat and
what to do about it, surprising everyone at the end by passing
around little sample bottles of Ban roll-on for us to put in our
gym lockers and use. Yawn is in this class, but I can't bring
myself to turn around to wave at her.

Today's topic is irresponsible social behavior, and the film
projector is set up; that's a good sign. Nagy runs through an
outline that's already been written on the board, using a
pointer and making it interesting by supplying stories about
people from her hometown who had things happen to them
through bad judgment: a girl who dove into a pond that was
only two feet deep, a boy who carried a firecracker and a cigarette lighter in the same pocket, another boy who tried to
spray-paint his girlfriend's name on a highway overpass by
hanging upside-down.

No matter how I try to connect the dots in Gretchen's note,
nothing that looks like anything appears; she didn't number
them, which is why. Once the film starts going, Miss Nagy
creeps up to crouch next to my desk.

"Do you have a permission slip?" she whispers.

"What?" I whisper back.

The film is so loud the voices are distorted. She runs to the projector, turns it down, and comes back to crouch again. "You need a slip if you're on the absence list, don't you?" She sounds uncertain.

"Um," I whisper, eyes on the screen, where a group of girls is gathered in a school corridor, also whispering. "I went to the office and Mrs. Knorr just told me to go to class."

"I thought you needed a signature or I couldn't let you in," she whispers, staring at the screen. Now there are boys in the film corridor, roughhousing; the whole big group of them is making plans for a party.

"Should I go back and tell Mrs. Knorr she has to give me a permission slip?" I ask. On the screen a boy student is seen slipping a bottle from his parents' liquor cabinet and holding it inside his coat.

Nagy bites her thumbnail. "No, it's okay," she whispers, getting up and fading to the back of the room as the boy's father gives him a lecture, putting an arm across his shoulder while holding a cigarette and a highball glass in the other hand. The mother comes out of the kitchen and looks worriedly from one to the other, but then swallows her misgivings and waves as the boy leaves the house.

Good luck ever seeing that kid again.

A tap on my shoulder and a note arrives, passed up the line from Yawn.

Hey Chikita: Everybody wonders where you been??? Wait for me after!!!! Luv, Jan p.s. We're all going to Flea's tonight—can you come?? p.p.s. This film is rediculus (sp?)

Followed by a hand in front of an open mouth.

On the screen, the kids convene in a parking lot and pool the bottles they collected from home. Before long they're glugging it down, boys and girls alike, lurching into one another and spilling all over their clothes from the 1950s. One girl, with a little chiffon scarf tied around her neck, clambers up and does the Watusi on a parked car, then falls into the arms of a waiting boy. Another girl sits on the ground in the middle of her big round skirt, mascara running down her face as she sobs, taking belts from a flask.

Jan — I been around! Today busy after school — dang! But see ya later! p.s. This party* looks like fun!
*in the film

Followed by a drawing of me as a bird, wearing a string tie.

I fold it into a triangle and send it backward just as the Galen Pierce kid drunkenly challenges the kid from the beginning to a drag race. The girls have lost all control and either are hanging on the boys, begging them to stop, or have thrown aside their cardigan sweaters and are cheering them on suggestively. What the film doesn't understand is that people in our grade don't drag-race; we can't even drive yet.

The bell ends up ringing before it's over, right when the kid from the beginning crashes into a tree and is thrown from his father's car, along with a girl who jumped in at the last minute for kicks. They don't show the wreck, just the dungareed heap that is the boy and then the girl, lying on her side in the grass with her head resting on one outstretched arm, her pale, scuffed face superimposed on the people in the first row as they collect their books and file out.

I feel like I remember her from somewhere.

Behind me, Yawn waits for the aisle to clear. I am kneeling to get my stuff out from under my desk—I'm still carrying around the big, flat art book for some reason, it's my new chest protector—when it comes to me suddenly, what it is about the girl. It isn't her face or her haystack bouffant, but the way they've arranged her, like Steerforth when David Copperfield found him washed up onshore, cold and still, lying with his head upon an outstretched arm, the way Davy had seen him so many times at school.

Yawn gets to my desk right as I stand, but she keeps moving, chin lifted, eyes straight ahead.

Just like that, I Reduce My Circle of Acquaintance.

Instead of haunting the halls, I go to Ringgold's class after school to tell him something before realizing I sort of can't talk. Not that it matters, since he isn't there, although his room is wide open, so I go sit at one of the tables for a while, clearing my throat and looking through his stack of books. When I try using my voice, all that comes out is a strangulated croak. Everything is abandoning me in the same week.

One of his books has nothing in it but black-and-white photographs of architecture and monuments, intermingled with writing. A wedge-shaped building in New York City, parting traffic like a rock in a stream, a foreign temple with a soufflélike dome, a leaning tower—not of pizza, it turns out, but of Pisa—and a lot of other things as well, castles, cathedrals, men sitting on girders amid clouds, modern houses built into rock faces. One looks slightly like the Melchers' house down the street.

Suddenly, whether I want to or not, I'm remembering our kittens from last summer: Ruffles, Blacky Strout, and Freckles.

Flea crying as she carried her half of the box through Monroe Park, me hammering on Lisa and Trent's door, the dark and fumy garage, Trent's pajama bottoms, Lisa's nightgown with the porch light shining through it, the foaming little creature she held up to her cheek for a moment. If only he were still alive somehow, living with the two of them, curled up on the blue patchwork afghan alongside Daniel, their big, quiet baby.

Out of nowhere, Van Leuven appears, gliding through the doorway before coming to a halt. "Oh!" she blurts out. "Is Phil here?"

"Khkkuh," I croak.

She looks different somehow than usual, looser and messier, her blouse untucked and knotted at her waist, hair pulled back so her cameo earrings are visible. "That's right, you missed today," she says, recovering herself. "Laryngitis?"

"Kkuh," I cough out.

"Well, we had a lively reading of Shakespeare, which you would have appreciated; maybe your friend can tell you about it."

I nod.

"Mr. Ringgold says you're quite interested in art," she mentions, tugging at her knotted blouse and then straightening her skirt.

I nod.

"Is he around, do you know?" she asks.

I shake my head.

"Well, I was just seeing if he had something," she says vaguely. She keeps standing there for a moment, not looking like herself, and then glides back out the way she came.

A minute later, Ringgold shows up, juggling tempera jars and some dirty brushes. "Mural repair," he explains, stopping to glance at the book I have open. "Oh yes: the twentieth century is to architecture what the Renaissance was to painting."

I nod.

"Ever seen a skyscraper?" he asks.

I shake my head.

"Well, it looks like you'll be able to—I just got approval for a field trip to the Art Institute. All people need are eight dollars and a sack lunch. How does that sound?"

Forget it for me. I have three dollars to my name.

"Great," I croak out.

My voice is back! This puts me nearly in a good mood.

"You'll see what wonders the elevator has wrought when you lay eyes on downtown Chicago. Mies van der Rohe apartments; the Marina City towers, which look like big ears of shucked corn; the John Hancock Center, a thousand feet and not topped out yet. Even the blasted old Civic Center—we'll get the driver to go by there—has got a Picasso sculpture out front," he tells me, lifting the window and whisking his bouquet of brushes stiffly back and forth to get the excess water out. His hair flies around as he does it.

I want to tell him something but I can't be sure whether my voice is really there without testing it. "Kkchck," I say. "I came up with an idea for a project."

The whole past hour, sitting out gym, I worked on a plan, based on one of the paintings in the book I borrowed. Instead of Loplop introducing a young girl, a young girl is going to introduce Loplop, and I'd like to use my own bird as Loplop.

"A bird like a bird?" he asks.

"Max Ernst drew the bird but used real things to represent the girl," I explain, showing him. "So I'd draw the girl but use a real thing as the bird."

"I think it's said *Mox* Ernst," he murmurs, looking closely at the painting in the book—Loplop in his sly, perky bow tie, presenting the ponytail, the egg, the red blob in a bottle—and then at my drawing of a flat panel with a girl figure on it, one hand reaching to hold a nail, from which a wire basket hangs. "How would you make this cagelike thing?"

"It's an egg basket with a lid, and I've already put my bird in it before and he likes it. I used to carry him around the block in it, so he could have a change of scenery."

I know it seems ridiculous—it's just a project for school—but this is all giving me a weird surge of comfort every time I think about it. Of using one of the blacksmith nails from the garage, of prying the hubcap off my old blue doll buggy, of painting a girl on a piece of wood, of wiring a perch into the egg basket, of getting the bird out of the house for a while.

"Uh-huh," Ringgold says excitedly, running his hands through his hair and then leaving it like that. "I don't want to say much more at this point except remember these names: Gorky, Klee, Duchamp, others that I'll talk about on the bus. Chagall, whose use of the ethereal will blow your mind."

I'm almost starting to wish I could go on his trip. It's turning dark outside, nearing time for cheerleading practice to be over. For a moment Ringgold stares at himself in the window, a man standing amid chaos. Leaning easels, jars bristling with brushes, his own upended hair. He clears his throat, as though there's something he wants to say, but then busies himself stacking drawings.

Everyone is over at Felicia's now, probably all sitting around her room, eating Ding Dongs, which her mom always buys. They keep them in the freezer, and sometimes when we used to feel mean we'd throw them at Stephanie, frozen aluminum-foiled hockey pucks. She couldn't complain because technically we were giving her Ding Dongs.

As I collect my things, Ringgold lifts off his denim apron and hangs it on a hook. Underneath it, there is yellow paint on his shirt. He seems to want to say something, but he's having trouble; it's turning him pink.

"Miss Van Leuven may help chaperone!" he blurts out finally, ears aflame, and then turns and disappears into his closet.

I have no idea which tree Cindy Falk meant, but I pick one and wait behind it, keeping an eye out for Cling, the cheerleading coach. It's not quite dark yet, the sky a royal, ethereal blue. Until Ringgold said it out loud, I always thought ethereal would be pronounced *ether-real*, like what it means: something foggy and atmospheric, like ether, but also real, like in this case the sky. On that same subject, Max Ernst is pronounced *Mox*. Somehow I'm sensing someone else out here, passing behind trees just as I turn to look, Loplop sneaking up on a young girl.

Man, is it cold.

There's the northern star, like an earring, and there's Jupiter or something, like another earring. There's the big round window above the banks of doors, glowing yellow from the gym lights. On the street side of the tree, where I'm standing, a variety of things have been carved into the bark, the word TIT appearing several times, probably because it's easy to carve.

When the gym doors pop open, the first one out is Coach Cling, who briefly scans the vicinity for hangers-on before shouldering her duffle and heading to the teacher's parking lot. The cheerleaders stand on the steps talking.

Am I supposed to go up there?

"You're behind the wrong tree," Cindy calls out suddenly, interrupting their conversation. "Cling could've seen you if she wasn't blind as an idiot."

When I step from behind the tree, Gretchen holds her arms out toward me and whimpers, like a toddler who wants to be picked up. "Me, me!" she says appealingly.

Kathy and Cathy give little waves and keep talking while Patterson tips her head to the side and purses her mouth for a moment, before remembering: *Oh yeah, it's you.*

Yeah, it's you too, you royal asshole.

"Hi," I say.

Cindy Falk is as tall as Felicia; I had forgotten that. "I'm sweating like a hog," she reports, flapping her jacket.

They're all overheated from whatever Cling was having them do — everyone has on an unbuttoned peacoat and a striped scarf. I'm wearing Meg's pea jacket over two sweaters, which makes it more or less fit if I keep my hands in the pockets; if I don't, the sleeves go down to my ankles. My scarf is striped too, but wrongly. It's made of variegated yarn, so the red stripe is really several different shades of red and the blue stripe several shades of blue, giving an overall impression of blurred purple. Nobody at John Deere wears purple if they can help it, but I can't, because my mother made it and because I actually chose the yarn without realizing what I was doing.

"Gay!" Patti calls, and a moment later Galen Pierce materializes, coatless except for a hooded sweatshirt. There's a boy with him, still in the shadows, wearing a dark stocking cap and a denim farm jacket. There's something about the wide, flat planes of the boy's face that reminds me of a cow, in a good way.

Galen grabs Patti and tries to jump on her back. She screams and takes a few staggering steps before dumping him off sideways. They pull on each other's clothes, laughing, and then Galen grabs her by the head and Patti slugs him for real. He leaps away and she follows.

"*Galen Pierce,*" Cindy says. "Either tell us about the stupid party or get lost."

"Tell her to get off me," Galen protests, laughing.

"You get off *me!*" Patti cries, jumping on him this time.

He walks around in a circle, her legs around his waist. "Saturday night at nine in the pavilion, everybody meet. There'll be a keg bought by me and got by Hector"—he tips his head in the direction of the other kid, who nods—"and there might be a fight around midnight, we don't know."

"He's paying off the cops!" Patti adds, kicking him in the side like a pony. He jumps, then squeezes her thighs until she screams. They gallop around in a circle.

The other boy drifts forward, his eyes on me. "Me and Galen're toting wood up there all week, two armloads a night. For a bonfire." He has a soft, lilting voice and a slight hillbilly accent. *Bon-fahr,* he pronounced it.

"Do you go to our school?" Cindy asks him.

He laughs, still looking at me.

"He just got out of Red Rock," Galen grunts, hoisting Patti up higher on his back. She puts her hands over his eyes.

Red Rock Farm is a reform school on the edge of town.

"I was framed," the boy says, grinning at me.

Kathy does a handstand up against the building, resting her heels lightly against the brick. Cathy stands back to assess. "I guess arch your back a little," she advises.

"*Don't* arch your back," Cindy interjects. "Cling has no idea what she's talking about."

The boy shifts his eyes to the upside-down Kathy for a moment and then back to me. "What kind of beer do you like?" he asks.

On the landing leading down to our basement is a case of brown bottles with red and gold labels. They say something, but I can't remember what. He watches me think.

"Any," I say finally.

At Red Rock, the boys learn how to farm whether they want to or not. All the grade schools take field trips out there so the children can see a working farm and what happens to boys who won't mind. I remember it was a lot cleaner than other farms, and everything was labeled, not just hooks where tools were to be hung, but everything. The water spigot outside the horse barn had a sign above it that said OUTSIDE WATER SPIGOT. The kid takes a step forward, pulling off his black cap and stuffing it into a pocket; he has a cowlick like a boy and sideburns like a man. Gray eyes, no gloves.

"That's a good brand," he says.

Hector. It means something, but I can't remember what. Drewrys, that's the beer they drink. Too late to say it.

Cindy drops her gym bag, tucks in her shirt, and kicks up into a handstand. She doesn't rest her feet on the building but hovers sturdily in midair, demonstrating how you don't arch your back except a little. "See?" She's speaking to her hands, but everyone nods, including me. "You have to reach up through your feet. Imagine someone is dangling you by the ankles."

Patterson breaks off from the handstand group to ask the Hector kid a question. "Can you get us lime vodka?"

He ignores her, taking his hat out of his pocket, giving it a shake, and putting it back on.

"Can you?" she asks again.

"You don't want that," he says to me.

Galen has Patti against a tree now, the one I was hiding behind earlier, and is kissing her madly, as a joke. She's kissing him madly back, also as a joke, but then all of a sudden she hooks a leg around him and he starts pushing against her in a realistic, involuntary-looking way.

Patterson looks me up and down, head tipped to the side. "Cute scarf," she says finally. "Is it purple?"

Imagine someone is dangling you by the ankles.

"Is it?" she asks again.

"Not really," I say to the boy.

One of the Red Rock kids escaped on a tractor a few years back, driving across fields and through fences all the way to the Mississippi, parking along Shore Drive and disappearing forever, either onto the interstate or into the current. That could be this kid, in his faded farmer coat and black cap, bare hands on the steering wheel, hauling along at two miles an hour, trailing barbed wire and posts. Another memory from the visit to Red Rock in sixth grade: a sign over a hook in the toolroom that read BOBWIRE CRIMPS. It had struck me, even as a twelve-year-old, that a hayseed had written the sign.

Patti wrenches free from Galen, who stands there with a dazed, sleepy expression on his face as she collects her gym bag. "Tell Felicia about the party," she commands me, and then grabs Galen by the hood of his sweatshirt and pulls him away into the night.

The boy looks after them uncertainly and then takes a step backward. *Wait, don't leave.*

"Nothing against your friend Fellatio, but do not tell her about the party," Cindy interjects, wrapping her scarf around her neck. She looks relaxed and clear eyed from being upside down. "Because not everyone can come—that's basically what a party is. Some can come and some can't."

"I'm pretty sure she already knows about it," I say.

I can't tell if the boy Hector is leaving or not. He looks like someone you'd never notice, not tall, not short.

"People can *know*," Patterson explains. "They just can't come if they're not invited."

"I don't think you can stop people from coming to a bon-fire in the middle of a closed park on a Saturday night," I inform her. My voice comes out sharper than I intended, and Deb and Cindy stare at me. "I mean, can you? It would be hard."

They consider this.

"True," Cindy admits.

Hector is fading away, out of the gym lights and into the darkness.

"We should wear our cheerleading jackets," Cindy says suddenly, and they all nod. "Since there might be people there from across the river." She turns to me. "You can wear Gretchen's last year's. Everything's the same but the cuffs."

A cheerleader jacket! Belonging to Gretchen Quist, who is my same size, so I won't have to twist my sister's long, long arm to get her peacoat and then keep my hands in my pockets all night, or wear my own crappy CPO and freeze.

"Three people can say they're staying at my house. I'll tell my parents we're going to a party but not what it is," Cindy goes on. "And here are the three."

She narrows her eyes, considering each of us in turn.

It's all the way night now and Hector has disappeared completely, leaving just us here, five girls watching Cindy Falk button her coat. Out on the street, a pizza delivery car creeps along with its dome light on, the guy inside trying to read something. Felicia and I ordered pizzas a few times and had them sent to the house of the parochial school kid, the one we used to spy on last summer through his bedroom window. Half-pepperoni and half-cheese, to make it seem specific.

"Maybe just two people," Cindy says, lifting her black hair and settling it around her shoulders. "You and you."

Gretchen and me.

"I couldn't anyway," Patterson blurts out. "I meant to say: I have church choir the next morning."

"Perfect then," Cindy says lightly.

Usually after we ordered pizza for the parochial kid, we'd walk over and sit behind the bushes across the street, waiting to see what they'd do when it showed up. A couple of times his mother paid and they ate it. Those were the good old days.

There's a one-sided fight going on when I get home, my dad sitting on a kitchen chair drunk, badgering my mother and my sister, who are in there trying to make cupcakes for some high school thing.

"I'll say this about that!" he keeps shouting.

"I hope you were at Yearbook," my mother says. "That's what I was telling myself."

"This about that!" he shouts.

"What?" I ask her.

"I said, '*This about that!*'" Even louder.

"Not *you*," my mother says to my dad. "I said, 'I hope you were at Yearbook,' and just ignore him."

"Oh," I answer. And then, even though it won't do any good: "Please make him shut up."

"*I'll say this about that!*" Louder still, fists clenched.

"Dad!" Meg cries. She's trying to frost a cupcake that isn't cool yet, and the top keeps peeling off. "Get out of here! Everyone in this house is sick of you!"

"Well," he mumbles, unclenching his fists and staring at his palms. One of them has a long scar on it, from a childhood accident with an old wood cookstove. "Look at that!" he murmurs, aghast, holding the melted palm out toward my mother.

"Oh, please!" my mother says.

"I have to take these *tomorrow!*" Meg cries, throwing the spatula across the room, where it slides down the side of the refrigerator on a trail of pink frosting. She runs out of the room, up the stairs, and into our bedroom, slamming the door.

"Now why don't you start throwing a fit," my mother says to me.

"Can't I even just walk in the house without being yelled at?" I ask, collecting the two ruined cupcakes on a plate.

My father bends his fingers over the stiff palm to make a fist and then tests it by pounding the table.

"Leave those alone," my mother says, taking the plate from my hand and putting it on the counter.

"Goddamn it!" he cries, pounding again, and then sits back to glare at us.

"Why?"

"Because I just said it," she answers. "You can eat dinner like a civilized person."

"I ate at school."

"What do you mean?"

"I don't know, they fed us."

"I'll say *this* about *that!*"

"Fed you what?"

"Pizza."

"I'LL SAY..."

"I *heard* what you said, you goddamned idiot!" she screams, standing over him with a cake-decorating tool, the one that looks like a giant metal syringe. "Drive me crazy all you want—nobody has an ounce of respect for me! But look at what you're doing to your kids!"

Tammy jumps down from my father's lap.

"See?" I say to him. "Even your own dog is sick of you."

"You can get out of my hair too," she shouts. "Now! Get upstairs."

"What did I do?" I ask, collecting the cupcakes and heading out of the kitchen, past Tammy, who has stopped to lick the frosting off the refrigerator.

Meg is sitting in bed with a book open and her eyes on the ceiling, trying to memorize something. There's a line down the middle of the bedroom, where my clean expanse ends and her rubble begins. I offer her one of the wrinkled cupcakes but she doesn't want it.

"Is she making the rest of them?" she asks.

"Trying to. She almost hit him with a metal thing," I report. "These are good."

"I wish she would hit him," Meg says. "It doesn't matter how good they are. They're for a bake sale, so it only matters what they look like. And they look like a mound of pink shit in a cupcake paper."

"I think she's putting white squiggles on the rest of them," I mention.

"What?" Meg cries. "I don't want anything on them!" She jumps up and runs out, slamming the door just as the phone rings.

The telephone is on my side of the room, sitting on the dresser with its cord in a neat coil next to it. Nobody downstairs will answer because of the bellowing.

"Hello?"

Silence.

"Hello?"

Silence. Muffled sounds in the background, of cars, or of people talking.

Suddenly, I know it's him, Hector, standing at the pay phone next to — where? — maybe the Dairy Mart, while Galen is inside shoplifting. Standing on the Dairy Mart corner with his cap off and his cold hands in his pockets, the receiver pressed to his shoulder, cars going past on Elm Ave. My heart begins pounding with the strangeness of it all; nobody has ever prank phone-called me before, and I don't know what to do.

Silence.

I set the phone back in the cradle.

In the dresser mirror, my face looks the same, but I feel something happening around me, some change as palpable as

weather. Stuck in the mirror are mementos from my childhood—
red and yellow ribbons for various underachievements, a brown
corsage from grade school graduation, a curling and faded picture of me petting a deer in Wisconsin—which is now over. I
wandered through it and came out the other side.

It's a stark feeling. Like getting to the last page of a book
and seeing "The End." Even if you didn't like the story that
much, or your childhood, you read it, you lived it. And now
it's over, book closed, that long-ago deer you petted in the
Dells as dead as the one in *The Yearling*.

I go across the hall and knock.

"What?" Raymond asks through his door. There's a thumping from downstairs and then some surprised yelling and
another thump. If my dad gets frustrated enough, he'll start
lunging from his chair, trying to grab at my mom.

"I have a present for you," I tell Ray, and he lets me in.

His room is smaller than ours, but better. It has a complicated closet, with slanted walls and a steeply pitched floor; a
four-poster double bed, which he's run three pieces of clothesline around so it looks like a boxing ring; outlets on all four
walls, each with its own nightlight; and a metal box under the
window with a fire escape ladder in it, the only one in the
house. We all seem to understand that if anything bad were to
happen, he's the one who should make it out alive.

"These are good," he says through the cupcake.

He's taken his bottom dresser drawer out, turned it over,
and thrown an old braided rug over it to create a hilly terrain
for his army men, some of them standing up and some fallen
over, all of them frozen in the throes of combat.

"It's the Battle of San Juan Hill," he explains. "All the men
try to get up any way they can, but they're shot down."

"Where's G.I. Joe when you need him?" I joke.

"He's in the cave," he answers, pointing to the space the dresser drawer normally occupies. Sure enough, G.I. Joe is in there conferring with a bendable Tonto.

"Would you go down and get me some Jell-O?"

"Dad's yelling," he says, moving his men around.

"He won't yell at you."

He moves a man so his bayonet is just touching another man's back. "Can't you?" he asks miserably.

"No, I told her I already ate and she believed me."

"She did?"

The hollering gets louder while he's down there, which I feel bad about. There's the sound of a scuffle, my sister crying out and my mother's shrill voice, berating my father, who bellows again. A minute later, Raymond comes back with a bowl of red Jell-O and a dinner roll with butter.

"Did you get a cupcake?"

He shakes his head and kneels next to his brown braided hill, staring at his men. While I'm eating my Jell-O, he starts to cry soundlessly, still playing, using the man with the bayonet to gently push all the other men over, until the whole army is defeated, and then he crawls under the bottom rope and gets in bed with his clothes on.

"It's okay," I say.

He grimaces, crying silently with his eyes closed. "I know," he whispers.

"Want me to tell you a story?"

He shakes his head. "Not right now," he whispers, so quietly I can barely hear him.

Just then the phone rings. Out the door, across the hall, into our room, and I grab it on the second ring. My heart is surging and stalling in my chest; I can't collect enough breath to say hello. Silence again over background noise, this time a distant, canned roar that sounds like television laughter. A television?

"Hello," I say.

The clattering of applause, and then Stephanie's voice in the background, demanding to turn the channel, followed by the phone being hung up.

Oh.

Of course.

I look at myself in the mirror. Why did I think it was that boy? He doesn't even know my name, and probably neither does Galen. Plus, I look like this. The person who prank phone called me is the only person I would care to talk to right now, but for some reason I can't. It isn't because Jed Jergestaad likes her and it isn't because Cindy Falk doesn't. It's something else.

On my dresser is a neat stack of books, *The Tempest* on top, with a painting on its cover of a storm-tossed ship. The rigging looks as fragile as a ship in a bottle, the wave rising up over the wooden deck like a gray petticoat. What I never saw before is the tiny man clinging to the mast, and all the other tiny men sliding into the water.

The shouting never stops, so I have to sleep with Raymond, whose bed is filled with what seems like sand. I bring my art book and he brings a handful of soldiers, and we keep the light on for a long time. I try to figure out what there is about the skyscrapers that Ringgold is so enthusiastic about — they just look like buildings to me. Maybe if I had the eight dollars and actually went on his field trip and saw them close up, but something tells me they would still look like buildings. I fall asleep at some point and dream that I'm standing under one of the lacy legs of the Eiffel Tower. Van Leuven is there, handing out valentines to everyone. "Sit down," she says as she gives each person a valentine. The girl next to me has hung hers from her ears. Stephanie is there, wearing my old blue pajamas, and the deaf janitor's assistant is there, carrying his bucket over his arm like a purse. "Look at the wonders the elevator has wrought," someone says, and then I'm in an elevator, going up very fast. Across from me is the girl with hearts hanging from her ears. Suddenly everything starts shaking. "The elevator has *rot*," she cries, and I know we're going to die.

It's Ray, pushing on me. "You're dreaming," he whispers. When I don't open my eyes, he gets up and turns the light off, climbs back under the rope, gathers up as many men as he can find, and then settles back down. When I open my eyes, the room has been cast into eeriness, dark on top but bright along the baseboards. Silence from downstairs. On the other pillow, Ray sleeps curled on his side clutching an army man next to his face, the plastic bayonet just touching his bottom lip. He used to be in love with a stuffed reindeer with a vinyl face, which he carried everywhere. My parents finally reasoned it away by talking him into storing it with the Christmas decorations one year. All spring and all summer he asked for updates on when it would be Christmas, and then gradually, by sometime in the fall, he had forgotten. When the reindeer was finally lifted ceremoniously from the box of balls and tinsel, Raymond held it awkwardly for a while, but you could see that something had changed, and when no one was paying attention, he set it down and never picked it up again.

I wonder where that stuffed reindeer is. Back in the attic,

probably, with the gun and the hip waders and the contraption I saw once when I was cleaning up there with my mother—a pink rubber thing that looked like a hot-water bottle with a hose that had a bulb on the end of it, stored in a flat white box stamped with a sprig of lilacs. Lilacs are usually a signal that you're dealing with feminine hygiene, but this looked more medical than menstrual.

"Mom, what is this?" I said, carrying it to where she sat on an old mattress, smoking cigarettes and sorting through pictures.

She lifted the lid, took a look, and then set it behind her on the bed. "I'll have to think about that and tell you later," she answered.

In other words, figure it out for yourself.

I'm tired of figuring things out for myself! Just tell me what the stupid contraption is. Just tell me why I look like this, feel like this, behave like this. Why am I awake when everyone else is asleep, and what if that boy doesn't know any better and ends up liking me? The same way Patti didn't know any better and invited Felicia and me to her slumber party, thereby ruining our friendship.

The very word *slumber* makes you tired. The perfect combination of *slump* and *lumber*, something that is dead to the world. I wish I were dead to the world, or the world were dead to me. Something. Because recently everything seems too alive, especially the boy Hector, with his naked what-seemed-like admiration. What if I end up marrying him and on the wedding night my mother hands over the contraption in the attic?

The heat kicks on, the house exhaling its hot breath. Over there on his pillow, Raymond squints in his sleep, dreaming whatever he dreams about, men crawling across braided rugs. Over here on my pillow, I'm finally starting to slide away from it all, my body taking my head with it. *Hector*. It means something, but I can't remember what.

What does *hector* mean? I ask the unknown somebody. No answer, but then just as I'm falling asleep another memory floats up from the long-ago visit to Red Rock Farm: Being last in a line of kids trooping past a pen full of pigs, and there was a boy in there washing them, using a broom dipped in soapy water. He had jumbled teeth, red hair, and, when he turned, a hand-lettered sign pinned to the back of his coat. BULLY, it said.

It's embarrassing to think about now, but when I was in about second grade, my parents held my birthday party at Prospect Point, right in the shelter where this Saturday night's beer party will be held. I have a picture of it, all little girls wearing dresses and patent leather shoes, our hair frizzed and held down with bows and headbands, everyone smiling with me in the middle, posing the way I always did back then, grinning into my own shoulder. *I know I'm not cute,* that pose seemed to say, *but I'm still having fun at this party.*

If only I could resurrect that attitude, put it on just for the night, like Gretchen Quist's cheerleader jacket. It's how Martha Van Dalle lives her whole life — our most popular girl, who is wild and tubby and likes everyone, including herself, it seems. The thing is, you *should* like yourself if you're Martha Van Dalle, a girl who first of all ran a pair of giant underpants up the school flagpole and second of all turned herself in when someone else got caught for it.

I was framed, Hector said, about being sent to Red Rock.

Me in my little blue dress with the see-through sleeves. *I'm still having fun at this party.*

*   *   *

Ringgold breaks the news to me on Thursday that I can't use my real bird as part of my art project. I'm hiding out during lunch, helping him prep canvases for the eighth graders to paint on.

"I thought I argued it pretty successfully, but in the end, it was no," Ringgold says regretfully. "It turns out there's a rule about having animals in school."

Somebody should tell that to the frogs in the science closet. The flat white paint we're using to prep the canvases is called gesso. I'm learning everything from Ringgold, good old teacher who lets me hang around his room even when he isn't here. Not that other teachers wouldn't—they all get excited if they think you like their subject—but who would want to hang around a civics room or a science lab, when you can come in here and figure out what else to put in the wire egg basket you're going to hang from your painting. If it can't be my real bird, can it be a drawing of a bird? A picture of a bird cut out of a magazine? The word BIRD written on a piece of paper?

"Why not for now just keep your mind open to possibilities," Ringgold says. "Remember, in a little over a week you'll be seeing things in the Art Institute of Chicago that could— or actually *will*—trigger new ideas."

Except I'm not going to the Art Institute of Chicago. At our house we don't have one dollar, let alone eight.

A lone feather? A human finger? An Easter egg? A doll's head?

The thing is, once you start thinking about surrealism, everything starts to seem both relevant and absurd. A pencil? A piece of twine? A fork? Air?

Suddenly air seems like the best thing to have in the egg

basket. Then I'm truly keeping my mind open to possibilities. The possibility of a bird. Should I say that out loud to Ringgold?

I can't explain it very well, but nevertheless, he slaps himself in the forehead. "See?" he asks me. "This is what happens when they look at art! Sure, you're captivated by Ernst, but then you *move beyond* his sphere of influence into something your own. The *possibility of a bird* is more beautiful than the bird itself—although I'm sure your own bird is a great one—because it exists only in the imagination of the viewer. That means the bird becomes both deeply specific *and* universal."

I know what it sounds like, but when you're in there talking to him, painting a whole row of white canvases white, it actually makes sense.

My father goes missing somewhere in there, between the night when he's downstairs roaring and the weekend. In a way this is good because it means my mother stops paying attention to her kids.

"I'm staying at Cindy Falk's on Saturday," I announce.

"You don't tell, you ask."

"Can I?"

She smokes a cigarette and pokes at a skillet full of hamburger and beans, the dinner she makes when she's tired of people not appreciating her cooking.

"I don't care what any of you do," she says finally.

Felicia doesn't show up for Van Leuven's class on Thursday, but I pass her in the hall later that day and she's wearing a vest I've never seen before. The front is a herringbone pattern and the back is plain brown; she wears it over a white blouse. Actually I may have seen it before, on Maroni. The skirt is familiar, bought at the Style with last summer's babysitting money.

"Hi," she says as we pass each other.

"Hi," I answer.

And that's it.

Friday morning, Gretchen Quist stops at my locker with the cheerleading jacket.

"It your," she says, handing it over in a paper grocery bag. She's being followed by a football player named Richard Manfredi, who everyone calls Freddy Man. He's carrying her books, leaving her free to flap around.

"Thanks," I say. It's heavier than I would have thought, I guess because of the leather sleeves.

"Bye, jackie!" Gretchen cries as I put the jacket in my locker, and she whirls off down the hall.

Friday afternoon I get called out of gym to go to the office.

"You're not in trouble," Mrs. Knorr says, using a razor blade to take tape off the window. "Just sit there and he'll be out in a minute."

I sit.

Mrs. Knorr gets a spray bottle and starts cleaning the glass. It's not that great to be in the principal's office in a gym suit; it's cold, my legs are all mottled, and a kid running the mimeograph machine is just turning the handle and staring at me.

The principal's door opens and out comes Patti Michaels, followed by the principal.

"So let's keep cheering," he tells her in a hearty voice.

"We will," she answers.

"Above a C," he says.

"I know," she answers.

"Not for anyone's good but yours," he says.

"I know," she answers.

"And you're next?" he asks me.

"This is the one with the math," Mrs. Knorr reminds him.

"Oh!" he says. "You're not in trouble."

His office has tall windows and is known for looking out over the parking lot, where people skipping can be spotted. On his desk there's a potted plant with an old ribbon stuck in the dirt, a wooden paddle that says EVERYONE SHOULD HAVE A TEACHER'S AIDE, and an ashtray filled with paper clips.

"The paddle is a gag," he says.

"I know," I say.

"Given to me by staff," he says. "Which brings me to... our math staffer, Mr. Lepkis... would like to see us move you out of gifted and back into regular."

"Okay," I say.

"Sometimes with these so-called gifted programs, people don't thrive as much as the powers that be would have you believe. So then you're in the position of moving a student around in a way that could make them feel they aren't smart. Or aren't learning at a rapid rate, say."

"Okay."

"Because in a regular class, I have a feeling you'd be right at the top."

"Okay."

"So from now on," he consults a piece of paper, "you'll have study hall, room 206, during gifted-math hour, and you'll have regular math, room 103, during your current study hall time."

"Okay."

Out in the hall, Patti is lurking until the end of the period, so she walks with me back to the gym.

"Were you in trouble?" she asks.

"No, but I thought I was at first," I tell her. "For keeping my admit slip the other day—they didn't put my name on it, the date, or a time, and Nagy didn't make me give it to her."

"Galen will buy that from you!" she exclaims.

We peek in the gym door. They're doing basketball drills, while Mr. Pettle sits on the sidelines, wedged into a student desk reading a paperback and pulling on his mustache.

"They should have that guy as our principal," Patti says.

A pair of hand-me-down suede boots arrives unexpectedly on Saturday, in a box of otherwise wrong clothes given to my mother by someone at work. They get offered first to Meg, who tries to jam her big feet in there but can't. Cinderella slips them on without any difficulty.

"Crap, are those cute," Meg says.

Are they ever. Almost eerily so. The way everything seems to be working out right now, I wouldn't be surprised if I ended up dead before the night is over. At the bottom of the box is a miniature purse containing love beads.

"We could hang those from our rearview mirror," Meg suggests.

"That I can do without," my mother answers, pushing the

box out of the way but not getting up from the couch. You never see her just sitting on a Saturday unless she's on the phone, and even then never here, on the couch. She looks around. "Where are my cigarettes?"

"In the kitchen, probably," I say, looking down at my new boots. In two hours I'll take a bath and then put on my burgundy shirt, long underwear, blue jeans, the cheerleader jacket, and these.

"I mean, where are they *go get them*," she says.

On the kitchen table, along with her cigarettes, is a tablet with my dad's notes to himself, mostly recording the weather, certain birds at the feeders, and things reported on the radio, all set off by wild punctuation, underlining, double underlining, anything to fight the utter boredom of it.

"Partly 'Cloudy' <u>Overnight</u> w/Snow SHOWERS (?) Likely By Morning*!!!!!!!!" [*!...<u>Sunrise</u> @ 6:10...!]

    Old Milly back from CALIFORNIA ₒₒₒ Gift for feeding "CURLY" ₒₒₒ {Orange Marmalade} !!

    "Gray SQUIRREL drives away 'red SQUIRREL' ~ {But... only to <u>Locust Tree</u>!!!}"

    [~ Black-capped Chickadees ~ ~~14~~ 15 in 1 minute!!]

Out the back window, birds land on the empty feeder and take off again. Tammy stands at the end of her chain, watching the house. Next door, Curly sits alertly, also staring at our house. Everyone is waiting for my dad to come back.

When the phone rings, I'm standing right there and I pick it up without thinking.

"I was going to see if you wanted to come over to Luekenfelter's and then go to that party," Maroni says.

All over the front of our refrigerator is grime. Fingerprints, smudged food. You don't see it unless you see it, and then you can't not see it. I get the dishrag and start scrubbing on it.

"What are you doing?" Maroni asks.

"Scrubbing at stuff on the refrigerator."

"Oh."

"Well...I might not be able to go to the party. My mom is in a bad mood, but if I can get out, I'll probably just go alone and run into people there."

"What do you mean, alone?" Maroni says. "By your*self*?"

"Yeah," I say, "or...maybe with Cindy Falk."

"That honky bitch!" Felicia pipes up.

"I knew you were on the extension," I say.

"How did you know?" Maroni asks.

"Get off, Gina," Felicia says.

"Bye," Maroni says, and hangs up.

Silence. The refrigerator is spotless now. Raymond comes in looking for the cigarettes and I hand them to him.

"You would never be going to a party alone in your *life*," Felicia says.

Silence.

"You pretend to be shy and backward but you aren't *at all*," she says.

Silence. Chickadees landing and taking off.

"This is so sad," Maroni says.

"Gina, *get off*," Felicia says in a strangled voice, and then one by one we all hang up.

"I wish someone would stay home here tonight," my mother says, watching while I search everywhere for first my mittens and then my scarf. There it is, under books on a dining room chair, just a corner of its purpleness showing.

"I can't," Meg says.

"I can't either," I say.

"No, nobody can," my mother says, sighing. Raymond is sleeping over at a kid's house and Meg is supposedly going to a surprise party, although that's not what it is—I know from hearing her talk on the phone.

"Are you taking a present?" my mother asks.

"We don't take presents, Mother," Meg answers. "People just say Surprise, and then Happy Birthday, and that's it."

"Well, will someone bring a cake?"

"That, I doubt," Meg answers, staring at herself in the shaving mirror hanging by the basement door.

"And I don't even know who this girl is you're staying with, or where you got that coat," my mother says to me. "Why don't my kids tell me anything?"

"We tell you but you don't listen," I say. "This girl is really nice, but a little quiet. The coat was given to me by another girl who wanted me to have it. What else do you want to know?"

"Nothing, I guess," she says, staring out the window toward the garage. It's nighttime, though, and the window is black. All she can see is her own kitchen.

The sky is immense and beautiful, more so than usual; it might have something to do with my boots. I sing while I'm walking in them, one of my old favorite songs:

Ooh, child things are gonna get easier
Ooh, child things'll get brighter...

At one point, Felicia and I liked this song so much that we named a rag doll after it. This was the rag doll that, if Felicia ever cleaned her room and made her bed, would be set picturesquely against the pillows. During moments of high hilarity, we were known to attack Ooh Child, kicking her around the room like a soccer ball.

The other song we liked was "Ben," a lullaby to a rat. If you were trying to get your rodent to fall asleep, that was the song to sing to him:

> *Ben, the two of us need look no more,*
> *We both found what we were looking for.*

Cindy Falk lives on the other side of Monroe Park, through the teacher part with the shrubbery and through the part where you have to walk in the street and through the part where you have to cut across three broad, manicured yards to arrive at a little lane leading to several houses on a bluff, including Cindy's, rambling brick and glass, which is supposedly shabby on the inside but turns out not to be at all—it's just extremely messy. Her dad is tall, with a straight spine and very short hair, like an army colonel.

"They're in her room playing records. Go on up and knock. You can just kick those to the side," he tells me as I try to step over dirty laundry that it looks like someone has dumped over the banister from upstairs. The part of the house that isn't messy is everything from head height to the tall canted ceilings— a large, airy space that makes you think of Chicago or Philadelphia, or some other place that isn't Zanesville.

Upstairs is a long corridor with closed doors, but I can hear where the music is coming from. *I started a joke which started the whole world crying.*

265

"Get in here," Cindy says, shutting the door behind me.

Huge, the room is, and clean, or cleaner. A canopied bed and a rocking chair, a vanity with a three-tiered mirror and a cushioned bench, a built-in cabinet with a stereo and records, a window seat, and its own bathroom, which Gretchen is in, peeing.

"Hi!" she calls, waving.

In the middle of the room, a grizzled wiener dog sits atop a basket of laundry. The rocking chair is filled with stuffed animals, and from one of the bedposts, toe shoes hang from pink ribbons. I've never seen toe shoes in person before; they're sturdy looking. The wiener dog hops down and comes over to greet me.

"What's your name?" I ask him.

"Heinzie," Cindy answers, sitting down at her vanity. "Do you want perfume? Because we're putting on perfume."

"No, thanks," I say.

"Me do!" Gretchen says, emerging from the bathroom. She's so cute it's unbelievable. Her hair is literally gold.

Cindy sprays her on the neck and then turns to me. "Give me your wrist," she orders.

I get sprayed on one wrist, rub it on the other, and then, when they're not looking, rub both on my pants. For some reason, I can't stand perfume — I'd rather smell a garden full of puke. All my other friends know that.

"Hey, Heinzie," I say, but he wanders back over to his basket and hops in.

They put their coats on and we look at ourselves in Cindy's mirror. Two extremely good-looking girls with me in the middle. Before we leave, Cindy tries a stocking cap on my head but then takes it off again, and I have to refluff my hair by bending over and swinging it down and then swinging it back up, leaving me with the sensation I had earlier in the week, of my hair floating around above my head.

"First we go into the living room, where my dad is, and then we go to wherever my mom is," Cindy says. "And whatever I say, you agree with. Just nod, don't even talk. Okay?"

We nod.

We're walking on a limestone path under the cold stars, taking the back way along the bluff to Prospect. The path gets skinny at one point and we have to go sideways, holding hands, until it widens again. I've seen this from below, the sheer rock face with a fringe of trees at the top, like a crew cut. It would be impossible during the day, but this is night and nothing is real. We creep along the rock's hairline, Minonk Road and the river roaring along somewhere below, and those two engaged in a conversation about how Jon G. treats Kathy Liddelmeyer like dirt.

"He alway make Liddy-biddy cry," Gretchen says.

"She makes herself cry," Cindy says.

I know one thing: this path is perfect. Wherever it leads, you want to follow. The trees, the pale strand we're walking on, the voices of the girls ahead of me. It's like passing through a black bead curtain, giving yourself over to the night, the sky. As soon as you do, things happen. Freddy Man materializes on a converging path, scaring us half out of our wits.

"Freddy, *shit*," Cindy cries.

Behind him is Tommy Walton, who nods at me.

"Hi," I say. He sits behind me in history.

"No boys allowed, Thomas," Cindy says primly. Sometimes they like each other and sometimes they don't.

"No boys!" Gretchen cries, running around behind me and peering over my shoulder at Freddy.

"What about men?" Freddy asks.

"Let us know if you see any," Cindy says, and pulls Gretchen and me along.

We have to go down a slope and through a frozen bog, the boys following, then up the other side of the slope, where a bonfire and a lot of flickering people come into view. Suddenly my shoulder is tapped.

I look back and Freddy Man points his thumb at Tommy.

"What?"

"Nothing," Tommy says. "How's the Magna Carta?"

We don't really talk in history, but occasionally he'll poke me with his pencil eraser and, when I turn around, show me things he's done to the pictures in his textbook. I never know what to say, just like now.

"You tell me," I try. "You're the one listening in there."

"I'm never listening!" he protests. "*You're* listening." And then Tommy Walton, the second-most-popular boy in our school, tugs on my hair.

People are just their faces and the fronts of their coats, whatever is lit up by the bonfire, nobody I know yet. Then we're there and it's like entering a dark forest except the trees start talking to you.

"Hi," says a girl I'm partners with in gym sometimes.

"Hi," I say.

"Hi," says someone else.

"Hi," I say.

"Hi," says Jackie Lopez. She's hanging on the arm of Whitey Pelletier, who moved to Springfield but is frequently seen back here. "Hi," he says.

"Hi, hi," I say.

"She saw me the other day with pie on my shirt," Jackie tells Whitey.

"Did it look good?" he asks me, and Jackie punches him in the arm.

"Ow," he says.

"Hey, where is everybody?" says Deb Patterson. She's wearing eyeliner and a hat like the one they tried on me. It looks good on her.

"Hi," I say.

"Where is everybody?"

"Hi," I say.

"*Hi*. Where is everybody?"

"Through there." I point to a knot of people, and Patterson shoves past me and into them. They scatter for a moment and then move back to where they were. One looks over, a girl in my Shakespeare class, and waves. In her other hand she's holding the same paper cup a lot of people are holding.

I wave back.

"Hi there," says a girl.

"Jane!" I say. She looks different somehow, now that her mother is dead. "How are you doing?"

"Fine," she says nervously, looking around. "Everyone's over by the fire, sitting on a log." She seems to be walking around with Mark Johansson, a boy who is very cute but obscure; there's some reason he isn't more popular, which nobody can put a finger on.

"Let's go," he says.

"We're looking for the punch," Jane explains.

"I like your hair," I say, because that's what's different— she has bangs now. They make her look like the picture in the locket her mother was wearing.

"Oh, it's just these," she says, touching the bangs, which are sort of short.

"Let's go," Mark the Obscure says.

Everyone is over by the fire, sitting on a log. If they see me in this jacket, we'll all feel terrible. Why didn't I figure something out, stow another coat behind the pavilion or something, or not come at all? That was the only real solution, and I could have done it—my mother needed me at home. She's alone there now, at the kitchen window, smoking and waiting for one of us to come back. The sky suddenly feels crowded and awful, too many stars, and now the moon too, which wasn't there before.

"Hi," says Freddy Man. "What did he call you?"

"Who?" I ask.

"Tommy—he called you Magnet, or something like that."

"Oh. Magna Carta. It's a thing from history," I say.

"Oh," Freddy Man says, nodding, and then just stands there.

The party mills around us, but it has a rustling quiet, like being in a field of cattle in the middle of the night. If it's dark enough, the cattle are just presences, big mounds shifting as you walk through them. Except for the cow pies, it's magical and strange.

"Did you see where Gretchen went?" Freddy asks.

"Maybe over there?" I point to a knot of people.

"I already looked over there," Freddy Man says.

"Maybe over there?" I point to the bonfire, and standing beside it, poking a stick into the flames, is the boy Hector. The same farm jacket and black cap, the same eyes.

"Where did you go?" Cindy says. "You were supposed to be following us." Behind her are Patterson, Kathy, Cathy, and Gretchen.

Where did I go. "I don't know," I say. Hector lifts a big piece of firewood and lays it on top of the bonfire, loosening a torrent of sparks. For a moment his face looks bright and hot.

"No boys!" Gretchen cries, running behind me to peek at Freddy Man, who looks horribly miserable all of a sudden, like he might cry.

"Where'd you get that punch?" Cindy asks Kathy.

"Over there," Kathy says, taking a sip. "By that log where people are sitting."

"Where Freddy Man?" Gretchen says, looking around.

Hector has disappeared too. There's the fire going strong, and where he was standing on the other side of it, nothing, just darkness.

"Come on," says Cindy, and they all turn at once, like a school of shining fish, and follow her.

Banner for a School of Monsters is the name of a Max Ernst painting that shows a creature in a black forest, head cracked open to better reveal its teeth. It's all sharp claws and primary colors, like a monster from a child's imagination. You can only wonder what's happening back at my house right now while I stand here alone.

"Hello," somebody says, gliding past.

"Hello," I say.

I wonder what my father does, adrift in the night, after the bars close. Nowhere to sleep but the backseat or a park bench.

And what if the park bench were in this very park, what if my dad came reeling through the crowd, looking for a place to pass out, what would I do? What would I do? My heart lurches in circles, looking for a way out of this thought.

"Hey, Galen's trying to find you," someone says.

He is?

"I'll give you money for that absence slip," Galen says, wandering up with Patti attached to him.

"I told him you had a slip from the office with no name, date, or time on it," Patti explains. Her hair is shining, as always, but her lips are sliding sideways on her face. I'm starting to realize people are drunk.

"I pay five dollars if they aren't folded," Galen says.

"I didn't fold it," I say. "It's in my health book."

"Put it in the vent of locker number 1202," Galen says, taking a bill out of his pocket and giving it to me.

"And drink!" Patti calls over her shoulder.

Drink, drank, drunk.

"Hi," says Tommy Walton.

"No," I answer.

He looks at me.

"I mean," I say, and then stand there. What do I mean?

A girl bumps into Tommy and sprawls on the ground. He helps her up; she's laughing with her hair across her face, and another girl drags her away. Tommy tips his spilled cup toward me — all gone — then takes my elbow and starts steering me toward the bonfire, the booze, the log.

As we pass the pavilion, he sets his cup on a ledge and pulls me inside. Picnic tables have been stacked in here for the winter, and I sense that kids have climbed them like scaffolding and are necking, though it's all just shapes in the blackness, faint rustling sounds. The thing about the nighttime cattle is that they always know where you are, even if you can't see them. Tommy leans against the wall, gathering me against him with one hand and pushing my hair back with the other.

I'm shorter than he is, so mostly what's happening is between me and his coat, a dark wool CPO. My face is pressed against the pocket; I can feel the button on my chin.

"You have beautiful hair," he whispers. "It just hangs there in history, right in front of me."

"Thank you," I whisper back. It's true, my hair is my one good thing.

He shifts slightly and his hand moves down to the small of my back, pressing me against him. Everything feels very focused all of a sudden, his breath in my ear, the warm starfish shape of the hand on my back, the contours of his leg. All I would have to do now is look up, instead of down, and I'd most likely be necking.

"Hey," he whispers. "Hey."

It's slightly delirious to stand here with his arms around me, my face pressed into his dark plaid, but I'm not going to lift my head. No matter what this feels like right now—the intimate, echoey sounds of feet shuffling on concrete as our bodies arrange themselves closer together, the party just steps away, all those other bodies out there, moving around, trampling the grass, his hands under the cheerleader jacket—Monday is only two days from now. Better to be the plain girl from history class who didn't kiss him than the plain girl from history class who did.

The Magnet Carta was enacted to limit the powers of the king. I wrench myself free from him. In the arched doorway of the pavilion, Tommy Walton squints at me.

"You're odd," he says.

He leaves his cup behind, so I hold it just for something to do with my hand. Someone yells and then someone else, and then a bunch of people make them be quiet. On the river side of the pavilion are two rocks with a bench between them. Sitting there is Petie, Martha Van Dalle's retarded neighbor. I perch on the bench for a moment, a few feet away, and try to look as though I'm finally getting a rest from the party.

"Where's Martha?" I ask her.

She kicks at her own shoe with the other shoe. "Kissing a kid," she answers loudly.

Okay.

"I used to have a bird named Petie," I mention, just for something to say.

She stares at me, her lips bunched up under her nose. "I used to have a bird named whatever your name is too," she answers.

It occurs to me that Petie may not be retarded at all; she may be obnoxious.

Someone peeks a head around the corner of the pavilion, and it's Hector.

"Oh," he says, seeing my cup. "You got punch."

"It's actually empty," I say, showing him.

He takes a long drag off a cigarette and flicks it out into the night, like a shooting star. "Because we got your beer over there, what you asked for."

"You do?"

"Yeah."

"Where did you get it?"

"All stole," he admits, grinning.

"Really?"

"From the back door of Walgreens. Me and Galen dragged a wagon over all these goddamned hills." His voice is softly slurred in its hillbilly cadences, and in the moonlight his face looks sharp and white, like it's been carved out of soap. Suddenly I feel nervous again. What if someone comes through, saying that there's a drunk man lurching around, looking for a park bench? It couldn't happen, but if it did, I guess I would just take off running.

"Hi," Petie says loudly.

Hector gives her a curious look—she's big, in a padded coat and a black knit cap, her lips pushed forward in a scowl—and then nods.

"Are you going to kiss him?" she asks me.

It's cold on the bench, but the boots are warm and the cheerleader jacket is warm. The sleeves are leather and the rest of it is boiled wool with a quilted lining. Nothing warmer than boiled wool, but how do they boil it? Just in water, like an egg?

"Yes," I say.

Petie the parakeet came from an elderly woman who lived down our street. I saw him for the first time in her house, after she got sick, on a day when my mother looked in on her. The old woman sat me down in her dark living room, had me hold out my finger, and set the bird on it. While my mother straightened up the house and gathered a load of sheets and towels, the old woman puttered around in the kitchen, protesting and making coffee. The whole time it took for them to sit around doing a wash and getting it hung up in the basement, the bird and I sat together on her brocade chair, him walking up and down my forearm and, when I touched the tips of my index fingers to each other, stepping across and walking up the other arm. At the top he sat on my shoulder, sorting through my hair until he came to my ear, which he gave a piercing jab to before crawling along my shirtfront to the other side. He got that ear too and then sat on my shoulder, leaning forward to look at my lips while I whistled. A few months later, he was brought to our house in his cage and given to me, but he pecked my finger every time I put it near him and then, not long after, died.

That was the story of that Petie.

This Petie seems to be crying.

For all I know, maybe my father finds a woman to stay with on the nights he doesn't come home, or maybe he sleeps on the ground—he and my mother did go camping a lot before they had kids. On their honeymoon, at the Wisconsin Dells, they caught an enormous northern pike that wouldn't be hauled to shore; in their old-fashioned fishing hats, they rowed in circles, trying to wear it out, but the northern wore them out instead. The photo my mother took on the dock is of my father holding up his finned and bloody hands in defeat.

That's how I picture it when I think of him out there alone—somehow younger than he is now, and exhausted, whatever he needed eluding him.

"Are you okay?" I ask Petie.

She won't answer but just keeps wrinkling her nose and grimacing. She's definitely crying.

"Hey," Hector says, and crouches in front of her. She looks away from him and shakes her head emphatically.

"Stand up," Hector says, pulling her to her feet.

She stands obediently, scowling at him, and then he dips his head down and kisses her on the lips.

"Now you're the one getting kissed," he tells her.

"No, sir!" she cries, her eyes wide.

"Yes," he says.

"Not me!" She puts both mittens over her mouth.

"You," he says.

After Petie runs away to find Martha and tell her the news, Hector tries to get me to go off in the dark with him.

"Come on," he says, tugging on my sleeve. "I want to show you something."

"Show me what?" I say, planting my feet.

"Just something." He puts his hand around my upper arm and tugs.

"But what?"

"Just something." He tugs harder.

"But something what?" I resist, digging my feet in.

"I'll *show* you," he says and just like that, yanks me down the hill.

I've even noticed this with Raymond, who only comes up to my shoulders—boys are strong. You don't think they are, but suddenly you realize: they are.

My heart is thudding in my chest. I don't know whether to go along with it and then bolt when he lets go, or whether to keep resisting and possibly wreck my boots. This kid was put in Red Rock for a reason.

The school of monsters, Max Ernst's dark forests and odd creatures, the cracked jawbone and a row of dinosaur teeth, Loplop perched on his scaly legs, the hubcaps, ponytails, doorbells, outhouses, garden gates, birds in egg baskets, a bottle with a blob in it, a girl holding a rusted blacksmith's nail. In the painting of two children threatened by a nightingale, one is being carried off by a man as the other screams for help.

Help, Felicia.

We used to be able to get each other's attention telepathically in class, she and I, by internally bellowing the other person's name while staring at their back or the side of their head, or even a sleeve, whatever was visible.

Felicia!

Now we're going downhill and I have to run to keep from falling; we're in the hollow, where you can't hear or see the party at all, and where there's old snow, gleaming in the inky blackness. We're heading to the overlook, the big rock with all the warning signs.

Help, Felicia!

My grandmother's house, the chicken shed I used to jump off into a pile of loose dirt, the ankle-turning plummet, and then a mouthful of grit. The stone, the leaf, the unfound door. The old stump with two nails pounded into it, the chicken's neck stretched between them, the eye that watches the ax come down, what happens afterward, never seen but read about—the body running in circles, terrified to be without its head. Hector pulls me up onto the big rock where no one is supposed to go.

Felicia!

"See?" he says, letting go of my hand.

And there it is, larger and brighter than I've ever seen it, floating above the Mississippi like a giant pearl. The moon over Zanesville.

* * *

All those years ago, at my birthday party in the pavilion, I got as my gift a pearl necklace from a jewelry store. The pearl in its filigreed setting rested on a piece of velvet cardboard bent to fit the box, its length of gold chain hidden below. It was from the whole family, minus Raymond, who wasn't born yet, but it was really from my dad.

"He saw this, and that's all there was to it," my mother told everyone as she fastened it around my neck. In the picture of me with all my friends, you can see the pearl against the blue collar of my dress.

"It's beautiful," I tell Hector.

From atop the dangerous rock, we gaze down at the inky void and back up at the starry sky until we're dizzy and then he turns and kisses me. No ceremony, no confusion of legs and arms. Just kisses me more or less like he did Petie.

I know I'm not cute, but I'm still having fun at this party.

"Is that you?" Felicia calls. "Are you okay?"

I step to the edge of the rock and there she is, bent over and panting, looking up through the late-night frizz of her hair. "Hi," I say.

"I thought you were in trouble," she says.

"Really?"

"Yes, *really*," she says, swiping at her nose. She squints past me, at Hector, who is smoking his cigarette and listening, or not listening. "Why did I think you were dying or something?"

"Mental telepathy," I confess.

"Out here?" she asks, looking around. "I thought it only worked in class."

"Me too."

"Wait—why did you?" she asks.

I widen my eyes.

"Oh," she says, nodding.

There's a long, thoughtful silence, during which a cloud passes over the moon, dimming us for a moment. Then the giant pearl is restored to its spot on the big sky-bosom.

"Anyhoo," I say.

"Well, I was having a heart attack," she says.

"I've been having one for this whole party," I admit.

"You have?" she asks.

"Yeah. I feel weird about this, for one thing," I say, indicating the cheerleader jacket.

"You do?"

"Yeah."

"I wouldn't feel weird—it looks cute."

"You wouldn't?"

"No," she says. "*I'd* feel weird about being an asshole."

"I think I'll go back up where the beer is," Hector says.

At my grandmother's house, during the era of jumping off sheds, there was a spare room that had a bed with a dark pink tufted bedspread and a doll leaning against the pillow. The doll was a baby with molded hair and a bottle with magic milk inside, which disappeared and reappeared, depending on how you held it. The bottle was kept jammed in the doll's mouth, jutting straight up in the air as though an imaginary person were holding it there. The magic bottle was highly prized among the girl cousins, and once, during a family gathering, I crept in there and took the bottle, keeping it in a deep, baggy pocket of my overalls all afternoon and into the evening, occasionally stepping into the bathroom to play with it by myself. Eventually I started feeling guilty and pressured by the fact that its disappearance was causing an uproar among the cousins, who had decided the culprit was an older, wry cousin named Deenie, who not only had no interest in dolls but would demonstrate her indifference to them by various means. Like putting them on the floor and stepping on their heads.

"Why would someone who hates dolls take a doll's *bottle*?" she continued to ask disgustedly.

"Because you're robbing a *doll*, that's why," I said nervously at one point, before retiring to the bathroom to tip the bottle back and forth and think about what to do.

My mother happened to be passing by when I came out of the bathroom for the tenth time.

"You got a problem?" she asked.

Sometimes when you're cruel to others, it's because you've gotten yourself into a situation you can't get out of.

I feel terrible.

"You should," Felicia says.

Hector jumps down off the rock and disappears. I do a combination of sliding and jumping, but I still kill my ankles. "Ouch, fuck," I say.

"Good," she says.

"Now who's the asshole?"

"Not me," she says. "I'm the victim."

"You're the one who abandoned me in my moment of greatest need!"

"How's that? Because somebody else wanted to *walk* with me that night? What about all those cheerleaders you're such good friends with—they weren't exactly holding your hand."

"I wasn't their sidekick!"

"I never wanted a sidekick!"

"You didn't?"

"No!"

"So you just abandoned me in my moment of need!"

"Why do you keep saying that? You just don't want to be friends with me anymore and you're looking for a way to make it my fault."

We stare at each other.

"I just feel strange," I say. "Like everything I was doing I can't do anymore."

"Why not?"

"I don't know," I admit. "And it's sort of going away."

"You are?"

"No, the *feeling* is sort of going away."

"Why are you acting so weird?" she asks, peering at me in the dark.

"I'm trying to tell you—this is how I am now. I'm weird."

She thinks about that.

"I'm weird too," she says finally.

We head up the hill, trudging along, me in my cheerleader jacket, her in her coat with the bottomless pockets. Once, we unstitched that coat's lining, removed over a dollar in change, and stitched it back up. We spent the money on penny candy.

"Remember that candy that looked like a record?"

"Not really," she says.

"Remember? It was a piece of black licorice wound into a circle with a candy dot in the center?"

"Oh yeah. You liked them, not me. I liked the little pop bottles with one sip inside them."

"Remember when *sip* was my favorite word?"

"Yeah."

"What was yours?"

"When yours was *sip*, I think mine was *crimp*. Now it's *eucalyptus*."

"I like the word, I don't like the smell."

"I think I like the word *because* of the smell," she says. "Where did you get those boots?"

"In a box of clothes my mom brought home."

"Anything else?"

"No, these were the only thing," I say. "Some love beads."

"Your sister should wear those, see if it does anything."

"It would be like putting garlic on a vampire."

"Ha. But actually she's nice," Felicia says primly.

"So's yours," I say primly back.

We climb the last hill, walking slower and slower. Either the bonfire is bigger or the party is; everywhere are flickering people.

"What's your favorite word right now?" Felicia asks.

"If it's just a word, then '*tis*. But if it can be a phrase, then '*Tis new to thee*. From Shakespeare."

"'*Tis new to thee*," she repeats. "If we can have Shakespeare, then mine is *Monster, I smell all horse-piss*, or whatever that was."

"Ha. Van Leuven and Ringgold are madly in love with each other."

"They are?"

"Maybe. Tommy Dalton tried to kiss me."

"Jed Jergestaad did kiss me, and now he's walking around with Martha Van Dalle again. It's so embarrassing."

"I was sitting with her neighbor Petie."

"You were?"

"She started crying because she was abandoned," I tell her. "Which is a terrible feeling."

"I didn't abandon you! You're the one who abandoned me!" She swipes at her nose.

"You're making your nose all red."

"I am?"

"Not *all* red," I say.

"Good thing it's dark out here," she says. "Who was that kid? He was cute."

"A friend of Galen Pierce's, from Red Rock. I know."

"Red Rock lets them out for the weekend?"

"I don't think he was let out, I think he got out."

"You mean escaped?"

"No, he just got out. He was done being there."

"Too bad he isn't an escapee."

"I know," I say. We're standing on the edge of the party now, throngs of people I don't recognize. "Where are we?"

"Insanesville," Felicia answers.

There's an abrupt scream that morphs into screaming laughter. Only a matter of time now before we're turned in to the cops or there's a fight, or both.

"Hi," someone says to Felicia.

"Hi," Felicia answers.

"Hi," the same person says to me.

"Hi," I answer.

"Who was that?" Felicia asks me.

I don't know; everybody is starting to blur together. Somebody pushes us and we almost fall over. Straight ahead is the pavilion, and then beyond it the glow of the bonfire, where Hector is, and probably everyone else: Cindy Falk, Maroni, Patterson, Luekenfelter, Gretchen Quist, Dunk. All of them mixed together like a bad salad.

"Where are we going?" I ask Felicia.

"We're following that kid back to the fire," she says, but neither of us takes a step.

"Have you had any of that punch?"

"Not yet. Didn't we all sign a vow in seventh-grade health not to drink or smoke?"

"Are you kidding?" I ask her.

"Maybe," she says. "But I did sign the vow."

"So did I, but I said 'today' to myself while I was signing it," I tell her. "That's what everybody did."

"They did?"

"Either way, no vow can last longer than that school year."

"It can't?"

"Otherwise what happens when you're thirty and you go to a cocktail party? Is the vow still in effect?"

A girl staggers past us and kneels on the ground, holding her long hair away from her face. She's staring at the ratty grass, concentrating.

"Are you okay?" Felicia calls.

The girl nods, still staring at the grass, and then she vomits.

It feels weird right at this moment to not be anybody's sidekick. Hard to explain, but when I look at the moon, it seems like it's paying attention to me, instead of me paying attention to it. It's way up there now. *Hi, moon,* I say silently to it. *Yes, I'm high,* it says back. The moon has a sense of humor.

"Do you guys have any gum?" the girl who vomited asks us.

"Sorry," Felicia answers, "these pockets don't work."

"I might have one Chiclet somewhere," I tell her.

"Can I have it?" she asks.

It ends up being in my front pants pocket, and I hand it over. Also in there is the five-dollar bill Galen Pierce gave me. I just realized: five dollars means I've got eight altogether.

"I'm going on a field trip to Chicago, for art," I tell Felicia, who looks aghast.

"What about the curse of the mummy?" she asks.

The thing I couldn't do I'm getting to do. Me, riding on the bus and staring out the window at downtown Chicago, me seeing buildings that look like ears of corn, me seeing stairways full of clouds and all the other things Ringgold is so excited about that are impossible to picture until you're there, having your mind blown. I'll probably wear what I have on right now, but I may put my hair in a French braid that day, just so I don't have to think about it.

Somehow the party has absorbed us, we're in the middle of a bunch of strangers, so we move on to the bonfire, which is blazing away with what looks like part of a picnic table in it.

"What happens when the cops come?" I ask Felicia.

She thinks. "The back way through yards, down to Twenty-first, and over the Grassy Knoll. Meet up under the buckeye tree."

"Going through yards is where we always have our problems."

"Because you don't stick with me," she says.

"It gets too confusing."

"Not if you just follow."

I don't want to follow.

"Which is why I said the buckeye tree."

"Hi," says Hector, handing each of us a bottle of beer.

Everybody we've ever known is at this bonfire, but none of them is paying any attention to us. Everyone is drinking. The beer I'm holding smells dark and awful but not unfamiliar.

Hector tips his bottle up and drinks it, inch by inch, until it's gone.

"Try that," he says.

It's like the magic baby bottle I used to love so much. I look at Felicia and she looks at me.

Bombs away.

Acknowledgments

I would like to express my gratitude to early readers of this manuscript: Mary Allen, Joe and Lucy Blair, Jill Ciment, and Peter Trachtenberg. Thank you as well to Elizabeth White, for a friendship that has spanned years and continents.

About the Author

Jo Ann Beard is the author of *The Boys of My Youth,* a collection of autobiographical essays, and other works of nonfiction that have appeared in the *New Yorker, Tin House, Best American Essays,* and other magazines and anthologies. She has received a Whiting Foundation Award and fellowships from the New York Foundation for the Arts and the John Simon Guggenheim Foundation.